TAL MACEY

Beacon Farm

Best Wishes,

Tal

GULL PRESS

This book was professionally typeset on Reedsy.
Find out more at reedsy.com

For Nana Newlyn
and Katie

Both of whom I certainly would not have written this book
without.

The Four Seasons

1944

Spring

The sensation of the tractor engine jolting and growling as she drove through the uneven tracks of the farm was like nothing Carolyn had ever felt before. As a child she had ridden on a tractor almost every single day, but since growing up those times had become very scarce. That was until the past few years when everything changed.

At first, nobody thought they would be able to do it, that they could never keep things going while the men were away, but Carolyn and her girls had proved every single one of the doubters wrong. It was a relatively warm day and she was certain that they were able to surpass anything that the boys had done before.

She felt proud as she rumbled into the field and saw the lines of girls working alongside each other. Together they had started something incredible. The boys were away defending the country, while they were here keeping the country going. Together they were all making sure the world never stopped turning.

When the war was first announced and she heard that it would not be like the first time round, Carolyn assumed that meant she would be allowed to fight. When that had turned out to not have been the case, she had been furious about the thought of sitting at home and twiddling her thumbs while the likes of her brother risked their lives.

But then her father had offered her a job.

Now Carolyn could not imagine any other way of life. In the fields you battled everything; the weather, the changing of the seasons, blight. These years had taught her more than she could ever have imagined and to see it all was a privilege. Carolyn ground the tractor to a halt and jumped down.

'Alright, girls?' She always unintentionally imitated her father while in the fields. 'How's it all going?'

'Won't lie to you.' Madge stretched her aching back. 'It's hard!'

'But you can do it, right?' Carolyn looked at all of the girls around her. 'You can all do it! We did it last year and the year before, so what's one more year, eh?'

'I hope it's only one more year.' Kerenza shoved her fork into the solid earth again with a groan.

'Even if it's not, we'll still be here,' Carolyn insisted. 'Feeding the nation.'

Madge and Kerenza exchanged glances of despair as Carolyn marched down the field, inspecting her gang's work.

'Spring's always the hardest time, but what we've all got to keep in mind is how proud we will feel when summer comes around and we'll see the results of today and every other day that we've spent in these fields! Now, hand me that fork!'

Madge tossed her over a fork and Carolyn began to dig. Less than a minute later, the bright sun disappeared and cast a dense shadow over the field.

'It's gonna rain!' Carolyn heard Kerenza moan and felt the first fresh drops hit her hand. *It's coming*, she thought, and looked up as the heavens opened. The rest of her group shuddered and cried out as Carolyn remained there, face up and drinking in the rain.

'Carolyn, can we go inside?' Kerenza cried.

Carolyn burst into childlike laughter. 'No way!' She beamed and began to dig again. 'Out in all seasons *and* all weather. That's what we pledged when we agreed to feed the nation!'

She knew that the girls were scowling and whispering behind her back, but Carolyn did not give a damn. It was out in the elements that she had found who she truly was. This was where Carolyn was supposed to be.

Summer

The shade from the hedge was a refreshing relief as she waited on the corner. The July sun felt particularly bright today and Rosie was wondering just how long she could stand in it before getting scorched. She had been waiting for quite a while now, but the post was always a little erratic these days. Still, she could not risk the postman delivering anything directly to the house, for if there was something addressed to her then questions would be asked and her secret would be spilled. Instead she now spent every morning loitering around the bottom of Beacon Lane waiting for the inevitable sound of the postman's bike.

Rosie just wanted the war to be over. For everything to go back to how it had been before – although perhaps not *everything*.

Finally she heard the sound of a bicycle bell dinging and peered down the lane to see the postman pedalling along. The lane was rather steep and he appeared to be suffering even more than usual in today's heat, his lined face red and beaded with sweat. As Rosie stepped out from the hedge with a smile, he almost toppled from his bike in shock.

'Morning, Morris.' She gave him a big smile. 'Is there any post for us?'

'Um, well…' The postman began fumbling about in his bag, 'I should really deliver it directly to the property.'

'I'm only thinking of you,' Rosie said innocently, 'It's such a hot day and I wouldn't want you suffering needlessly, trying to cycle up that hill when I'm going that way anyway.'

An anxious smile flashed across the postman's face. 'You're a kind girl, Rosie, but if my boss found out that I don't take my post right to the farm then I'll be in trouble.'

'OK, fine.' Rosie tossed her blonde hair over her shoulders and turned back to the hill. 'If you want to struggle. I was just trying to be nice.'

'Wait.' The postman began rummaging around his satchel again, pulling out a handful of envelopes. 'Here you go.'

Rosie took them with glee and gave him another of her smiles. 'See you tomorrow.'

The postman blushed as he began cycling away again.

'Thank you!' Rosie called and watched as he disappeared back down the road. She then tightened her clutch of the letters and began running up the lane.

Fortunately for her, Beacon's farmyard was empty as she reached her home. As it was the height of the summer, all of the help were out in the fields, including her father and sister. Rosie walked into one of the barns and, clamping the letters between her white teeth, climbed up the ladder and onto the loft. There she made her way through the loose hay to the pitching door, where a stream of scorching sun was shining through. Making herself comfortable in the warm light, Rosie began sifting through the letters. Most of them were for her father and a couple for her mother. There was one for Inez, but finally she reached it; the letter that she had spent days waiting for.

His handwriting really was dreadful, and Rosie often wondered how his letters even reached her. But that messy scrawl across the envelope was just another reason why she loved him.

Rosie turned the letter over to discover it had been sealed with a kiss and smiled to herself as she opened the envelope, careful not to rip his kisses.

Then she removed the pages and began to read. And while she read, Rosie was content.

As long as she kept reading his words, he would still be with her.

Autumn

It had always been her favourite time of the year, when things began to quieten down after a season of heat and hysteria. Her family were always on a high after a bountiful summer and they could now begin looking forward to Christmas. Inez loved every season, but autumn held a special place in her heart. She and Charlie would walk for miles on crisp afternoons when the weather was just beginning to turn. One of her favourite things was how everything changed. What, a few weeks ago, had been lush green, was now full of browns and golds and oranges and as she walked through the village Inez wished with every bone that Charlie could see the trees alongside her. Despite enjoying change, for Inez, these past few years had changed too much. Rarely a minute went by that she did not miss Charlie and she had re-read his letters so much that she was certain that she could quote them word for word. When Charlie returned, things would change once again – but this time for the better. They had been nineteen when he first left to fight, barely more than children. But now she felt older, wiser even, and when Charlie finally returned, Inez believed that she would be ready. Ready to grow up and begin her own new life. She and Charlie had barely been blossom when he left, but now she was ready for her life to turn brown and orange with him.

Inez came this way every day on her walk home from her work. It had been his final request before going to fight. Charlie did not want his grandmother to be lonely. Inez reached Myrtle House and began to walk up the path. The garden had always been Mrs Howard's pride and joy, and even now it was beautiful, with the orange leaves scattering the path and lawn. The thick trees had begun to shed their leaves and their spindly branches looked like arms beckoning to her in the breeze. She liked to imagine it was the Howards welcoming her into the family, for Inez had always suspected that they would. She had known Charlie since childhood and Mrs Howard had made no secret of her joy over their friendship. As they grew older and Inez would visit for tea, Charlie's grandmother could never resist dropping hints about the future and great-grandchildren. It had embarrassed her at first, and even embarrassed her at nineteen. But now it did not.

As she made her way up the path, Inez plunged her hand into her coat pocket. It was a mustard-yellow one – a birthday present from her parents one year – and she had been meaning to buy a new one. She rummaged around in her pocket for a moment before feeling her heart rising to her throat as her fingers stumbled across a hole. The hole had been there for a while, but never as big as this. Then the panic began to set in as she realised that it was gone. Inez turned on her heels and began scanning the path. She knew that she had it when she came into the village, so it could not have fallen out too far away. She pushed her thick hair back and began retracing her steps.

Finally her eyes fell upon it, sitting at the bottom of the gatepost. Inez realised that she must have caught her coat on the gate as she came through and crouched down to retrieve the key. As she did, however, something else caught her eye.

It was only because it was so unusual to see. A glint of pinkish white amongst the brown leaves.

A piece of fallen blossom.

Winter

It was always so cold. *He* was always so cold. Even in the summer he was cold, so as Fred lay in the freezing silence, he knew that sleep would be an impossibility. They had found the house late in the afternoon and decided to use it as a pit stop for the night. They had been walking for what felt like weeks with their packs and weapons and all Fred wanted was his own bed back at Beacon Farm – a world away from this abandoned house somewhere in France. The only comforting thing about this situation was knowing that Jimmy was barely a foot away from him. They had been through everything together in life, and this was no different.

'What's the time?' he heard his old friend whisper and frowned. He was too exhausted to know where they were let alone what time it was.

'I don't know.'

'Half past one,' came another voice as Edward rolled over to face them.

'You know what day it is then, don't you?' Jimmy asked. When neither of the boys answered, he said, 'Christmas Day.'

'Is it?' Fred pulled his thin blanket further around himself as he shuddered.

'Yeah.'

Fred closed his eyes and tried to sleep, but all that he could see were his family.

Christmas was always a big occasion at the farm with his father slaughtering the biggest bird that he could find out of the flock. Then his mother cooked it. If Fred had to say what he missed the most, he would say his mother's cooking in a heartbeat. The turkey, so succulent that it practically danced its way into your mouth; the light glowing through the crisp shell of the potatoes as you cracked through it and into the cloud-like centre. She even made the sprouts edible. Fred's tortured stomach began to growl as Jimmy laughed. 'I know what you're thinking about, your mother's roast!'

Fred forced a laugh out as he fought his tears back, 'How d'you guess?'

'Ever had one of Mrs Tregidden's roasts, Ed?' Jimmy asked.

'Don't think so.'

'When we all get home, I'm sure she'll make one for us.' Fred thought back to all the hours as a child that he would sit at the table and watch his mother working her magic at the stove.

'With gravy?'

'Course.'

'And all the trimmings?'

'The lot!'

'What about you, Ed?' Jimmy asked, 'What would your lot be doing today?'

Edward's reply was more of a grunt. 'Goin' church, then Mother's overboiled roast, then back to church in the evening.'

'Jesus,' Fred laughed, 'Come to mine anytime!'

'What about you, Jim?' Edward asked.

'D'you really need to ask?'

The three fell into silence.

'He'll be on his own today.'

'D'you reckon he'll spend all day in the Lion?' Fred asked.

'Nah, they'll kick him out.' Jimmy then said, 'I'd rather be here!'

'Here?'

'Yeah,' Jimmy said, 'At least I'm with my family here.'

He reached out into the darkness and placed a hand on both Fred and Edward, patting them. 'I love you boys, I really do. Merry Christmas.'

'Merry Christmas, Jim.'

'Merry Christmas.' Fred rolled over and tried his hardest to slip into sleep, but yet found it even more impossible than before. The images of his parents and sisters and grandfather all opening their gifts and then sitting down to dinner flashed through his mind in a continuous cycle. Fred worried that he would never see them again, let alone celebrate another Christmas with them. He could not relate to Jimmy in the slightest. He would rather be anywhere in the world than here. But nowhere more than back at home on Beacon Farm.

Beacon Farm

1945

Chapter 1

Today was going to be a good day, George could feel it. From the moment he had woken up and opened the curtains, gazing out at the bright dawn sky, he knew today was going to be a special one. Fred was coming home.

Helen got up not long after her husband and went straight into the kitchen. She had so much to do, a lot to prepare for. The cake needed icing and his bed still needed making. She felt a tingle of excitement run through her veins as she set about her tasks and did not mind one bit at doing her daily chores, for she knew what the afternoon would bring. Her son. Fred was coming home.

George spent all morning out in the fields; the cabbages were coming along nicely, yet he thought he would give it another week before doing something about it. After years of uncertainty and panic, things finally appeared to be looking up. The war was in its final days, that's what Mr Churchill had promised them. And George was sure they were certain, why else would Fred be allowed to come home – apparently for good this time as well!

This time tomorrow things were going to be back to normal. He would have his family around him, all of his children under one roof. Fred and the other village boys would all be back in the fields, helping to provide the locals with their produce. George could not wait to hear them all laughing and shouting to each other across the muddy banks, all winding each other up with their jokes and comments that went over his aging head. When they were here George felt young, he felt like one of them, like he could do anything. This war had aged him. It was not like the other one three decades ago; he had been forced to watch it unfold from the farm. He was not fighting, but instead watching his son. He was so proud, more proud than he had ever been before, though never more scared either. This war had been longer as well. Six years. Six years of struggle and worry. The entire world had changed, and there would be no going back to the way it had been before.

Even the village had changed for good. Families had been destroyed and people that George had seen growing up, he would never see again. He tried to push these invading thoughts from his mind to focus on the positive. He had not lost anything, or anyone. His girls were up the house, while his son was on his way back home.

What more could a man ask for?

Chapter 2

'What time's he getting here?' Carolyn carried the basket of freshly collected eggs into the farmhouse kitchen.

'His train gets in at two.' Her mother smiled contently to herself.

''Spect he'll be tired.' Carolyn placed the basket down and began distributing the eggs into boxes of twelve. 'I'll go and see if Da needs a hand in the field when I've finished here.'

'Oh, don't worry 'bout that, sweetheart,' Helen said. 'Why don't you help me with the food? Rosie's already offered to decorate the cake for me, she always makes them look so pretty. But I still need to peel all the potatoes for the pasties, you can do that if you like?'

Carolyn fought her instinct to turn her nose. 'No thanks, I think I'll go and help Da. The girl's ain't coming up today, so he'll be there all alone.'

Helen closed her eyes, not wanting to be the one to break the news; she knew how Carolyn would take it. 'Actually, I think your father wanted to talk to you about that—' she began, but was unable to finish, for at that moment a crash sounded against the doorframe.

'Grandad!' Carolyn ran to the kitchen door. Frank Tregid-

4

den stood wobbling in the doorway, gathering himself before taking another step. His coarse fingers clung to the wooden doorframe as he held himself up. Carolyn took her grandfather's arm and led him slowly into the kitchen.

'Where's your stick?'

'Don't need no bleddy stick!'

Helen pulled a chair out from under the table and Frank collapsed into it. 'Stop fussing!' he snapped, swatting Carolyn away.

'Frank, you need to be careful,' Helen said. 'We don't want you falling down the stairs again.'

'This is my farm!' Frank hit the table with his palm, 'I should be out in the fields working! Not sitting in the kitchen surrounded by…' He looked around at the ingredients covering the table.

'Wha's all this anyway?'

'Food for the party,' Helen said.

Frank dropped his head wearily into his hand. 'We ain't having a party, are we? What for?'

'Cos Fred's coming home,' Carolyn said, 'We told you that yesterday.'

Frank's head suddenly shot up again as he stared at the two women. His blue eyes were wide and now sparkled with life.

'Frederick?' His voice was a hoarse rumble.

'Yes.' Helen smiled at her father-in-law.

'Little Freddie's coming home?"

Frank found that he had no choice but to repeat the news in as many different ways as possible, otherwise he could not quite convince himself to believe it. The old man snorted and pressed his head into his hands again.

Carolyn gave her mother a sympathetic smile and planted a

kiss on her grandfather's bald head.

'Is ev'rything alright?'

They looked up to see Inez walking in from the yard.

'Grandad, are you OK?' Inez asked, noticing his swollen red eyes.

'I ain't crying!' Frank said loudly.

'I never said you were…' Inez glanced around the kitchen and began to laugh. 'I'm guessing all of this is about Fred?'

Helen had been saving up most of her rations just for today. 'We're so excited about Freddie returning.' Helen beamed.

'So am I! But just remember that he ain't been on holiday, he's been fighting in a war. He'll prob'ly be quite tired and, you know, not himself.'

'Ev'rything'll be back to normal.' Frank sat back in his chair and smiled triumphantly. 'All four'a my grandchildren back under one roof, Fred helping your father and me out in the field. Bliss!'

'Grandad, you can't work in the fields, I keep telling you.' Carolyn was growing tired of her grandfather's denial. 'But I'll be helping out there as much as I can, of course.'

'We got Fred now.' Frank smiled to himself, 'Freddie's coming home.'

Chapter 3

T he journey had been a long and tiring one and Fred began to wonder if this was all in fact a dream. He did not allow himself to believe it. Not when he stepped off the train and saw his father's beaming smile amongst the crowds of people, not even when he sat in the front of the old Land Rover, his head bumping repetitively against the window as they drove along the uneven village roads. George had been telling him all of the news from the farm, although Fred barely took any of it in. He was home and apparently for good this time.

'You must be tired,' he finally heard George say.

'No.' He shifted in his seat, straightening his back.

'No, I'm fine.'

'There's no shame in it, Son.' George said, 'You been fightin' for King and Country, there's no shame in bein' a little tired at all. I remember it took it out of me as well.'

'I just can't believe I'm home.' Fred looked out of the window at the map of fields and woodlands around them. He knew each of them like the back of his hand. To him they were the patches of his childhood blanket. The blanket that had been torn from him six years ago, when he had been forced to face reality. Forced to grow up. ''Specially since some of the others ain't.'

He felt his father's eyes as George glanced at him before saying, 'Don't go thinkin' about that now. Just be relieved that you're back here.'

Fred nodded. 'I am. Of course I am.'

As they pulled into the farmyard, Fred felt his breath catch in the back of his throat. Everything was exactly the same as when he first left. The pothole-filled ground, dusty with a layer of mud that had dried over the summer; the barns filled with equipment and freshly baled hay.

'It looks no different,' Fred found himself saying as he climbed from the car.

'Your sisters have all been a huge help – and some of the other girls from the village.'

'I bet Carrie loved it.' Fred smiled. When they were children, all he and Carolyn wanted to do was follow George, Frank and whoever else happened to be working on the farm around, copying everything they did.

'Oh, she did. Couldn't get her off the back of that tractor.'

At the sound of a very familiar bark, Fred felt his breath catch again. Seemingly from nowhere, an old sheepdog appeared; his fur was greying and tufty, but he moved like a puppy as he scampered across the yard, pawing at Fred's legs and licking his hands.

'Hello, boy!' Fred began ruffling the dog's fur, 'Hello, Jessop!'

'Jessop!' At George's sharp voice, Jessop stepped back and stared at his owner, waiting for his next command.

'Freddie!' The shrill voice startled Fred, who looked up to see a blur of blonde hair hurtling towards him as Rosie leapt into his arms.

'Here she is!' Fred laughed and spun his younger sister

around. 'You've grown!'

'Do you think so?' Rosie linked her arm through his as they walked towards the house, leaving their father to get his bag. 'Carolyn still towers above both Inez and me. How are the others? Are Jimmy and Edward home as well?'

'Yeah, we dropped them home on the way here.'

'Oh, are they coming up here later?'

'I shouldn't think so,' Fred said as he opened the kitchen door.

He was immediately met with a blast of noise when three voices all yelled, 'Freddie!'

For a moment everything went black and Fred struggled to breathe, although the sight of the kitchen flooded him with a warm glow. He was home. His mother and sisters rushed to him and smothered him with hugs and kisses.

'Oh, my darling!' Helen gasped over and over, sobbing and tightening her grip on Fred by the second.

'Careful, Mum.' Fred laughed. 'I got away with no injuries in the war, you don't want me suffering a broken spine the moment I set foot home.'

'I'm sorry, but I'm never letting you go again!'

'Nor are we!' Inez was the next to engulf him in a hug. Hers was softer, yet just as embracing. It had the same comforting warmth that Fred had always been used to. Yet there was a quality to his sister that appeared to be missing. Her joy. Fred was not surprised, however, given the last few years…

'I've missed you, my little brother!' she whispered into his brown hair.

'Don't forget about me!' Carolyn was as tall as Fred, maybe even taller, with long willowy arms that she folded around him, trailing a line of hard kisses along his forehead. Once the fuss was over and he had finally been released, Fred was unsure of what to say. It was as though his ability to speak had vanished, and all he could think about was his breathing. In and out, in and out. He rammed his hands inside his trouser pockets, not wanting his family to see the tremors. He had to pull himself together; he was home now and with his family.

'What about Grandad?' he finally found he was able to ask.

'I'll go and get him!' Carolyn ran from the room, back into the long, narrow farmhouse.

Fred glanced around, giving each of his family member's a beaming smile.

'Take a seat!' Helen finally said, 'And when your Grandad comes down we'll cut the cake!'

'The cake?' Fred collapsed into a chair at the table – *his* chair at the table.

'Yes!' Helen scurried from the room.

'I tried to make her promise that there wouldn't be a huge fuss,' Inez said quietly, sitting down beside him, 'But you know what Mum's like, she loves a party at the best of times, 'specially when she finally has us all back together.'

'A party?' Fred was so tired.

'Yes!' Rosie took the seat on his other side. 'We've made you a cake and even managed to find some of that beer you love. You know, the one that you drink at the summer festival?'

'I'm looking forward to it,' Fred said, feeling Inez's hand squeeze his arm.

'We got more than we needed,' Rosie continued. 'We thought some of the boys might be coming up.'

'Rosie, why don't you see where Da's got to?' Inez suggested.

Rosie stood up and rolled her eyes. 'I'm just excited to have Fred back!'

10

'I know you are.' Fred gave her a smile, 'I'm so happy to be back, Rose.'

'Taa-daa!' Helen came walking in, carrying her best china tray. On it sat the biggest Victoria sponge that Fred had ever seen. 'Saved up all my rations to make this, I did!' she grinned proudly.

'Thanks, Mum.' Fred's cheeks were getting sore from all this smiling, 'You didn't have to go to all this trouble!'

'Nothing's trouble if it means my little's boy's home.' Helen placed her hand on Fred's cheek and kissed his head. 'Where have you been?' she suddenly asked as George came walking in.

'Sorry, I was just checking on Delilah,' George said. 'Reckon she's gonna give birth any time now.' He added, for Fred's benefit, 'It'll be all hands on deck then. Thank god you're home, boy!'

'You said that Carolyn's been a good help, didn't you—'

'Where is 'e? Where is 'e?' Frank Tregidden was getting old. His spine was curving and his limbs did things that he did not intend for them to do. He found that he could no longer walk as fast as he wanted to and could not pick things up that he had been able to before. He blinked rapidly, scouring the faces of his family until he saw him. Fred. What a sight he was after all this time, sitting at the dining room table. It was as though nothing had happened at all.

'He's here, Grandad,' Inez said.

As Fred crossed the room, his grandfather lurched forward, sending a chair crashing to the ground. The sound pierced Fred's ears and he drew back, a cold sweat running down his face and spine. The tremors had returned in his hands and he could no longer breathe.

11

'Freddie?' His mother's voice was lost in the abyss that was his mind. 'Freddie?'

He turned to her.

'Are you alright?' Carolyn asked her brother, having helped Frank to regain his balance. 'Fred?' she repeated, 'You don't look very well.'

Fred forced that automatic smile. 'Yeah. Yeah, I'm just a bit tired that's all.'

'Course you are.' George said, 'Tell you what, I'll give you a few days off to catch up on your sleep, then it's back to real hard work in the fields!' He started to laugh, and Fred joined in, though he was not really sure why.

Chapter 4

Henrietta Howard had lived what some might call a rather tragic life, for the old woman's adulthood had been almost entirely defined by death. First was her husband James at a horrendously young age. It happened not long after they had moved to the village with their two young sons, when James had started his new job as a teacher at the village school. One night he never came home and in the morning Henrietta learnt the tragic news that James had fallen into the river and drowned, having tried to save a dog from the bank.

The worst thing that Henrietta had ever endured was sitting down to explain to Richard and Michael why their daddy would not be coming home. Together the three of them had survived the tragedy and Richard and Michael had grown into decent human beings. Richard had been the brains of the family, while Michael bore such a vibrant personality that you could not help but sob with laughter at almost anything he said. At the age of eighteen, Richard moved away to London to train to be a lawyer, something which Henrietta could not help but boast about to anyone who would listen. Little did she know that her pride in Richard would only set in motion another tragedy.

Michael grew jealous of the attention his brother got from their mother as he worked as a farmhand on Frank Tregidden's farm. He and his good friend George often exchanged complaints about their brothers, both of whom had run away and left them to take care of their families. During this time the fury in Michael grew until, during one of Richard's annual visits, he finally exploded. Henrietta was never sure why, but that fateful summer had seen her sons fall out, never to speak again. Richard rarely returned, while Michael refused to speak his name, not when either of them married, nor when they began families of their own.

Henrietta had been over the moon when Michael's wife Olive gave birth to a son, little baby Charlie. She had one other grandson, but, due to Richard refusing to come back home, she rarely got the chance to see him. So having little Charlie living at home with her every day was a dream come true.

Richard did return once, but only out of duty. During that very dark time when poor Charlie was made an orphan. Michael and Olive had been out for the day, leaving Charlie in the care of Henrietta. Though like James all those years ago, Michael and Olive never came home. A larger vehicle, a tractor, had collided with their small car head on. The doctors said that it had been quick; that neither of them would have known a thing.

So there it was, Henrietta and Charlie, alone in Myrtle House. They were devoted to one another, even as Charlie grew up, just he and Granny, and Inez Tregidden on occasion.

Henrietta liked Inez, she was a sweet girl and had been a real help recently since her latest tragedy occurred, a tragedy that so many other people around the world had suffered. The sight of the postman walking up the path, a telegram in his hand, still plagued Henrietta day and night.

Charlie's ship had been sunk. And, just like that, with that one piece of paper, Henrietta's heart shattered once again. Charlie James Howard, her lovely grandson, the boy who had inherited his father's cheeky tongue, the boy who had worked hard at Beacon Farm, the boy she had hoped might marry Inez Tregidden, was dead.

Despite her delight at having Fred home, Inez could not help but feel a little relieved to find an excuse to finally slip away from their often chaotic house. The walk through the village was a quiet and peaceful one, its narrow streets warmly lit by the late afternoon sun. With no sound other than the leaves and river – and the occasional seagull cry, it was the perfect time for Inez to think. This war had ruined people's lives, as had the last one. Charlie, the boy that she cared for so much, was gone. She visited Mrs Howard once a day; at first at Charlie's request when he went to sea, but now for no reason other than the fact that she enjoyed it. Mrs Howard was good company. Despite everything that she had been through in her life, she still had spark. She could take a joke and no one in the village would dare boss her around. That is why it pained Inez so much to think about her sitting alone in Myrtle House. It was one of the biggest houses in the village, and with no one to share it with, Inez could imagine it feeling isolated and cold.

The lawn of Myrtle House's small boxed garden was always very neatly cut. Charlie always did it, but he had shown Inez how to just before he left. There were lots of things that he had done in that last week he spent at home, almost as if he knew that he was not going to return. He fixed the leaking roof in the spare bedroom and took his granny into the town for dinner a few times. On his final night in the village he took Inez to the pictures. The film was not particularly memorable to Inez, but then maybe that was because she was too focused on what Charlie had whispered into her ear halfway through the film. Those words that every person wishes to hear at least once in their life – and, unfortunately for Inez and Charlie, those words would only be uttered between them that once. On the way home, as they reached Beacon Lane, Charlie had tugged Inez back lightly by the hand and combed back her dark-blonde hair from her face.

'Will you do something for me?'

Inez said she would.

'Take care of Granny, please.' And, with a grin, he added, 'She loves you.'

'And I love her.' Inez had smiled. Charlie had then taken Inez's hand and slipped something onto her palm. A key.

Inez used this key now, as she let herself into Myrtle House. 'It's just me, Mrs Howard.' She hung her old coat up on the peg inside the door.

'Hello, love,' the old lady called from the living room, 'I've just put the kettle on for us both.'

Inez stood in the doorway and smiled. Mrs Howard was sitting in her favourite floral armchair as she leafed her way through a romantic novel.

'How did you know I'd be coming?'

'I always know you'll be down,' Mrs Howard said, 'That should have boiled by now…' She shifted in the chair, trying to heave herself up, but Inez was already back out in the hall.

'Don't worry, I'll get it.' And she disappeared into the kitchen.

The two women sat chatting for a long time; their conversation usually centred around the goings-on of village life, each tentatively dancing around the subject that neither wanted to discuss. It was hard for Inez to think about Charlie, so she could scarcely imagine what it must be like for Mrs Howard.

'How's your grandad?' This was always one of the old woman's favourite questions.

'He's fine,' Inez replied with a coy smile. Her grandfather had always had a soft spot for Mrs Howard.

'Frank Tregidden.' Mrs Howard sat back in her armchair. 'He was a dishy man when I first met him.'

This was another of her favourite lines. 'He always thought something was going to happen between us after my James passed over, and I used to say to him, "What about your Lizzie?" and he used to laugh and say, "What Lizzie don't know won't hurt her" and then he'd give me that wink of his!'

Inez felt rather uncomfortable at this; she had always thought her grandparents had loved each other dearly.

'Course he never meant it.' Mrs Howard sipped her tea and Inez relaxed. 'But I mightn't have said no if it werent for me having the boys here.'

Inez spluttered as Mrs Howard chuckled to herself, lost in the good old days.

'And what about your brother?' she finally asked, and Inez felt her back straighten. She had not wanted to raise the subject of him. Not today.

'Little Fred? He was always such a sweet boy when you were all growing up. Did he make it home safely today?'

Inez watched her carefully, before giving her a small nod. 'He's up at the house now.'

'Then what are you doing here with me?' Mrs Howard cried, throwing her spindly hands in the air, 'You should be with him, celebrating his safe return!'

'I know…' Inez began. 'But I thought I'd come and see you. You know, like we always do.'

Mrs Howard scoffed. 'I'm sure you'd much rather be doing a lot of stuff than watching an old lady spilling tea down her cardy.'

'That's not true,' Inez insisted. 'I enjoy our chats, I really do.'

'Because when you're here you think of him?' Mrs Howard asked. 'Our Charlie – because he was *ours*, you know, mine and yours.'

Inez felt her throat growing thick and focused on the dregs of tea at the bottom of her china cup propped carefully in the lap of her skirt.

'I know that he told you to come here and look after me,' Mrs Howard said. 'But I promise you, my dear, I'm fine.' She placed her cup on the coffee table and reached her shaky hands out, clasping them around Inez's own soft ones. 'Look at me, sweet'eart,' she said and Inez glanced into her pale, bloodshot eyes. 'Charlie loved us both very much. *Very* much. But he ent here anymore.'

Inez clenched her jaw; she never allowed herself to cry in front of anyone and was not going to start now. 'But your brother *is*. And so many other young men are. Don't be sad because Charlie isn't here, be happy that they are.'

Inez inhaled, steadying her breathing, and nodded.

'Good girl.' Mrs Howard sat back in her armchair with a proud smile on her lined face. 'Now, you go home and celebrate the fact that you still have a brother. What's your mother doing for tea?'

Inez laughed. 'Pasties.'

Mrs Howard closed her eyes and licked her lips.

'Mmm… I do like a pasty.'

Chapter 5

U p at the farm, Fred was trying his hardest to follow the frantic conversations of his family. He had been away for so long, he had forgotten how loud they could be, all of them talking at once and changing the subject halfway through sentences. He had never realised how exhausting this was before, in fact he had never realised how exhausting any of this was before. While he was away all that he wanted was to be back here on the farm surrounded by the people that he loved the most. And while he was definitely relieved to be home, he could not help but feel strange, anxious even at the sound of the Tregiddens' constant noise. Life had gone on whilst he had been away and now he had to slot back in as seamlessly as possible.

'Alright there, boy?' He heard his father ask and looked up to see George watching him from across the kitchen. 'Looking like you might nod off there.'

Fred forced a smile; this could be his excuse to escape, for he had not had a moment alone for as long as he could remember. He just wanted silence.

'It's been a really long…' He was going to say 'day', but it had been longer. The longest years of his life. Even his visits home had always seemed manic, seeing as many people as he was possibly able to, taking Madge Pascoe to dances, and then being whisked away again to wherever else in the world he was needed. But now things seemed slower. He had been promised that this would be it, he would never have to leave again. He had all the time in the world to listen to his family, but for now all he wanted was to be by himself. 'I think I need a sleep before tea if that's alright?'

'Course,' Helen said.

As Fred crossed the room, his grandfather took his hand and gave it a weak squeeze. He seemed a lot older than when he had last been here. Fred smiled slightly and squeezed back before leaving the room, longing for nothing more than bed.

'You know, I think I'm a bit tired m'self.' Frank let out a long yawn as he tried to finish his sentence.

'Go to bed then, you lazy tuss,' George said. Frank grumbled something in reply as he hauled himself from his chair.

'I've got you, Grandad.' Carolyn hastily stood up after him.

'I'm fine!' Frank insisted.

'I'll just help you up the stairs then.'

'Rose, give your grandad a hand, will you?' said George. 'I need to speak to Carrie about something.'

Rosie obediently put the hat that she had been mending down, and headed towards Frank. Placing one hand on the old man's back and the other on his elbow, she slowly led him out of the kitchen. George waited until their voices drifted upstairs, with Frank fiercely insisting that he could walk alone while Rosie calmly agreed, guiding him along.

'Is ev'rything alright?' Carolyn leant against the wall and inspected her father carefully. He had the look on his face that he always bore when about to deliver bad news.

'Yeah, there's just a few things I thought I should discuss

with you.'

Carolyn waited for him to continue, though she knew what it was that he was going to say.

'I just thought I'd say thanks,' her father said. 'For ev'rything you've done to help during all this.'

Carolyn nodded. She had loved every single second of it.

'You've kept things going so well. So when the boys all start again we'll be able to take over perfectly.'

This was the moment that Carolyn had been dreading – yet expecting. She decided to play ignorant, just to see how far she could take things.

'What d'you mean?'

'Well.' George rubbed the back of his sunburnt neck as he sighed. 'You know, the boys are back now and I can't really afford to keep all of you on at once.'

'You want me to give up my job?' Carolyn stared in disgust at her father across the kitchen.

'It won't just be you, I'm gonna have to let Madge and Kerenza go as well. In fact, all the girls.'

'Why?' Carolyn snapped.

''Cos Fred and the others are back now. I can't afford to keep you all on.'

'I understand that,' Carolyn said. 'But *I'm* your daughter.'

'I know it's hard for you to understand, after ev'rything that you've done for the past few years—'

'You make it sound like I've been on holiday or taken up a new hobby. I've been working for *you*, and working bleddy hard as well, to keep your farm running.'

'And, like I said, I appreciate ev'rything that you've done,' George explained. 'But Fred's back now.'

'You can see what he's like, he's a nervous wreck. There's

22

no way he can go back to work, not yet anyway. Why can't I carry on?'

'Because…' George began and let out a long sigh. 'At the end of the day, it's men's work, ent it?' He watched as a wave of fury passed over his daughter. Carolyn was always the most fiery of his children, never letting go of things easily. She had been a great deal of help during the war, but, now that it was over, things had to go back to normal.

'But I've been doing it.' Carolyn would not give up so easily. 'I've been doing ev'rything that Fred did before the war. I weren't allowed to fight for my country, so I stepped in here. Inez and Rosie helped out in their own ways, but my thing was *this*! Da, I don't think you understand what these past few years have meant to me. And now you want to put me back in the kitchen with my knitting? For Christ's sake!'

'I'm sorry if you feel that way, Carrie.' George stood up with a sigh. 'But it were Fred's job first, so it has to go back to him.'

He picked up Carolyn's cup from the table. It was still full of stone-cold tea. She refused to look at him, still staring straight ahead at the granite wall, seething at this bombshell. Why should she have to give everything up just because the men had come home? This was not fair, on her or Fred.

Meanwhile, upstairs, Fred lay in his bed trying his hardest to sleep. From the room next door he heard banging through the walls as Rosie tried to help a clumsy Frank into bed. Every bump and bang echoed in Fred's head. He was not in bed, he was in the middle of a war zone. No. He was not. He was safe. He was lying in his bed at Beacon Farm.

Chapter 6

Rosie Tregidden was as relieved as anyone that the war was over. She had only been young, twelve years old, when the war was first announced and remembered that moment vividly. They had all been gathered in the kitchen, hunched round the wireless. She had not been quite sure what the voice on the radio was talking about, but knew it had to be serious. Her grandad had his head in his hands as the voice droned on, while her father hugged Inez and Carolyn close. All of the colour had drained from Fred's face – clearly he knew what was in store for him. It was only when her mother started crying that Rosie knew things were seriously bad. She had only ever seen Helen cry once, when George's mother Lizzie had passed away. But that was so long ago.

It was strange now that, six years later, things were starting to get back to normal. Rosie walked through the farmyard seeing all of the young men back working hard, as if nothing had happened at all. It had only been a week since they had all returned and it was still not a sight she was used to.

'Mornin', Rosie,' one of them called, nodding to her from up on the barn roof.

Carolyn had spent the past week refusing to speak to

anyone, and Rosie could see why. Until now it had been her sister doing this; mending roofs and ploughing fields. She had never seen Carolyn so alive and happy, despite everything else going on in the world.

Rosie smoothed down her new mint-green dress as she casually looked around the farm, trying her hardest to find him. He had to be here; her father had said that all of the boys would be back to work on the farm today, yet Rosie was unable to find him. She had made a special effort; today was the day that the war finally ended for her. The day that everything she wanted returned.

Finally giving up, Rosie began making her way back to the house, passing the empty barns on the way.

'Pssssst!'

The sharp hiss made her jump and she looked around.

'Psssssst!' This time she realised where it was coming from and, suppressing her smile, entered one of the barns.

It had once been used to store the tractors, but was now used for the hay. Rosie stepped inside and looked around, spotting him almost immediately. There he was, amongst the hay bales and old rusting parts of machinery. Her boy.

She did not remember crossing the barn, but found herself entangled in his arms, her face buried in his chest and taking in the scent that she had craved to smell again for what had felt like for ever. As Jimmy released her, she looked up and gazed at him, taking in every inch of the him; his light-brown hair swept back out of the way and his bright-green eyes staring into hers. The two did not say anything for a long time; there was no need to, for their looks and embraces of one another said it all. Then Jimmy kissed her and Rosie felt complete. She had him back, and for good this time.

It had been hard, seeing him fleetingly every now and again, stealing kisses at the back of dances and watching him from afar as he boarded the train with her brother again. But that was all over. Jimmy had returned.

'You've no idea how much I've missed you!' She was finally able to release the breath that she had been holding onto since Jimmy first went away.

'I think I do.' Jimmy brushed her golden-blonde hair back over her shoulders. 'I am never leaving you again.'

'I won't let you.' Rosie linked her fingers between Jimmy's and clenched his hand tightly. She would never let him go if she had it her way. 'Why haven't you been up yet? Fred said that you might've come up for his party?'

'I'm sorry,' Jimmy said. 'My old man wanted me to stay with him. He missed me – 'parently.'

'Well, I've missed you.' Rosie smiled, wrapping her arms around his neck. 'I have *so* much!'

'We've got all the time in the world now.' Jimmy beamed at her. 'Things are going to change.'

Rosie glanced away from him, her hand playing with the sleeve of his shirt.

'Your parents don't know about us, do they?' Jimmy asked.

Rosie shook her head. 'Maybe they'll be OK with us now?' she suggested. 'You fought alongside Fred. You served King and Country.'

Jimmy looked at her doubtfully. 'Fred's one of my best friends and your father's my boss… I can't see them accepting it somehow. 'Specially with what my old man's like.'

'But like you said…' Rosie reached up and gave Jimmy a light kiss. 'Things are going to change now.'

Rosie had known Jimmy Worthing her entire life, first as a school friend of Fred's and then, when he got older, as a farmhand working for her father. The Tregiddens and the Worthings were both ancient families who had lived in the village for generations, although over the years the two families had drifted apart – particularly when Jimmy's father, Samuel-the-drunk (as he was known in the village), committed his terrible deed. Although that was all long before the birth of Jimmy or Rosie and her siblings, and the Tregiddens did not hold Jimmy responsible for his father's actions.

Jimmy, in turn, was very grateful for the kindness that they had shown him over the years, having him around for tea and giving him Fred's hand-me-downs, for as children Fred had been plump and rosy, while Jimmy grew up always hearing the term 'bag of bones' associated with him. It had only been natural for Jimmy to begin working on the farm alongside Fred when they finished school, for he had always been treated as though he were their fifth child. Jimmy had a distinct memory from school. He could not have been more than eight years old when he saw a list of names on the headmaster's desk one lunchtime, having been called in for fighting. As he read down through them he saw the names of his favourite family, in alphabetical order, just below the Roskelleys:

Carolyn Tregidden
Frederick Tregidden
Inez Tregidden
Rosenwyn Tregidden

And then at the bottom of the list all alone:

James Worthing

How he had longed to be up there with them, to be part of a happy family with siblings and a father that was not drunk from dawn till dusk. But alas, he was not and he and Rosie often worried about what her family might have to say if they found that their youngest daughter was getting herself involved with a Worthing. They treated Jimmy well, but would they want a Worthing as part of their family? Or, more to the point, would they want their daughter becoming a Worthing? Jimmy doubted it highly.

He had not always loved Rosie; until a couple of years ago he had not seen her as being anything more than Fred's little sister. But then he came back from war on a visit and saw her at a dance. She had been abandoned by her date and left humiliated on the dance floor, so Jimmy offered to stand in. During that dance things changed and the two seemed to connect. For she was no longer Fred's younger sister, but Rosie Tregidden, the most beautiful girl he had ever seen. He thought about this dance as he went back to work in the field; since then nothing had changed. Rosie Tregidden was still the most beautiful girl he had ever seen.

Chapter 7

Fred wanted to help. He wanted to be better. The war was over and he was no longer in any danger, so why was he finding it so hard to get back to work? His father had put him in the field today helping to harvest the potatoes. The constant rumbling and spluttering of the tractor engine was setting Fred's teeth on edge and he was unable to concentrate. The other lads were all working hard, chatting and laughing; why were they finding it so easy when he was not? Fred could feel himself shaking again, the same way he had done his first evening back and hastily rammed his hands into the pockets of his overalls. As he made his way across the field, Jimmy caught sight of him from over by the hedge and called him over. Fred wanted to run, but decided against it. Maybe if he fought against his instincts then he might be all right after all. As he reached Jimmy, his friend held out a pack of cigarettes.

'No thanks,' Fred said.

Jimmy took a long drag on his cigarette as he leant back against a tree stump protruding from the hedge.

'It's strange, ent it? Being back here in the fields like nothing's happened.'

Fred nodded.

'You alright, Freddie? Barely heard two words from you since we came back.'

'Course.' Fred nodded vigorously. 'Just – like you said, ent it strange being back.'

The two remained in silence until another voice sounded beside them. 'Alright?'

They glanced to their side to find Edward Pascoe standing there.

'Yeah, you?' Fred asked.

Edward glanced at Jimmy, who had not replied. 'Alright, Jim?'

Jimmy merely nodded.

'Either of you got a spare smoke? I'm gasping?'

'Jim does.' Fred said and Jimmy scowled at him. He pulled the carton out of his pocket again and held it out to Edward, who took one graciously.

Edward began patting himself down and added. 'You ain't got a light, have you?'

Once again Jimmy begrudgingly pulled a box of matches from his pocket and struck one. Edward leant in while Jimmy lit the end of the cigarette. Fred was beginning to feel rather uncomfortable with Jimmy's frosty attitude to Edward. The three had always been close, having grown up together, and Jimmy and Edward had spent the majority of the war together as well.

As Edward stood back up, he inhaled. 'Cheers.' He glanced at them both again. 'Interrupting something, am I?'

'No,' Jimmy replied, a little more sharply than Fred had expected.

Edward seemed to take the hint that he was not wanted and began to walk away, although then stopped and turned back to them. 'Oh, Fred, I think Madge was hoping to see you later today? Reckon she's gonna come up here this evening. Said I'd let you know.'

'Thanks.' Fred had been casually seeing Edward's twin sister Madge on his visits home over the past couple of years, though had been deliberately avoiding her since his return.

Once Edward was out of earshot, he turned to Jimmy.

'What was all that about?'

'Dunno what you mean.' Jimmy flicked his cigarette butt away.

'Course you do.' Fred rolled his eyes. 'Ed only wanted a fag, nothing too strenuous! What's he done for you to be such a tuss to him?'

Jimmy let out an indignant scoff and crossed his arms firmly across his chest. 'I ain't told anyone,' he said, keeping his voice quiet, 'He made me swear not to. But he...You know.'

Fred frowned, he most certainly did not know.

'When we were away. One night, we were alone outside and he tried to...*you know*,'

Jimmy craned his neck to make sure they were alone before leaning into Fred and whispering, 'He tried to kiss me.'

Fred frowned, starting to laugh. 'Ed did?' He looked across to Edward, who had resumed work amongst the crops. 'Are you sure?'

'I think I'd know if someone was throwing themselves at me!' Jimmy insisted.

'What did he say?'

'He told me it were an "accident" and that he werent thinking straight.'

'Makes sense,' Fred said. 'It was a funny old time out there. Don't think any of us really knew what we were doing.' He

31

thought about all the things he had experienced while at war; strange visions and blackouts. None of them were in their right minds at war. 'Besides, Ed don't seem the type, ent he courting Kerenza Roskelley?'

'He was before he tried it on with me anyway,' Jimmy said.

'Why don't you let it go? If he said it were a mistake, I'd believe him.'

Jimmy took this advice on board and nodded.

'Don't lose a mate over a stupid mistake,' Fred said, adding, 'He prob'ly just missed Kerenza and wanted to kiss something.'

'You're right.' Jimmy tossed his second cigarette butt into the hedge and stood up. 'Ed!' he called as he made his way over to him, 'Gimme that spade!'

Fred watched as his friends continued to work and began to feel a little more at ease. At least he was not the only one struggling.

Later that evening, as Fred headed towards the farmhouse, he saw her through the window, sitting at the kitchen table and immediately felt a sense of dread. Madge appeared to be laughing about something with Helen. As Fred reached the door, he took a deep, steady breath to prepare himself.

It was not that he did not like Madge; he had enjoyed her company very much before and during the war, it was just now he felt uneasy whenever he thought about her and the commitment that she was inevitably expecting him to make. How could he be the person that she needed him to be, when he was unsure who he was himself anymore? Since being home there had not been a day that he had felt normal and the last thing that he wanted was to subject Madge to that. Not when she could have the pick of whoever she wanted.

Upon entering the kitchen, Madge turned to him, giving him a beaming smile as her pale face lit up. 'Hello, Fred.'

'Hello, Madge.' Fred forced himself to look at her. She had made an effort, curling the thick black hair that she had tied back neatly and was wearing what looked like a brand-new outfit. Fred felt a pang of guilt. She had made this effort for him.

'Tell you what.' Helen hastily made her way to the door. 'I'll leave you two to it. You've pro'bly got a lot to catch up on.'

Once they were alone, Madge smiled again, while Fred wrung his broad hands together, still standing in the doorway.

'Ain't you gonna sit down?' Madge asked, and Fred obliged, pulling out the chair beside her and sitting down. Madge reached over and clasped one of Fred's hands in her own warm ones.

'You're shaking.'

'It's gone a bit cold out there.'

'You've changed.' Madge studied Fred closely; his face, his eyes. He tensed as she ran her hand over his short brown hair. 'You didn't come to see me,' Madge said, before blushing instantly. 'I just, you know, thought you might…you know – Ed did with Renza.'

'I'm really sorry.' Fred stared at her, unsure what he was going to say next. 'It's been busy here. Da's been trying to get me up to speed with ev'rything Carolyn and the rest of you have been doing while we've been away.'

'And do you reckon it's all up to scratch?' Madge asked with a smile.

'Oh, definitely.' Fred laughed. 'It's like I ain't been away.'

'I'm glad to hear it.' Madge smiled and the two fell into

33

silence again.

'I like your frock,' Fred finally said, nodding to Madge's outfit. It was a pale-purple dress with a matching cardigan. On her breast she had pinned a jewelled brooch in the shape of some heather.

'Thanks,' Madge smoothed it down, blushing again. 'I got it in Polglaze's with Rosie a couple of weeks ago. She got a new frock as well. Thought we'd treat ourselves with you all coming home.'

'Who did Rosie get hers for?' Fred asked, confused. As far as he knew, his sister was not trying to impress any of the local boys – he would know, surely?

'Oh, no one in particular.' Madge gazed out of the window. 'It's still beautiful out there, ent it? Fancy going for a walk?'

'A walk?' Fred repeated. Madge turned to him and smiled again.

'Yeah, a walk. You put one foot in front of the other and see where you end up.' Fred let out a small laugh. He had forgotten how it felt to laugh with Madge.

'Come on then,' he finally said, standing up. 'Let's go.'

Chapter 8

Despite Mrs Howard having told her that she needed to start moving forward with her life, Inez still called on her every afternoon. She enjoyed spending time in her quiet house, a world away from reality, a world in which Charlie could still exist.

As Inez walked up the garden path towards the front door of Myrtle House, she made a mental note to offer to cut back the fuchsia bushes, which were beginning to take over. She reached the door and gave it a courteous knock, before rummaging in her bag for the key. As she searched through the contents of her small blue bag, she heard the door click open. She looked up expecting to see Mrs Howard, although instead of the elderly woman that she had grown to care for, Inez found herself face to face with a man.

He was tall and looked nearer to thirty than twenty.

'Oh?' Inez took a step back in surprise.

'Hello?' the man asked.

'Hello.' Inez was still stunned. This man was a stranger to her and the village. Surely he was not a burglar because burglars did not answer doors when they were knocked.

'Can I help you?' He had strong features, which seemed to grow harsher when he frowned.

'I've come to see Mrs Howard.'

'She's busy.' The man seemed irritated, like Inez was intruding and he was far too busy to speak to her.

'Oh. Well can I see her?'

'Like I said, she's busy.' Who was this man and why would he not let her see Mrs Howard?

'It's just…' Inez would not give up that easily. She had made a promise to Charlie and one that she was not willing to break. 'I come to see her ev'ry afternoon. We have tea.'

'I'm afraid she's having tea with me right now,' the man said. 'I'm her grandson.'

Inez frowned.

'You're a relative of Charlie's, then?' She had not seen him at Charlie's memorial service. In fact, no other Howard was there, only his grandmother.

The man nodded in his brisk way. 'He was my cousin. You knew him?'

'Very well.' Inez finally felt like this conversation might take a turn for the better. 'I'm Inez Tregidden, I live at Beacon Farm…'

'Ralph Howard.' He thrust out a large hand, which Inez took. After a very sharp shake, Ralph released her and stepped back inside. 'I'll tell Granny that you called by.'

And without so much as another word, the door of Myrtle House was closed on Inez. She remained in shock for a moment, utterly bemused by the abruptness of Ralph Howard. She could not understand why she had not heard of him before, nor why he was so much ruder than the kind Mrs Howard and Charlie that she had grown up with. Slowly, she turned on her heels and began walking away. If Ralph Howard was here to stay, then she was going to have to keep her promise in another way.

Fred and Madge had finished their walk and were beginning to make their way back to the house. Fred had finally managed to pluck up the courage and allowed Madge to hold his hand, finding the warmth from her decreased his shaking.

'Are you cold?' Madge asked, concerned. To her the evening air still felt warm.

'No, I…' Fred thought about what else to say and decided to correct himself. 'I am a bit.'

Madge watched him carefully as they strolled along. Every step Fred took seemed to take so much effort. He was tense as he gripped her hand and she could see his jaw working back and forth as he clenched his teeth.

'Fred?' She pulled his hand closer to herself, 'I'm sorry.'

Fred glanced at her and frowned. 'What d'you mean?'

'Ev'rything that you must have seen and been through,' Madge said. 'I'm sorry.'

'It weren't your fault, was it? Anyway, it weren't just me. Hundreds of lads like me went through it. Your brother did.'

Madge nodded. 'I know. And he's struggling more than he's letting on to anyone, I'm sure.'

That was an understatement. For the past two nights Edward had awoken screaming, soaked in a cold sweat and woken the entire house up. Like Fred, he was putting on a brave act.

From over the brow of the field, the two saw Carolyn appear. She was tall with long limbs, extenuated by the glow of the setting sun. She had tucked her blonde hair up into a blue headscarf, her usual, self-proclaimed 'practical' style. As she saw the two of them, she raised one slender arm and waved.

'Look at you two lovebirds!' she beamed as she strode over to them.

Madge had always found Carolyn to be the intimidating member of the Tregidden family. She was unconventional and argumentative, never taking 'no' for an answer. These were all qualities Madge had never experienced, growing up in a quiet Christian family like her own. However, having spent the past few years working on the farm, Madge had seen Carolyn in a new light. She was no longer Fred's scary older sister, but a resourceful and strong-willed woman who was more than capable of running the farm herself.

'I've been looking for you.' Carolyn smiled breathlessly as she reached them. 'I wanted to have a quick word.'

'Go on?' Fred said, but Carolyn shook her head.

'No, with Madge.'

The couple glanced at each other, confused, and Fred finally released Madge's hand. Carolyn waited for Fred to walk away before saying anything. Once her brother was out of earshot, she turned to Madge and began to explain. 'I need your help.'

'Is ev'rything alright?'

'It will be,' Carolyn said. 'We had fun, didn't we, working on the farm?'

'Yeah, of course...' Madge had a feeling that she knew where this conversation was heading.

'Well, my dad's sacking us all.'

'I know, he told me last week that he was gonna have to let us go.'

'It's completely unfair, ain't it!' Carolyn cried. 'But I was thinking that if we all make a stand then he'll have no choice but to change his mind. He can't just sack us!'

'Carolyn.' Madge closed her eyes and let out a sigh. 'I'm sorry, but I really don't mind that he's sacked me.'

'You don't have to say that—'

'No, you don't understand. I never wanted to work on the farm in the first place. It was only to lend a hand while the war was on. Yes, it was fun, but not the job that I want to do for ever. I have plans. I've been working on them with Mrs Jelbert and won't be able to make them happen if I'm stuck here baling hay or digging potatoes my whole life!'

Carolyn stared at her for a moment, hurt. She thought that they had had fun working in the fields, all the girls together.

'You don't want to stay?'

'I'm sorry,' Madge sighed. 'But if you feel so passionately about it then you should definitely make a stand. It's not fair if you lose the job you love.' She gave Carolyn a sympathetic smile. 'I'd better go and find Fred to say bye, I'm late for tea.'

Carolyn watched as Madge walked away. Once again it turned out that she was on her own.

Chapter 9

The war had been hard on the village and all who inhabited it. George liked to think of Beacon Farm as a beacon of hope, somewhere that the locals could always find solace, whether that be a couple of extra eggs or just a friendly face or two. He was proud of how successfully they had kept the farm going over the past six years, with everyone doing their bit to make sure it remained the success it had always been.

'We survived through the first war,' George always said. 'So this should be a piece of cake.' He had begun saying this in 1939, when the war was just breaking out. *Surely this one would be different*, he thought to himself, *in no way could it be like the one before, four years of Hell.* George had fought in the trenches, lying about his age – as so many of his friends had done also. He had been so proud lining up in the town hall alongside the others waiting to sign up to fight. Little did he know what they were all in store for, naive fifteen year olds believing that they were heading towards eternal glory…

This time around he felt guilty, seeing his son and the youngsters he had watched grow up all going off to meet that dark fate. Even the ones who returned, like Fred thankfully, were changed. Because war changed everyone and George could not help but feel that the likes of Charlie Howard had been the lucky ones in some strange, twisted way.

As he stood in the field, watching all of his boys back at work, he felt proud of all he had accomplished. They had all done their bit and were successful. The war was over and they could all hold their heads high. There they all were, Edward Pascoe, the Bolitho brothers – only one was missing.

'Where's Jimmy?' George called across the field.

'Dunno,' Alf Bolitho called back. 'Ain't seen 'im since this morning.'

'Said 'e had an 'eadache,' Edward said.

'Right,' George grumbled. 'You lot carry on here. I'm gonna find 'im.'

Rosie rolled over, resting her hand on Jimmy's lightly heaving chest as he slept. She could not imagine being more happy than she was now. They were together again and it was just how she had dreamt it would be. She reached up, brushing Jimmy's brown fringe from his eyes and rested her head down on his chest. He absentmindedly wrapped his arm around her, pulling her in closer, but their tranquillity barely lasted a minute before there was a noise downstairs. Rosie sprung to life, sitting up in bed hastily. The noise was growing closer; someone was making their way up the stairs.

'Jimmy!' she hissed, shaking him. Jimmy stirred. 'Jimmy! Wake up!'

Jimmy's eyes opened lazily as he gazed up at her.

'Jimmy, someone's coming.'

He was suddenly alert as well. 'I thought you said everyone was out?'

'They were!' Rosie insisted as Jimmy tumbled from the bed and began dressing himself. She had been certain that they would have the house to themselves for at least a couple of hours. Her father and Fred were working, while her mother and Inez had gone shopping in Penzance. Carolyn had disappeared just after breakfast – something about going to speak to Kerenza – and her grandfather had been taken out for the day by his friend Dick Jenkins. As the footsteps drew nearer, it became apparent that whoever this person was, was heading towards her bedroom door.

'If it's your old man, I'm done for,' Jimmy said in hushed tones, 'Rosie, I can't lose my job!'

'You won't.' Rosie pulled her dress up and hastily buttoned the front. The footsteps reached them and a knock sounded on the door. 'Who is it?' Rosie's voice came out a strangled cry as she pushed Jimmy down the side of her bed, where he lay like a cat ready to pounce.

'It's just me,' Inez's voice replied, 'Can I come in?'

'I'm just getting changed.' Rosie glanced in the mirror and hastily began fanning her face with her hand, trying to reduce its red flush. 'I thought you were in town with Mum?'

'We're about to go,' Inez said, 'But I've got enough coupons for that coat I wanted from Polglaze's, thought that you might like to come and help me choose one? I could do with your advice.'

Rosie knew that her sister would become suspicious if she declined to join her, so, in the breeziest voice she could muster said, 'Course! I'll be down in just a second.'

The footsteps retreated. Glancing at Jimmy, whose head was poking up from down the side of her bed, she mouthed, 'Sorry.' Jimmy rolled his eyes, but with a smile. It seemed this was the way it was always going to be, sneaking around and stealing moments when they could. He climbed back onto the bed and watched as Rosie finished dressing. She crossed over to the mirror where she began fussing with her hair, making sure that each glossy curl fell just how she intended it. After she finished powdering her nose, she glanced at Jimmy in the mirror.

'How do I look?' she asked, running a red lipstick over her lips, which she pushed together.

'Beautiful.' Jimmy leant back on the pillow. 'As always.'

Rosie blushed again as she stood up, stepping into her shoes.

'Do I get another kiss before you leave?' he asked. Rosie leant in, but, before she reached Jimmy, paused and gave him a wink. 'I've just done my lipstick.' She smirked and stepped back, then walked across the room and glanced over her shoulder, blowing Jimmy a kiss before darting out the door and closing it behind her again.

'I'm coming!' Jimmy heard her voice calling down the corridor and lay back, waiting. Then he climbed from the bed, finished dressing and left the room – making sure to leave no trace of himself behind. The Tregiddens had always treated him like family, although he felt that this might change if they ever found out what was going on between Rosie and himself. If he had fallen for Inez, or even Carolyn, then he felt things would be different. Rosie was the youngest, the baby of the family, only eighteen, and George was hellbent on keeping her in the nest for as long as possible. He could propose, Jimmy always knew that, but there was something exciting about not doing things the 'proper way', and he knew that Rosie felt it too. For now it was just the two of them in their relationship, but as soon as they went public then everyone else would have entered their bubble, all of the Tregiddens – as well as his father.

Walking through the empty farmhouse felt strange. Jimmy had been coming here since he was a little child and it had always been busy and bustling with the large family that lived there, as well as many of the villagers who popped in and out for an array of reasons. He had never been there alone before and as this dawned on him, his feelings for the house changed. It no longer felt like his second home but a museum preserving the Tregiddens' lives within it.

Jimmy left the house, pulling the heavy wooden door closed. 'Oi! Worthing!'

Jimmy felt a shiver run down his spine and felt like laughing at himself. After everything he had seen over the past six years, why was he still afraid of George Tregidden's temper?

Jimmy turned to see George marching across the yard towards him, his stocky arms swinging from side to side and his signature harsh scowl on his face.

'Where yeh been?'

'Sorry, Mr Tregidden.' Jimmy scratched the back of his head, 'I were just checkin' on Delilah, heard she weren't doing very well.'

'The horse?' George frowned. Jimmy nodded, thanking his lucky star that Rosie had mentioned in passing that Delilah the mare had not been herself since the birth of her offspring.

'Yeah, just thought I'd make sure she was alright, not ill or nothin'.'

'I heard you had an 'eadache,' George said.

'I did.' Jimmy began thinking on his feet. 'I went to get a drink and stopped off to see Delilah on the way back.'

George grunted in reply. 'You're like your old man, you

44

know? An opportunist.'

Jimmy was not sure what that meant, but, judging by the tone that George said it in, he thought it could not be good.

'What d'you mean?'

'I know you ain't been with the horses,' George said. 'I sent Fred to look after 'em this morning. Went in to see him then and he said he ain't seen you all day.'

Jimmy twitched, instantly coming up with a new excuse.

As he opened his mouth, however, George said, 'I don't care where you were. Just make sure that while I'm paying you, you're where I tell you to be. And right now, that's in the field.'

Chapter 10

C arolyn had a plan. A plan that she had spent the morning convincing Kerenza Roskelley to be a crucial part of. Kerenza had been working on the farm for the past few years as well, and, like Carolyn, was determined to keep her job.

The war had been hard on the Roskelley family. Both Mr and Mrs Roskelley had lost their jobs and further tragedy struck in 1941 when they lost Mr Roskelley in one of the Penzance bombings. Poor old Bernard Roskelley had been a very kind man, always the loudest one to laugh and the first to buy a round in the pub. His death had been a big loss in the family, especially as he left behind a widowed wife and their five daughters, with Kerenza being the second eldest. It had been up to her and Rowenna to support their mother, both emotionally and financially, and both began taking on any work that they possibly could. Rowenna began working at the school, offering extra support for evacuees, while Kerenza took a job up at Beacon Farm. Everything had been going well until Rowenna fell in love. A soldier named David Cardy whom she met at a dance. The two married the next time he came home and before any of the Roskelleys had known it, Rowenna had run away to St Austell, to help David's parents run their pub. Before she left, she had sworn to Kerenza that this was not her abandoning them and promised to continue sending money down to help support their mother and little sisters. But it was not long until Kerenza's wages were the only income that they saw. So, much like Carolyn, she had been furious when George had given her her notice. While Madge had accepted the news politely, Kerenza had been unable to bow into submission, arguing with George until she was blue in the face. Immediately after, she felt foolish; there was no way George would have her back now, not after the things she had said to him. But Carolyn insisted that this would not be the case, and that if their plan worked then George would have no choice but to take them back.

As the two of them marched towards the farm, however, Kerenza was beginning to get cold feet.

'Are you sure this is a good idea?' she asked. 'Only it seems like somethin' that might blow up in our faces.'

'I promise you, it'll work. We just have to make sure we don't back down. No matter what anyone says, alright?'

'I s'pose…'

It was not the fact that Kerenza particularly enjoyed working on the farm, because she did not enjoy it much at all. It was hard and cold and dirty and tiring – but it was a job. And, right now, that was all she wanted.

Over the brow of the hill, the field emerged. In it the girls could see the workers digging the potatoes.

'They're our potatoes,' Carolyn insisted. 'We're the ones who took all that time planting them. Us!'

She handed Kerenza a headscarf, much like the one her own hair was tucked up in. 'Here.'

Kerenza silently took it, tying it around her long copper

hair.

'Carolyn...' she began as they reached the gate.

'Don't back down,' Carolyn said passionately. She opened the gate and the two marched into the field. All of the men stopped what they were doing to watch. Some wolf-whistled, while others stared at them, utterly confused.

'Carolyn? Renza?' Edward began walking towards them. 'What you doing?'

'Working.' Carolyn picked up a large rusting fork from the ground, which she tossed to Kerenza, who hastily caught it. Carolyn carried on walking across the field – right towards the tractor.

'Carolyn, I don't think this is such a good idea after all,' Kerenza called after her.

'What's she doing?' Edward asked as Carolyn climbed into the tractor and started the engine.

'Carolyn, stop!' Edward suddenly cried, joining a few of the farmhands who were running towards her. Carolyn refused to listen; it was as though she was in a trance. Slowly, the tractor began to move.

'Carolyn!' Kerenza joined in the chase after the tractor. No matter how many people joined them, or fast they ran, Carolyn would not stop.

'Ed, do something,' Kerenza begged. Something caught her eye and she glanced over her shoulder to see George marching down the field with Jimmy at his side.

'CAROLYN!' he bellowed fiercely and took flight after her as well. Jimmy joined Kerenza, an amused smile on his face.

'What's going on?'

'Carolyn's hijacked the tractor.' Kerenza heard a breathy laugh come from him. 'It ent funny, Jim!'

'Sorry.' Jimmy grinned as he watched dumpy George bobbing up and down, trying desperately to grab hold of the tractor.

Finally George caught up with it. 'What d'you think you're doing?'

'Working.' Carolyn refused to look at her father and stared straight ahead.

'But this ent your job!' George was out of breath. 'Someone stop 'er, for Christ' sake!'

It was Walt Bolitho who finally climbed into the tractor and ground it to a halt. Carolyn glared at him.

'Geroff, Walt!' she cried as George stood in front of the tractor, slamming his hands down on the tyre.

'Get. Down. Now!' he ordered.

Carolyn glanced from her father to Walt, and then at the farmhands who had gathered around the tractor, blocking her way. Amongst them all she saw Kerenza, looking up at her sheepishly. Slowly, Carolyn hauled herself from the tractor. Her fight was far from over.

Helen was blissfully ignorant to the dramas of her family at the farm, and was instead enjoying spending time shopping with her daughters. It was not very often that she found an excuse to enter the dress shop in Penzance, let alone spend any time in it. She was usually so busy up at the farm or helping out in the village, and it was not like any of her daughters needed their mother to chaperone them around anymore, more the pity. So to spend time with both Rosie and Inez as they asked for her advice was pure joy. Inez had been certain on the coat that she wanted as they came into town, but now that they were here, she was not so sure. There were two in starkly different colours and she was unsure which one she liked the most. 'You could always get one, save up again and get the other?' Rosie suggested, 'That's what I'd do.'

'I know you would,' Inez rolled her eyes as she ran her down the red coat's sleeve, 'But I don't need two coats, do I?'

'I'd go for the red one personally,' Helen put in, coming over from the reels of fabric on the wall. 'White would pick up a lot of dirt.'

'I know, but you don't see white ones very often, do you?'

'White would make you look rich,' Rosie smiled wistfully. 'I could imagine Scarlett O'Hara wearing it.'

'I can't imagine Scarlett O'Hara shopping in Polgaze's, can you?' Inez said. 'Sorry,' she hastily added to the shop girl who came walking past. 'Actually, which would you choose?'

The girl turned back to her, 'Sorry?'

'Which one of these coats would you choose? I can't decide between them.' The girl walked towards them and glanced at Rosie, who scowled back; they had attended school together and did not get along. 'I think the red would suit your colouring,' the girl said, 'You have dark-blonde hair and fair skin, I think the red coat would complement that.'

'Thank you,' Inez said and began studying the red coat closely, 'Yes, I think I'll take this one please.'

After paying, Rosie became distracted by a floral dress that she wished she had bought instead of her green one and was trying to convince the girl to let her swap it. Inez was beginning to grow bored. Yes, she liked clothes, but nowhere near to the extent that Rosie did; always buying and altering and swapping. Inez barely saw her sister in the same outfit twice before it was tweaked and changed and eventually given to a friend so that she could wear something new. She instead found herself drawn to the array of multicoloured ribbon hanging in the window which she ran her fingers through, allowing them to swing back in formation. It was only then that she noticed him, his face contorted as he stared through the window, completely oblivious to her. Ralph Howard. Without really thinking why, Inez found herself stepping out of the shop and into the damp mizzle that had begun. Ralph was wearing a brown coat with its collar turned up to shelter him and was concentrating so much that he did not notice Inez until she spoke. 'Hello again.'

At this Ralph jumped and turned to face her. 'Oh!' He was evidently startled, 'Iris! I was miles away.'

'Inez,' she corrected and Ralph blushed.

'Sorry, Inez, of course. It's Spanish, isn't it?'

'I'm not sure,' Inez said, 'Mother read it in a book 'parently.'

Well, I'll remember it now, I promise.'

He seemed friendlier than before; more talkative and much less stern. Inez even felt that she might have been able to joke with him.

'Shall I ask why you're staring through a dress shop window with such intent, or just pretend that I havent noticed?'

'Oh!' Ralph began to laugh. This was the first time that Inez had seen him smile; she had to admit that he did not look completely unpleasant. 'Granny sent me out for some wool, I wasn't sure if they sold any in there?'

''Fraid not,' Inez said, 'You'd be better trying Buttons and Bows, it's just around the corner.'

'Right, thank you.' For a moment it looked as though Ralph was going to leave, then he turned back to her. He appeared smaller and much less proud than before. 'I just wanted to

51

apologise for the way I acted when we met. I had just finished a long and rather stressful train journey from London and I didn't know who you were – I know that's no excuse for being rude, but still. What I'm trying to say is, could we possibly start again?'

Inez watched him for a moment before holding out her hand. 'I'm Inez,' she said with a smile, 'Nice to meet you.'

Ralph began to laugh and shook her hand. 'Ralph.'

'So your granny told you who I am then?'

'Oh yes.' Ralph nodded sheepishly, 'She was furious when she found out I'd shut the door on you, said that you've been a huge help since, well, you know…'

'We all loved Charlie a lot… Were the two of you close?'

'I only ever met him a handful of times, I wish I'd known him better.'

'He was very special.'

The two fell into a silence, neither sure how to break it. Thankfully, the arrival of Helen and Rosie brought a new subject. 'Hello,' Ralph smiled politely.

'This is my mother,' Inez said. 'And my little sister. This is Ralph, Mrs Howard's grandson.'

'Charlie's cousin?' said Rosie.

'That's right.' Ralph nodded, avoiding Inez's eye.

'Oh.' Helen beamed and shook his hand, 'Inez is very fond of your granny, we all are!'

'Granny's very fond of all of you,' Ralph said. 'She's always talking about Inez Tregidden and her family. In fact,'

At this he turned his attention solely to Inez and she felt the sensation of being a horse at a gymkhana with all eyes on her. 'I was wondering whether you would like to come around for tea this afternoon?'

'Oh.'

'Or it doesn't have to be this afternoon,' Ralph added hastily. 'Anytime at all really!'

'No, this afternoon's perfect,' Inez said in a hurried manner and she saw Ralph's mouth twitch into a smile.

'Excellent,' he said, 'I'll see you this afternoon then – four o'clock?'

'Four o'clock,' Inez nodded. With a courteous goodbye to Helen and Rosie, Ralph walked off down the street.

'I think he likes you!' Rosie grinned, clinging onto her sister's arm.

'Don't be daft,' Inez said. 'He don't know me.'

But, all the same, she couldn't help glancing over her shoulder at Ralph. Maybe he was not so bad after all.

Chapter 11

Delilah the mare was the daughter of Lady, who had been a Christmas present to the four Tregidden children in 1931. The family all loved the horses, but none more than Fred who found that he could spend all day with them in the stables and not grow bored. This is why, when Delilah had had complications following her first foaling, which the family had been shocked to discover were twins, he had volunteered to stay with the mare and make sure she recovered well.

For a horse to have twins was rare – and for the twins to both survive was even rarer. Despite the odds, however, both Delilah and her foals had survived the ordeal, though were all still rather weak. The two foals were black, much darker than their grey-black mother, though one had the same cream smudge on its nose as her. They were both small, with legs like needles, shaking under the weight of them as they stood. They were male, so Fred knew that at least one of them would have to go at some point – that's if they survived. George was confident that they would, so confident in fact that he had arranged an interview with a journalist from the local gazette to celebrate this victorious occasion – the war being over and twin foals barely a fortnight from one another.

54

All George had talked about for days was this interview, so Fred was confused as to why his father had not shown up. The journalist had come and gone and Fred had been left to conduct the interview all on his own. Though he had not minded. He spoke about the birthing process, Delilah's heritage, the father of the foals and finally their names – Winston and Nelson, named after two great victors according to Helen. When he was with the horses, Fred found that nothing seemed to matter at all; the war and his experiences felt miles away, like they had all been a dream. Encouraging Delilah to feed the foals, mucking out the stables and cleaning Lady; they all made him feel calm. They were easy and quiet and it was just him and the horses.

He was concerned, however. It was not like his father to miss an occasion such as an interview with the *Gazette*. Eventually, when it occurred to him that he had not seen his father since his search for Jimmy that morning, he decided to go and look for him himself.

Approaching the farmhouse, Fred could already hear faint yet strong voices, one was his father's and the other sounded like Carolyn.

As he walked into the kitchen he found himself intruding on a blazing row between the two.

'Don't you *ever* do *anything* like that again!' George shouted.

'Then stop treating me like a child!' Carolyn screeched back. Fred could feel his chest tightening.

'What's going on?' He turned to see his mother, Inez and Rosie coming in behind him.

'Are you going to tell her or shall I?' George asked.

'What's happened?' Helen repeated.

'Carolyn here decided to try and steal my tractor this

mornin'—'

'I didn't steal it, I was working!'

'It ent your job, Carolyn!' George looked like he was about to explode. 'I don't employ you anymore!'

'Why not? I'm excellent at the job! Better than *he* is at the moment!'

At this she threw her hand out at Fred, who shrunk back into the wall, that uncontrollable shaking having come over him again.

'Don't you talk to your brother like that!' George growled. 'He fought for King and Country!'

'Look at him, Da.' Carolyn pointed at Fred again.

He was pale and shining with sweat, struggling to breathe.

'Anyone can see he ent well!'

'This ent about Fred, it's about you not doing what you're told!'

Fred felt Inez's hand on his shoulder and jumped.

'It's OK,' she whispered. 'You're fine.'

'It's because I'm not going to let you bully me,' Carolyn snapped. 'Fred has been allowed to do whatever he wants, while we, your daughters, have to sit still quietly and look pretty!'

'Carrie, that's not true—' Helen began.

'Carolyn, you can do whatever you like with your life, you know that,' George said. 'But this is different! This ent a hobby, it's a career! And a career that I have trained Fred in, not you.'

'BUT I CAN RUN THIS FARM!' In her rage, Carolyn swept the ceramic fruit bowl from the table, sending it shattering onto the kitchen floor. This and Rosie's scream that followed sent Fred's mind into overdrive. Everything went black and he felt himself sinking to the floor. 'Fred?' Inez desperately attempted to help him stand as he trembled in her arms. 'Freddie!'

'Fred!' Helen ran to them to help.

Carolyn and George fell silent as they watched the events unfold.

'Is he OK?' Rosie was on the verge of tears. 'Is-is he OK?'

'He'll be fine.' George took her hand and tugged her towards him, out of the way as Helen and Inez helped Fred calm down.

Slowly his vision came back and Fred saw his family all watching him, each with their own anxious expression. He felt a wave of embarrassment replace his panic as he stood back up.

'Are you OK, sweetheart?' Helen brushed his hair away from his damp forehead.

'Yeah, yeah.' Fred shrugged away from her, 'I'm fine. Really, I'm fine, Mum.'

'You sure, boy?' George asked.

'Yes, I'm just going to…' Without finishing his sentence he walked into the living room and began running up the stairs.

Helen went to move after him, but Inez said, 'Leave him. I think he wants to be alone.'

'I told you,' Carolyn said quietly, 'He ent right.'

'Neither are you,' Inez argued. 'Screaming and shouting and smashing things!'

'I think we've had enough arguing.' Helen silenced her daughters. 'Leave that, darling, I'll do it,' she added to Rosie, who had begun gathering the pieces of broken china on the floor. 'Carolyn, apologise to your father for disobeying him.'

Carolyn looked at her mother in despair before turning reluctantly to her father and muttering, 'Sorry.'

'George?' Helen asked when he failed to reply and saw that he was still stuck staring at the door, which Fred had just disappeared through.

'George?'

George snapped from his trance.

'Carrie just apologised.'

'Oh,' George said slowly. 'OK.' He turned to walk to the porch.

'Where are you going?' Helen asked.

'Just…to check on Delilah.' And George left the house.

As he walked across the yard, he vaguely noticed his father hobbling towards the house on his walking stick, in his hand a bag of mackerel.

''Ere, Georgie!' Frank waved the mackerel proudly, 'Look what I won from Dick Jenkins!'

But George was not listening. He had seen people have attacks like Fred's the last time. Some of them were better now, but others weren't. He needed to find a way to make sure Fred would be all right.

Chapter 12

'What are you gonna wear?' Rosie tossed herself into a chair at the table as Inez tipped the broken china from the dustpan and into the bin.

'What d'you mean?' she asked.

'When you go to the Howards' house, it's almost three o'clock now!'

'Oh… I probably won't go. Not now.'

'What d'you mean? Ralph invited you!'

'I know, but I feel guilty. How can I go to their house for tea when you all need me here.'

'Don't be silly, you can't not go just 'cos Carolyn got teasy.'

'What's going on?' Carolyn asked as she joined her sisters in the kitchen.

Rosie blushed. 'Inez was invited to tea by Mrs Howard's grandson, but now she's saying that she don't want to go.'

'Charlie's cousin? Won't that be a bit, I don't know, weird?'

'What d'you mean?' Inez asked, her defences flying up.

'I mean…after ev'rything between you and Charlie, won't it seem a bit…odd to be moving on with his cousin?'

'He invited me to tea! He ain't proposed!'

'Did Charlie propose?' Rosie asked suddenly and Inez looked away. 'He proposed?'

'No,' Inez said. 'Not proposed exactly, but…before he went away he said that…he said he loved me.'

'And did you love him?' Carolyn asked. 'Do you, I mean?'

Inez turned away from them and began scrubbing the worktop, despite it being clean. 'I just think it would feel odd being there with a stranger when I was so used to Charlie. You were right, Carolyn.'

'No I weren't.' Her sister sighed. 'Inez, you should go. Rosie's right, I'm just teasy. Don't let me ruin your afternoon.'

Inez turned to them. 'OK.' She gave them both a weak smile. 'OK, I'll go.'

'Right!' Rosie clasped her hands together. 'Now, tell me what you're gonna wear.'

It took Ralph a long time to finally find everything that he needed. He had only ever been to Penzance twice in his life, and both of those times had been as a child, so to him the town and neighbouring village were utterly alien. Though finally with all of his items, and most importantly his granny's wool, he made his way back home. Checking his watch, he realised that he was five minutes late, although by the looks of things Inez was too. He felt very guilty about the way he had treated her and his granny had scolded him like he was a child when she found out about the conversation that they had had on her doorstep. It was only then that he realised who Inez Tregidden was, a close friend of his cousin Charlie – possibly something more judging by the way his granny spoke about her, and a loyal companion to her.

Myrtle House still felt unfamiliar, nothing like the home it was supposed to be. Still, he thought, it had only been a week or so, there was plenty of time for him to settle in.

He walked up the path and took his key out, only to find that the door was already unlocked.

After much tutting and rolling of his eyes, he stepped inside and took his coat off. 'Granny, I keep telling you not to leave the door unlocked when you're home alone. You never know who might come wandering in.' He walked into the living room and was stunned.

'It's OK,' Inez said brightly. 'I unlocked it, I let myself in.' She was sitting on the sofa with a cup of tea, opposite his granny in her chair.

'Oh.' Ralph looked at her in confusion. 'Do you have a key then?'

'Charlie gave me one. Your granny's been telling me all about your life in London.'

'Uh-oh.' Ralph perched on the other end of the sofa as Inez poured him a cup of tea, 'All good, I hope?'

'Course.' Inez laughed. 'Although maybe I won't tell my grandad that you're a lawyer, don't trust 'em apparently.'

'I swear I'm trustworthy!'

'I don't doubt it.' Inez sipped her tea with a smile.

'Gets his brains from his father, he does.' Mrs Howard beamed proudly. 'Richard was always the smartest in this family. He takes after his father as well.'

'Dad says that,' Ralph said, before hastily adding, 'Not saying that he doesn't think that you aren't smart!'

'Ah, I have thick skin!' His granny smiled. 'No, he's right, my James was the teacher and I was the housewife. That's what things were back then, but I think that they're changing.'

'You should speak to Carolyn,' Inez said, 'She's hellbent on running the farm. Da's not so impressed though.'

61

'Good for her,' Mrs Howard declared, sloshing tea down from her cup.

'Why shouldn't she run the farm if she wants to? I can see her doing it; she's certainly strong enough! I remember when you were all tiny – you and Charlie couldn't have been, my, more than eight? – and he came running in in tears, said he'd been attacked by someone. "Who did that to you?" I remember asking. "Carolyn Tregidden!" he wailed back. I just laughed, I remember, a six-year-old girl beating up a boy two years her age!' She raised her cup to her lips. 'You might be the oldest child, Inez, but your Carolyn certainly knows how to take care of herself.'

'I know that all too well.' Inez laughed.

'Carolyn?' Ralph was feeling a little excluded from the conversation, 'That's not the sister I met earlier, is it?'

'No,' Inez said, 'That was Rosie.'

'A sweet little bird.' Mrs Howard commented.

'She's my youngest sister,' Inez explained. 'There're four of us: me, Carolyn, Fred and Rosie.'

'And you live up on the farm?' Ralph asked. 'Where Charlie worked?'

That's right.'

'And his dad before him,' Mrs Howard added. 'When I first moved here, Beacon Farm ran this village and, of course, your grandad, Frank, was the head! He was brand new, you know. His father died young, didn't he? Left it all to Frank to run.'

'And he's still trying to run it single-handedly at his age,' Inez said.

'Well, that's the thing about us elderly folk,' Mrs Howard smiled, 'we don't like to be reminded that we're getting old.'

'So what about you?' Inez turned her attention to Ralph.

'Tell me about your life in big old London. I've only been once, and that was just to visit my uncle.'

Ralph shifted in his seat. London was very different to here where everyone seemed to know one another. 'It's, um, well, it's different to here. It's rather busy and loud and everybody seems to have somewhere very important that they need to be at all times.'

'It must be exciting though, being a lawyer in London?'

'It's just my job,' Ralph said. 'I only really got into it because of my father – he's a lawyer as well. But I suppose it is interesting sometimes.'

'How are you going to cope down here with work?'

'I have it all figured out.' Ralph lit up at the chance to explain his plan. 'I'm going to commute. It won't be all the time, only for trials and meetings sometimes. The rest of the time I can correspond via post. And, anyway, I might pick up some clientele here.'

'What made you move down?'

'Well, it was for Granny. The two of us rarely get to see each other, and after Charlie... I just couldn't stand the thought of her sitting in this empty house alone. So when I realised that I had the opportunity to relocate, I had no commitment to London other than work, I thought why not?'

'I'm so glad you're here.' Mrs Howard reached out to him and beamed.

The three chatted for a long time, Mrs Howard telling anecdotes about both Ralph and Inez when they were children, while the two opened up to one another more and more. Finally, when the clock in the hallway chimed seven, Inez almost jumped out of her seat.

'I didn't realise the time! I'd better be getting back or they'll wonder where I am.'

'Are you sure you won't stay for dinner?' Ralph asked.

'Thank you, but I'd better not.' Inez stood up and smoothed her dress out. 'My mother's loving cooking for the seven of us at the moment. It's the first time she's been able to for years. Thank you for having me. I'll see you soon, Mrs Howard.'

'God bless, love.' Mrs Howard kissed Inez's cheek.

'I'll show you out,' Ralph replied and the two walked into the hall where Inez put on her new red coat and pulled on her hat. 'Thank you,' Ralph said as he pulled the door closed. 'For taking such good care of Granny.'

Inez smiled. 'She's a wonderful person.'

Ralph opened the front door and Inez stepped out into the cool evening air. The mizzle had ceased and the air finally felt clear. 'By the way...' Ralph scratched his neck. 'Could I take that key back?'

Inez frowned, 'Sorry?'

'The key that Charlie gave you. It's just, well, he only gave it to you so that you could help Granny, didn't he? And I'm here now.'

Inez stared at him. She thought that she had misjudged Ralph on their first meeting, but was now certain she had been correct all along. Ralph Howard did not understand anything. She pulled the key from her pocket and slammed it into Ralph's palm, who seemed rather confused at her anger. Without another word, Inez turned on her heels and stormed away. Ralph watched her go in confusion; he'd thought they were having a nice time.

Chapter 13

Things were growing tense in the Tregidden household. Carolyn and George were refusing to talk while Inez refused to tell anyone about her visit to the Howards' – no matter how many times Rosie asked. Fred was keeping quiet as well, retreating further into himself, and Rosie was growing lonely. The only company she had now were her stolen moments with Jimmy. While she had always loved and craved them, this was never truer than now, for Jimmy was the only person who she felt she could truly speak to. Despite trying to hide her delight whenever thinking of Jimmy, she was never able to completely suppress her cheerful mood.

'That's a pretty song sweet'eart,' Frank said one day as he sat in his armchair listening to Rosie quietly singing to herself while tidying the living room.

'I didn't realise I was singing.' Rosie immediately stopped and blushed.

'No, carry on.' Frank closed his eyes and settled back into his chair. 'Nice to hear someone in this house in a good mood.'

Rosie smiled to herself; she was in a good mood. Jimmy had a half-day and they were going to go for a walk this afternoon. 'I'm sure the others'll cheer up.' She plumped the cushions behind her grandfather. 'I heard Carrie and Da talking this morning and Fred seems loads better! Dunno what's put Inez in her mood though.'

'A broken 'eart is a terrible thing.' Frank sighed. 'She loved that Howard boy, anyone could see it.'

'D'you reckon she was using her visits to Mrs Howard to feel close to Charlie again?' Rosie asked.

'Prob'ly. Mind you, any excuse to see Hetty Howard and I'd be down there like a shot! She were a fine one in 'er day – still is whenever I see 'er! Got nice legs still!'

'Grandad.' Rosie gave him a look of comedic disgust. 'You shouldn't talk about her like that, I don't want to know about Mrs Howard's legs!'

'Ah, the feeling was mutual,' Frank gave a toothy grin as he remembered the good old days. 'I used to see her looking when me and the boys were working in the village, partic'ly in the summer, all of us topless and brown!'

'I don't want to think about you topless and brown.' Although, Rosie was now thinking about Jimmy out in the fields in the height of the summer. 'Besides, what about Nana?'

'It were all a bit'a fun,' Frank said. 'Your Nana and Hetty loved each other like sisters! No one could compare to my Lizzie, you know that, not even Hetty Howard!'

Rosie smiled, she always loved hearing her grandad talk about her nana.

'Yeah…' Frank muttered to himself, 'Hetty Howard. I should give her a visit soon.'

Rosie sighed and rolled her eyes, before looking at the clock on the wall – half past one. She hastily put the cushion down.

'I didn't realise that was the time.'

'Got somewhere you need to be?' Frank asked.

66

'No…' Rosie began as she crossed the room.

'Got a little fella 'ave you?'

'No!' Rosie replied hastily, but Frank merely laughed.

'Your secret's safe with me.' He gave her a wink.

'I don't have any secrets,' Rosie replied indignantly and walked out.

Frank sat back in his armchair and waited; it was never long before someone else came through and stopped to have a chat with him. Now he had been banned from the fields, it was the only thing he had to look forward to. The next person to arrive was Carolyn. She had been bearing a moody scowl on her face ever since her infamously explosive argument with George.

'Looking pretty, sweet'eart.' Frank nodded to her clothes. She was wearing a polka-dot dress and Inez's hand-me-down dark-blue hat.

Carolyn scoffed and tossed her bag onto the sofa, before following it with a muffled thud. 'I borrowed 'em from Inez.' She took the hat off and shook her blonde hair back down to her shoulders. 'I went for a job interview in the tea rooms on the seafront.'

'Do a bleddy 'ansome cream tea in there, they do,' Frank said, 'My Lizzie used to love goin' there.'

''S'not exactly the sort of place you could imagine me working in though, is it, Grandad?' Carolyn slumped back on the cushions with a sigh.

'Why not? You'd be perfect for it!'

'With my face? It makes expressions without me knowing! I scowl too much.'

'You've got a lovely face, m'bird,' Frank said, 'The customers will all love you.'

'I don't wanna be a waitress, I want to work on the farm!'

'So do I, m'bird,' Frank gave her a weak smile. 'So do I.'

Rosie found Jimmy walking across the farmyard alone. The other boys had headed off already and Fred said that he was going to check on Delilah and the foals.

'Hello.' Jimmy smiled as Rosie reached him.

'Where d'you want to go?' Rosie asked. 'The yarrows have started blooming in the woods and look like thick snow, we could go there? Or down Lamorna Way?'

She saw that Jimmy had glanced away.

'What?'

'Well…' Jimmy began, 'It's just some of the lads are going down the prom. Having one last swim before the summer ends, you know?'

'And you've said you'll go?' There was a stung tone in Rosie's voice.

'*We* could go?' Jimmy caught her hand, 'I think Madge and Kerenza are going, a few others as well? Fred an' all. What d'you think?'

'I was hoping we'd be alone,' Rosie said quietly.

'Don't you want one final swim?' Jimmy asked. 'Think about it, we have all autumn and winter to walk through the woods together, just you and me, but in a few weeks it'll be too cold to go in the water again.'

'When we're there I have to pretend I don't love you.' Rosie said, ''Specially if Fred's gonna be there. I hate that.'

'Please come, it'll be fun, I promise! Oh, wait a second…' From his back pocket, he produced a cluster of red campion and daisies. 'Here, I saw 'em growing down the lane and thought you'd like them.'

Rosie took them and smiled. 'Is this a bribe?'

'It's an invitation. Besides, Fred'll have Madge, Ed'll have Renza, they won't notice us, I'm sure.'

Rosie finally nodded. 'OK, when are you heading down?'

'Now.'

'Alright, I'll go and get changed and head down with Fred when he's ready.'

Jimmy closed his arms around Rosie and kissed her, unaware of Edward watching them from a few feet away.

Edward waited for Jimmy to leave and hastily caught up to Rosie as she walked back to the house.

'Alright, Rose?'

'Oh, hello.' Rosie smiled. 'I just heard about ev'ryone going down the prom, so I'm going to get changed and join you.'

'Jimmy tell you, did he?'

Rosie looked at Edward. *What did he know?*

'Yeah…' she said slowly. 'Yeah, he did.'

'I know about the two of you,' he said, and Rosie opened her mouth to protest. Before she could get a word out, however, Edward carried on. 'I won't tell anyone, don't worry. It's just…be careful of Jimmy, alright?'

'What d'you mean?'

'I don't know.' Edward shifted awkwardly. 'Just, don't put all your trust in him. I'm only thinking'a you! I don't want you getting hurt.'

Rosie suppressed a smile. Kerenza had told her that she and Edward were not as close as they once were. Edward was not bad-looking at all, but, unfortunately for him, she only had eyes for Jimmy. Besides, he was still apparently courting her best friend.

'Thank you,' she said, 'for caring about me. But I'm a big girl and I reckon I can look after myself. It's nice to know you care though, Ed.'

She gave his arm a squeeze and Edward watched her enter the house. There was only one person that Jimmy should be with. And it was not Rosie Tregidden.

Chapter 14

I t had always been a tradition that when the boys at the
farm were given a half-day at the end of the summer,
they would all go down to the rocks behind Penzance
promenade and swim, for who knew when the next time they
would go in the sea would be? Next week or next year?

The tradition had been something Frank Tregidden had
done in his youth; it was on one of those swims that he had
finally declared his love for Lizzie Polgreen, then George's
generation had followed suit. He, Michael Howard, Samuel
Worthing and all of the others made sure that no one would
ever be left behind – apart from Helen Rowe who was scared
of the sea, having watched her uncle's fishing boat go down
as a child.

Now it was gospel. Every farmworker and his friends *had*
to go for that last swim of the season. It was practically law!

The boys always got there first, stripping off their work
clothes and plunging into the sea, still bitterly cold despite
it being at its warmest. By the time the girls arrived in their
swimsuits, each of them egging the others to go in first, the
boys were usually fully clothed again.

It had been different in Frank's times, when the girls would
look away and blush, barely dipping more than a toe in the

water. No one cared anymore; they knew each other well enough and were all virtually family.

This year felt even more special. They had not had a half-day swim for six years! At least not all of them together and Jimmy felt a little emotional as he leapt into the sea amongst his friends, all of them shivering and yelling as they splashed their way through the waves. The icy water made him feel alive, it made him feel complete. This was where he was supposed to be; these people were his family. Not that sorry excuse for a father he had left at home too drunk to even stand. He had barely a moment to dwell on this, however, for it was not long until the mayhem began.

It was like in the sea they were able to shed their civilized shells and become their true animalistic forms that no one ever saw, all pushing and pulling each other under the water, leaping on one another, and all the while shouting as loud as they could.

As Jimmy swam out from under Edward, he heard a splash beside him and turned to see Fred in the water as well.

'FREDDIE!' he called and the boys all descended on him.

Fred felt his vision turn black as he was forced down under the water and began to fight back, viciously. He screamed and wailed, lashing out at whoever had hold of him.

Jimmy broke free from him and looked up at the group of girls who had gathered together up on the rocks. Amongst them stood Rosie, who was watching them in concern. Something about her expression chilled Jimmy; he had never seen her so panicked before. Suddenly she began to scream. 'GET OFF HIM! GET OFF MY BROTHER! GET OFF HIM!'

Without a second thought, Jimmy complied, tearing the boys away from Fred, each of them confused by the sudden end to their game. Fred popped up from the water, gasping for breath as he flailed around.

'I've got you!' Jimmy held onto Fred tightly and swam over to the rocks where Rosie and Madge helped pull him up out of the water. He was pale and shaking.

'What happened?' Madge took Fred's frozen face in her hands, attempting to warm him again.

'We were just messing around,' Jimmy directed this to Rosie, who was drying her brother with the towel from her bag. 'I didn't realise that anything was wrong, I promise!'

Finally Fred began to talk. 'It's OK,' he said. 'It's OK, I-I think it was just the shock of the water, haven't been in it for a while, have I?' He said this with a weak attempt at a laugh. Rosie still looked concerned. 'Freddie…' she began.

'It was the water!' Fred said loudly. 'It was *just* the water.'

'Are you gonna be OK?' Jimmy asked.

Fred nodded. 'I think I'll just sit here for a minute.'

Rosie stood up and walked away without a word. Jimmy had the uneasy feeling that he was in trouble, so went after her, pulling on his trousers.

Madge sat down beside Fred and continued to dry his shoulders.

'Are you sure you're alright?'

'Yes,' Fred insisted. 'I don't think I expected the water to be so cold, that's all.'

'You would tell me if something was wrong, wouldn't you?' Madge watched him carefully and Fred nodded.

He felt guilty. Madge sounded hurt and the last thing that he wanted to do was hurt her.

'Of course. Look, Madge, I'm sorry I ent been myself since I got back.'

At this Madge laughed, her pale cheeks turning red. 'Fred, you ent been on holiday. You know I'd be surprised if you were the same. Just…' She began drying his head now. 'Let me help. Yeah?'

Fred nodded, though had no intentions of burdening Madge with his problems. How would he even begin to describe it if he wanted to? The fact that for him the war was still going on, only this time it was confined to his head? Just the thought of it made him feel stupid. He wanted to be normal. He wanted to be able to laugh with his mates and do everything that he had done before. He had to try. 'Do you fancy going to the dance next week?' he found himself asking.

'Are you sure?'

'Course.' Though it was the last thing that he felt like doing, just the look on Madge's face as it lit up made Fred feel slightly better.

'Alright then.' she beamed.

'Rosie!' Jimmy chased her along the rocks. 'Rose!' His wet hair was flopping in his eyes and the jagged rocks were cutting into his bare feet. 'Rose, please! Let me explain! I di'n't mean to hurt Fred! Surely you know that?'

Rosie stopped a few feet ahead of him and turned, crossing her arms over her chest. Her wide eyes were shining and it looked like she was about to cry.

'It ent you.' Her voice was thick with tears. 'It's Fred. He's – he's not well.'

'What d'you mean?' Jimmy walked towards her slowly.

'Since he's been back he – he has these blackouts and shakes and ev'rything. It's really scary and no one can understand him at all until he comes round again. But he won't talk about them and just pretends that they ain't happening, but they are! They're happening to my brother!'

'Can I tell you something?' Jimmy looked to the sea rather than her. 'Sometimes I cry. I dunno why, I just do. The first week I was back, I couldn't stop. Me and my old man would be listening to the wireless and I would just feel a lump in my throat rising and rising 'til I started crying.'

'What did your father say?' Rosie asked, catching hold of Jimmy's hand.

'Nothing,' Jimmy said. 'He cries all the time when he's drunk. Reckon he thought that's what was wrong with me, I s'pose. But it weren't. I would think about things that I saw and did – I dunno… I just wanted to make sure you know that Freddie ent weird. He's just like the rest of us. None of us know what's going on, but we're getting better. I promise you, Rose.'

Chapter 15

The days leading up to the local dance were always rather stressful. Who was going, who was not going, who was wearing what, could they borrow something from you? Carolyn hated it. She hated the fuss and how much panic a silly little evening could cause. She had understood a little more during the war for the highs seemed very high against the lows, which felt incredibly low. But now that was over, she had no interest in dressing up and sitting in the village hall waiting for someone to ask her to dance, for no one ever did. That morning Inez had come walking into her room and began searching through her minimal selection of dresses.

'Have you decided what you're gonna wear?' she asked.

Carolyn had frowned. 'What d'you mean? What am I gonna wear?'

'To the dance.'

At this Carolyn had scoffed. 'I ent going to that.'

'Yes you are,' Inez had said. 'Because I want to go, but I don't have anyone to go with, so I'll go with you.'

'So that we can sit like two old biddies in the corner watching ev'ryone else get hysterical? Sounds fun!'

'Well I said to Mrs Green that we would help out.'

'You volunteered me?'

'What's the point in sitting at home all evening when Fred and Rosie are going to be having fun?'

'Fine!' Carolyn rolled her eyes and lay back on her bed.

'OK, well, what are you gonna wear, then?'

'I dunno, what about my red dress?'

Inez removed the dress from the wardrobe and groaned. 'Carrie, there's a hole in it! A huge one on the skirt!'

'Oh yeah, I did that climbing over a wall.'

Inez was going to ask for a further explanation, but decided against it. Instead she took her sister by the hand and dragged her down into the town in order to find something to cover the hole.

'Look, Inez, if I don't have anything suitable to wear then I just won't go!' Carolyn groaned. 'It's not a big deal!'

'I can't go on my own. And, like I said, I told Mrs Green that we would help out!'

'I already have to serve people at my new job! I don't want to spend my evening doing it as well!'

She hated her new job at the tea rooms, just as she had suspected. The customers were often rude and demanding and it took all of Carolyn's strength not to hurl something back at them.

'But this is different,' Inez said. 'We can dance and chat to people as well, it'll be fun.'

'I know why you want to go.' Carolyn rolled her eyes. 'You want to meet someone, don't you? You think that a handsome prince is gonna walk through the doors and sweep you off your feet? You're twenty-four. You know all of the men around here and also know that none of them are anything special.'

77

'I'm not looking for a prince,' Inez retorted. 'All I'm saying is that it will be nice to do something sociable.'

'You work in a shop and I work in a cafe, we are literally paid to be sociable.' As they rounded the corner, they found Ralph Howard once again staring with intent, though this time through the bookshop window. Immediately, Inez felt an unpleasant tingle down her spine. She decided that she was going to walk past him without a word, but, all of a sudden, found herself saying, 'We keep meeting like this.'

Furious at herself for saying anything, she drew up beside him as Ralph jumped.

'Hello,' he said, before turning to Carolyn. 'You must be the infamous Carolyn?'

'Infamous?' Carolyn laughed.

'According to the stories my granny tells anyway.' Ralph smiled. 'Something about you beating up my cousin when you were children?'

'Oh.' Carolyn began to laugh again at the memory. 'I can't believe Mrs Howard remembers that! You know it's funny you looking in that window, Inez works in there.'

'Do you?' Ralph said to Inez. 'I always assumed that you worked up at the farm?'

'Oh no,' Inez said, 'We're George Tregidden's daughters, we're kept as far away from the farm work as possible!'

Ralph's eyes lingered on her for a moment, an absent-minded smile on his face. 'Well, I was actually planning on popping in to order a book, only they seem to be closed. Would you be able to put the order in for me?' he asked, breaking from his trance and Inez felt her heart sink a little.

'Of course, I'm working tomorrow so pop in with the name. I'll see what I can do.'

'Thank you, Inez. Sorry, I don't want to keep you both if you're busy.'

'Only buying something to cover a hole in my dress.' Carolyn wrinkled her nose. 'There's a dance on Friday that she's making me attend.'

'Stop complaining, you always have fun at them.'

'Do I?'

'A dance?' Ralph asked. 'Where's that?'

'In the village hall,' Inez said. 'Mrs Green always organises it. It's for kids like our Rosie really, but we're lending a helping hand.'

'I might have to have a little look at it.' Ralph smiled.

'Really?' There was a distinct tone of surprise in Inez's voice.

'If I do, would you have a dance with me?'

Inez smiled slightly. 'You could save me from the tea stand.'

'And apologise for upsetting you the other day,' Ralph said. Inez felt herself blushing.

'You didn't upset me,' she said innocently.

'Of course I did,' Ralph scratched the back of his neck. Inez had noticed he did this frequently in uncomfortable situations. 'I didn't mean to sound cold when I asked for the key to the house back. I know that Charlie gave it to you with good reason.'

'Oh, that.' Inez pretended as though she had not been thinking about it every day since. 'Honestly, don't worry. All water under the bridge.'

Ralph gave her a smile again before clasping his hands together. 'OK then, I'd best be off. See you both soon. Good luck with the hole covering.'

'Bye,' Carolyn smiled. 'See you at the dance.'

'Maybe,' Ralph replied and walked away.

Carolyn glanced at her sister, who was watching Ralph walk away, and started to laugh. Inez turned to her, suddenly embarrassed. 'Come on,' she said sharply, taking Carolyn's arm. 'We still need to find something!'

Chapter 16

The dance seemed to take a long time to come around, with each day bringing yet more dread for Fred, who was regretting ever asking Madge.

'Why don't you want to go?' Jimmy asked on Thursday afternoon as he and Fred untied more bales. There had been a delivery of hay from a neighbouring farm and the two had been put in charge of unbaling and breaking up the mounds. Edward had begun with them, but for some reason had disappeared.

'I'm just tired,' Fred replied. Since his turn in the sea a few days ago, he had been feeling better and was scared of doing anything that might set him off again.

'You've told Madge that you'll go now,' Jimmy pointed out, ''Parently she's really excited, 'cording to Ed.'

'I know.' Fred groaned. 'I don't know what's worse, not going and disappointing her or going and disappointing her.'

'How about you try going and *not* disappointing her?' Jimmy asked. 'Might be easier, you never know?'

'Are you taking anyone?' Before the war Jimmy had courted almost every girl in the village at one point or another, but since being back he never mentioned any girl at all. Fred wondered if there was something Jimmy was not telling him;

that he was struggling more than he was letting on possibly?

'No,' Jimmy answered quickly. 'No one in particular anyway.'

'Well Rosie's going. So just be warned that she'll prob'ly try and get a dance outta you!'

'I don't mind.' Jimmy smiled to himself.

'I think she has her eye on someone though.' Fred continued. 'I just can't work out who. She keeps disappearing for hours on end with no explanation. Whoever he is had better keep away from my da though!'

'What makes you say that?' Jimmy suddenly felt slightly warmer than before around his collar.

'Well Rosie's his little girl,' Fred said. 'And she's my little sister. Da don't want her growing up yet.'

'She is eighteen, though,' Jimmy pointed out.

'But she's the last of the nest, ent she? You'd understand if you had a sister.'

Jimmy fell silent and Fred hastily added. 'Sorry, mate, you're practic'ly family. Obviously Rosie's like a sister to you as well.'

Jimmy cringed. 'But she's not though, is she?'

The two carried on their work, oblivious to Edward who was up in the loft of the barn, untying the bales up there and listening to their conversation. He had assumed that Rosie would have convinced Jimmy to take her to the dance and was pleased to hear that apparently Fred and the rest of the Tregiddens thought that Rosie was not right for him either. There had to be a way for him to make Jimmy realise what a huge mistake he was making.

From outside he heard the gruff voice of George as he called in. 'Fred? Come 'ere a minute!' and the sound of Fred tossing down his fork and leaving the barn. Edward and Jimmy were alone.

Fred found his father waiting for him with the tractor and began growing more anxious the closer he drew. There was a strangely warm expression on the farmer's face.

'Alright there, boy?' George asked. 'Just wanted a hand with the tractor. Just needs a bit'a tinkering, I reckon.'

'Weren't Alf doin' that?' Fred frowned.

'Sent him to the field with that brother of his,' George replied. 'Plus, thought we could have a bit of a chat anyway.'

He opened his toolbox and peered at the engine. 'Ain't been right since your sister decided to take it hostage. Pass me that spanner, will you?'

Fred obliged. 'I don't think Carolyn could have damaged it. She knows how to drive a tractor at the end of the day, don't she? Better than me prob'ly!'

'Don't say that!' It sounded like George was in pain. He turned to Fred, a stern look in his tired eyes. 'You need to have more faith in yourself,' he said. 'I know that you've been through hell and it's torn you to shreds, but you *have* to build yourself back up again, Fred. If not for yourself then for the farm.'

'Carolyn's right, though,' Fred said. 'Da, I'm broken. How can I run this place one day if I can't even jump in the sea?'

'See, this is what I mean,' George turned back to the engine and began tinkering with it. 'You need to believe in yourself more. One day Beacon Farm will be yours and you'll be the boss of a group of lads like all you lot. But I need to know that you can do it.'

'I thought I could,' Fred replied. 'Six years ago, I wanted nothing more! I'd just finished school and wanted to be here all the time – I wanted to be just like you. But now I'm different. I'm not as strong as you or Carolyn or Jim or Ed. I can't do this, Da. I – I think there's something wrong with me.'

'Shellshock,' George muttered, 'I saw lads with it last time round.'

'I weren't like this until I got back though.' Fred sat down on the steps with his head in his hands.

'I saw other lads getting sent back home 'cause of it.'

'The important thing to do is move on,' George said. 'Try and forget ev'rything, alright? You're back home with us now, boy.'

'It's hard!'

'I know. But you have to at least try. Cos you're my son, Fred, my only boy, and I can't lose you.'

'I'm still your boy,' Fred insisted, 'I've just…changed.'

'But don't go telling anyone that!' George said, his voice now hushed, 'OK? Make me a promise that you won't tell anyone else about this? Cos I don't wanna lose you.'

Fred slowly nodded. There was so much more that he wanted to say. Though there was no time as the two of them were suddenly interrupted by Edward's frantic cries as he came sprinting from the barn.

'HELP! QUICK! SOMEONE HELP!'

'Ed?' Fred shot up from the steps. Edward reached them, his face flushed in panic.

'Quick, I need your help! It's Jimmy!'

Chapter 17

Upon entering the barn, the three found a bale of hay in the middle of the room and underneath it Jimmy. He was face down and unconscious.

'Jimmy!' George ran to the boy and threw himself down beside him.

'What happened?' Fred asked.

'We were talking and one of the bales must have come loose from the loft!' Edward was shaking, he looked traumatised. 'It fell off and landed on him!'

'He's alive.' George pressed his ear in closely and listened to Jimmy's struggling breaths. 'We need to get him out, *now!*'

The boys ran to the bale and grabbed either side. 'Don't drag it!' George yelled, 'If it ain't broken his spine already, then draggin' it certainly will!'

'What do we do then?' Fred asked.

'Lift!'

'We need more people than us,' Edward cried. 'It's a ton bale!'

'Do it, yeh tuss!' George roared. 'It's crushing his bleddy lungs!'

This boy was his employee, he was his boss; not only that, but Jimmy felt like family. He had watched him grow up, and, despite what he thought about Samuel Worthing, George could not bring himself to imagine having to break the news that his son had died.

Edward and Fred looked at each other; they had no choice. They both crouched down and grabbed hold of the bottom of the bale, clasping the twine for support.

'Ready?' George asked, sliding his hands under Jimmy's arms.

'Ready,' Fred answered.

'Ready,' said Edward.

'NOW!' George bellowed. The two boys lifted, the bale inching up slightly. The twine cut into their fingers and they cried out from the pain and strain.

'MORE!' George ordered. Edward's side came up further and Fred almost lost his balance. He regained it and let out a roar as he too heaved up his end of the bale. He could not feel his fingers and for a moment wondered if the twine had cut them clean off. His arms gave up just about the same time as Edward's and they both sent the bale crashing back down. Stepping back they looked at each other, both were drenched in sweat and breathless. George sat a foot away, his ear pressed against Jimmy's chest. He had turned him onto his back and Jimmy lay free from the bale. He could have been sleeping.

'Is he alright?' The colour had drained from Edward's face now and he looked incredibly pale. 'Is he gonna be alright?'

'His breathing's better,' George said. 'But we need to get him to hospital.'

Jimmy was still out cold, but between the three of them, they lifted him up and carried him out of the barn.

'We'll get him home and call Dr Drake,' George said and they carried Jimmy towards the Land Rover. As they did, Helen and Rosie came out of the farmhouse.

'What's happened?' Helen asked.

'Is that Jimmy?' Rosie exclaimed.

'He had an accident in the barn.'

Rosie clamped her hand to her mouth as she fought back her tears. 'Is he going to be OK?'

'We need to get him home,' George said. Helen ran to the Land Rover and opened the door. The three men slid Jimmy in carefully.

'Fred, get in the back with him.' George said. 'Ed, call Dr Drake and tell him to get to Laurel Cottage as soon as he can.'

'Right.' Edward nodded.

'And make sure to say it's for *Jimmy* Worthing, not Samuel.' George added, 'He might not come if it's for Samuel.'

George climbed into the driver's seat and started the engine. Rosie turned away, hiding her tears as the car pulled away. Edward placed his hand on her shoulder. 'Jimmy's gonna be fine,' he said quietly, though more to himself than to her. For the colour had still not returned to his face.

'Da?' Fred asked as they drove along the lane. 'Why are we taking Jimmy back home if you said Dr Drake won't attend Mr Worthing?'

'Cos whether I like it or not, Jimmy's Samuel's son,' George replied. 'And if Dr Drake finds anything wrong with him then he should be with his father.'

Jimmy began to stir.

'Jim?' Fred asked, holding him back onto the seat. 'Jim, it's alright.'

Jimmy suddenly cried out in pain and Fred tried to hush him.

'Hold on, Worthing!' George called to him. 'You're gonna be fine!'

Laurel Cottage was not far from Beacon Farm, though it seemed a world away. It was only a very small house, two rooms up and two rooms down. The garden was overgrown and one of the windows had been smashed by local kids a few years ago. Jimmy had boarded it up, but Samuel had never bothered to get it fixed.

'Wait here,' George said as he pulled up and climbed from the car. He walked along the overgrown path and knocked on the door. He waited for a moment, before realising that no one would be answering it. Instead he tried the door and found that it was unlocked. Stepping immediately into the kitchen, George held his breath – the house was worse than he had remembered. The walls were damp and blackening in the corners and there was an unpleasant smell lingering in the air.

'Hello?' George called softly. 'Sam? It's George, George Tregidden.'

He walked through into the sitting room where he found Samuel slumped in a fraying armchair. In his hand was half a bottle of cheap whisky. Samuel Worthing was a small, wiry man. He had lost almost all of his unwashed hair and his chin was covered in straggly strands that he had missed whilst shaving. He looked a good ten years older than George, despite them having grown up together.

'Hello, Sam,' George said, keeping his voice light.

'Georgie Tregidden,' Samuel's grin was just as unpleasant as ever. Black and yellow. 'What do I owe this pleasure?' His voice was slow and claggy and set George on edge as the memories of why the village despised Samuel Worthing returned.

'I got your boy in my car,' George explained. 'Jimmy's had a bit of an accident, see?'

Samuel began rocking in his seat as he tried to stand. 'My Jim – my Jimmy? 'E wha'? Where's 'e?'

'In my car, Sam,' George replied. 'He had a bit of a knock up at the farm. Doctor's on his way, though. I'm just gonna bring him in and take him to bed, OK?'

'Wha' you done wi' my boy?' Samuel slurred, lurching towards George who held him back easily.

'He's fine, Sam. Just sit down, OK? I'll be just a minute, alright?'

Confused, Samuel stumbled back to his chair and sat down.

When George and Fred carried Jimmy in, Samuel tried to fight them again. 'My boy!' he wailed, 'My... James!'

When Dr Drake arrived, he studied Jimmy closely, all the while trying to ignore Samuel Worthing's drunken cries and curses from downstairs. He came to the conclusion that Jimmy was suffering from severe concussion, but nothing more. News that George could have wept at.

'He needs rest,' Dr Drake explained, 'But he'll be fine.'

When he left with George and Fred, they promised to visit Jimmy soon – mainly so he did not have to spend too long alone with his drunken father as his only company. However, Jimmy was not alone for long as less than an hour after George and Fred had left, Edward paid him a visit.

Edward walked into the Worthing house to find Samuel passed out in his chair, while upon entering Jimmy's room, he found him deep asleep also.

'Jim.' He took the seat beside Jimmy's bed and closed his eyes. 'I never meant for this to happen! I just – just wanted to scare you, see? I weren't thinking straight! All I knew was that I didn't want you goin' with *her*!' He reached out and gently brushed his hand across Jimmy's cheek. Jimmy began to stir and Edward retreated instantly.

'Ed?' Jimmy murmured. But before Edward could reply, he heard the sound of footsteps running up the stairs and Rosie appeared in the doorway.

'Jimmy?' She instantly welled up at the sight of him.

'Knew I'd get your attention somehow.' Jimmy gave her a dopey grin and she crossed the room to him, perching on the edge of the bed and kissing his forehead.

'I was so scared!'

Edward walked from the room, unable to bear listening to another of their conversations. He had messed up today, but tomorrow was another day.

Chapter 18

By Friday morning, Jimmy insisted that he was feeling better, more than well enough to attend the dance that evening.

'Are you sure?' Rosie asked for the seventh time since she first came to visit. The two were cleaning some of the dishes that Samuel had left behind the night before.

'Positive! Rose, nothing could stop me dancing with you tonight.'

'Apart from my brother…'

'Don't worry about Fred,' Jimmy said.

'I'm not.'

'Just…maybe don't tell your father that I'm going.'

'Why not?'

'He's giving me time off until Monday and paying me full! Don't want him taking it back if he finds out I took you dancing.'

Rosie began to laugh, 'Don't worry, I won't.'

'How you getting there?'

'Said I'd go with Kerenza.' Rosie said. 'Ed's 'parently not feeling well or something. He did look dreadful when I came here yesterday.'

'Ed was here?' Jimmy frowned, handing her a plate to dry.

'I don't remember that.'

'You were only just coming 'round when I arrived, he left soon after. You were prob'ly out of it.'

'Yeah,' Jimmy absentmindedly scratched his cheek. 'Still don't remember nothing about it.'

'Dr Drake said that you might never remember,' Rosie said, ''Parently you hit your head proper hard.'

'So a hay bale fell off the loft and landed on me?'

'That's what Da said.'

'See, I just don't understand!' Jimmy shook the water off another plate. 'Me and Fred tied them down up there.'

'Maybe one came loose?' Rosie suggested, 'Or maybe you missed one? Either way, you're fine and that's all that matters.'

''Ow's my li'l boy?' Samuel came stumbling in, falling against the doorframe. The way he walked reminded Rosie of her grandfather, but Frank's wobbling was not his own fault.

'Fine, Da.' Jimmy turned back to Rosie. 'He kept crying last night and tryna come into my room to tell me he loved me.'

'That's nice though,' Rosie said.

'No it ent, he were pissed! Said it were to "calm his nerves". There's always another excuse.'

'How are you, Mr Worthing?' Rosie pulled out the only stable chair at the table and Samuel collapsed into it.

'The better for seein' you, Helen,' Samuel grinned, 'Wha' you doin' wi' tha' Georgie, eh? Perfeck couple, you an' me.'

He reached out, but Rosie whipped the skirt of her dress away, before backing away to Jimmy.

'You dirty pervert!' Jimmy snapped. 'She ent Helen, she's her daughter!'

'Jussas beau'ful though.' Samuel gave Rosie a wink and she picked up her bag from the table.

'I'm so sorry,' Jimmy groaned.

'It's fine.'

'No it ent.'

'I'll see you at the dance.' Rosie held her breath as she crossed the kitchen and darted out of the house, back into the fresh early autumn air.

Rosie felt sorry for Jimmy having to live with a brute like Samuel. No matter what he did to try and help both his father and the house, Samuel always managed to ruin it again. She had always felt a strange sense of shame around Samuel Worthing despite this. As far as she could see, Samuel was the village's own creation – their very own Frankenstein. Samuel had been shunned when she was just a toddler and since then, his rejection by the village had made him worse. It was as though he put on a show; the village saw him as a disgusting creature so that was exactly what he decided to be. They never spoke about what it was that Samuel did; to this day Rosie was unsure. She had heard rumours, whisperings between folks in The White Lion when Samuel would come stumbling in begging for another drink. The landlord, Henry Bolitho, had even barred him. This ban extended to Jimmy also for a while, but soon Henry's wife Poll managed to convince him that he should not have to suffer for his father's sins. Rosie knew how much Jimmy resented his father and knew that this was part of the reason that he wanted to keep their relationship a secret. While the village did not have a problem with Jimmy, they both knew how people would talk when they discovered a Tregidden was involved with a Worthing.

When the evening came, Fred reluctantly found himself walking up the path towards Birch Cottage in which the Pascoe family lived. He had decided to take Jimmy's advice, to take Madge to the dance and try and have a good time. Jimmy's accident yesterday had made Fred think. Jimmy was someone who always lived life to the full, but could he say the same? As Jimmy lay in the back of the car unconscious yesterday, all that Fred had been able to think was that Jimmy had stories and that people had opinions on him, while he spent his own life anticipating the worst. He did not want to take Madge to the dance in fear of disappointing her, so tonight he was going to try something new. He was going to try and relax. Fred reached the door and knocked. After a few moments he saw movement behind the frosted glass and the door opened, revealing Madge's father. He was a slim man with neat grey hair and matching moustache.

'Afternoon, Frederick,' he said, holding out a hand.

'Hello, Mr Pascoe.' Fred gave him a smile as he shook his remarkably cold hand.

'Margaret's just finishing getting ready, I believe,' Mr Pascoe said, 'Come on in.'

'Thanks.' Fred stepped past Mr Pascoe and into the house. Birch Cottage was always very tidy, with everything kept in just the right place. Fred remembered attending a birthday party for Edward and Madge when they were six years old. Jimmy had stood on the sofa and Fred remembered wondering if Mrs Pascoe was going to cry.

'Take a seat,' Mr Pascoe said and Fred sat down on the very same sofa. On the floor sat the Pascoe's youngest child, Matty, who was drawing a picture. He was only eight years old and had the same dark hair and pale skin as his siblings. The picture that he was drawing appeared to be a boat. A pirate ship? Fred assumed, or maybe one of the naval ships that had been in and out of Penzance harbour throughout the war.

'That's good,' he said, giving Matty a smile.

'Thanks, it's Noah's Ark.'

'He's doing it for Sunday School, aren't you, Matthew?' Mr Pascoe said and Matty nodded.

'Well I'm sure Mrs Jelbert will love it.' Though Fred was not met with a reply from Matty, who had turned his attention back to his ship.

'Haven't seen you in church recently,' Mr Pascoe said, 'In fact, I haven't seen any of your siblings either, just your mother and father; not even your grandfather.'

'Grandad can't leave the house very much anymore,' Fred replied. 'He has trouble walking and won't use his stick.'

'I'll pray for him,' Mr Pascoe said.

'Thank you. And, um, well, I can't speak for my sisters, but I've found myself rather busy since I've been back. I know that Rosie goes sometimes, and so does Inez. But me and Carolyn have been rather busy.'

'I understand.' Mr Pascoe gave him a knowing nod. 'The Lord works in mysterious ways. It is natural for some young folk to lose their faith on occasion – I think our Edward is going through that right now – just so long as you know that God loves you and will find you again one day.'

'I ent a heathen!' Fred blurted, before biting his tongue, 'Sorry, I just mean… I think I know what I'm doing.'

Before Mr Pascoe had a chance to respond, the two were joined by Edward. 'Alright?' He gave Fred a friendly nod.

'I've just been telling Frederick that your belief's been wavering, boy,' Mr Pascoe said and Edward blushed.

'I'm sure Fred don't want to hear about that, Father. He's only come for Madge.'

'He's been point blank refusing to attend church at all,' Mr Pascoe informed Fred, who was beginning to feel a little uncomfortable.

'I know what I'm doing,' Edward said quietly.

'Your mother's over there now talking to the reverend about it,' Mr Pascoe insisted, 'You know how it's upsetting her.'

'Like I said, I know what I'm doing.' At this they fell quiet until Mr Pascoe clasped his hands together. 'Let me go and find that daughter of mine, don't wanna keep you waiting for too long.'

He turned and walked out of the room to the stairs, leaving Fred and Edward.

'Don't listen to him,' Edward said suddenly. 'I'm not doing anything wrong!'

'I ain't judging you,' Fred said, 'I haven't gone for a while either.'

'I've been reading it,' Edward explained. 'The Bible. There's just…some things that I want to understand first.'

'You don't need to explain,' Fred said. 'We all have our secrets.'

Edward smiled weakly. How right he was.

Fred decided to change the subject to an easier one. 'Why ain't you going to the dance? 'Parently Kerenza's not very happy about it.'

'Yeah, I just weren't feeling up to it,' Edward said.

'Oh, please come!' Fred begged. 'Jimmy ain't coming and I need at least one of my mates there.'

Edward's interest piqued at this. 'It's a bit late though,' he pointed out.

96

'No it ain't.' Fred shook his head, 'Go and get ready and me and Madge will meet you there, OK?'

Edward rolled his eyes.

'For you.'

'And Kerenza.'

'Course,' Edward muttered as he left the room.

It was not long until Madge appeared down the stairs, her father close behind. She was wearing a floral black tea dress and had her dark hair tied back simply. 'Are you ready?' she asked, her pale cheeks flushed.

'Of course.' Fred glanced at Mr Pascoe, who had a moody look on his face. 'You look lovely.'

'Thank you.' Madge shot a fierce look at her father, who returned it with disapproval.

'Is ev'rything alright?' Fred asked as they walked down the path, her arm linked through his.

'I'll tell you on the way,' Madge sighed. ''Parently I'm not dressed "appropriately enough".'

Fred began to laugh.

'What's so funny?' Madge asked. 'He might as well have called me a whore!'

'Your father really thinks that you ain't dressed appropriately? Has he seen what the Roskelley sisters wear?'

Madge started laughing at this, swatting Fred's arm. 'Kerenza's my friend and she could be his daughter-in-law one day, so watch what you say!'

'We're going to have fun tonight,' Fred grinned. 'I can feel it!'

Chapter 19

When Inez and Carolyn entered the village hall, the only other people there were Mrs Green, Mrs Jelbert and a few other older residents in the village, who volunteered their time when the dances were going on.

'Why have we come so early?' Carolyn groaned. They had been unable to find anything suitable to cover the hole in her dress, so Inez had hastily altered one of her own dresses to fit her much taller sister.

'Because we're helping out - Hello, Mrs Green, we're here.'

'Hello, Inez dear.' Mrs Green took both their hands warmly. 'Thank you ever so much for agreeing to help out tonight. My two would have come but they already had plans to go to the Winter Gardens tonight.'

The Winter Gardens was the local club in Penzance and Carolyn shot a furious look at her sister as Mrs Green shuffled away. 'That's where we should be, not here!'

'Give it a rest for one night, please!' Inez snapped back. She heard the sound of the first people entering and glanced over at the door.

'Even if he was coming, he wouldn't be here this early.' Carolyn sat down at a table and slumped back in the chair.

Inez stuck her tongue out at her and began pouring some tea.

By the time that Rosie and Kerenza arrived at the dance, it was already rather busy.

'Is there anyone that you have your eye on tonight?' Kerenza was already gazing around the room, looking for potential candidates.

'No one in particular.' Rosie had already scanned the room; Jimmy was not yet here.

'Hello.' Inez smiled at her sister. 'Would you like some tea?'

'Not yet, thank you.' Rosie glanced at the door again. She had a feeling that Jimmy would come walking in at any given moment. 'Maybe a little bit later.'

'How about you, Kerenza?'

But Kerenza was not listening. She had already spied someone across the room. He was taller than everyone else, so very easy to notice.

'Is that Edward?' she asked indignantly, causing both Rosie and Inez to follow her gaze. 'He came in with Madge and Fred.' Inez said.

'Who's he dancing with?' Kerenza stood on the tips of her toes to see. 'He told me that he wasn't coming because he weren't well!'

'I don't think he's dancing with anyone…' Rosie began, but it was too late as Kerenza was already marching across the hall, barging dancing couples out the way as she did. She reached Edward and forcefully tapped him on the shoulder.

Edward jumped and turned to face her. 'Renza!'

'Hello.' Kerenza's tone was so harsh that it caught him off guard. 'You told me that you weren't coming, said you didn't feel well. Well, you look fine to me.'

'I know.' Edward attempted to cobble together a hasty answer. 'I didn't feel well, honest! I weren't gonna come but then Fred convinced me to, you know, so that you had someone to dance with.'

Kerenza's face turned almost as red as her hair as she said, 'I could've had my pick of anyone, you know.'

'I know.'

'But I s'pose that now that you're here...' Kerenza held her hand out to him and Edward took it. 'You may as well have a dance with me.'

Edward laughed to himself and the two began to dance. This was better than he had been expecting; just a dance and nothing more. Kerenza did not expect anything else and he was delighted. He would dance with her all night if she wanted him to.

Madge was already exhausted from all the dancing. They had not stopped since they had arrived. She had not expected Fred to be in such a good mood given the past couple of months, but he was like his old self again; full of love and laughter as they spun around the floor.

'Freddie?' she cried over the music. 'Shall we have a rest?'

'Never!' Fred's face was shining as he beamed at her and Madge laughed, tossing her head back as they danced across the hall.

With still no sign of Jimmy, Rosie had found a seat beside Carolyn and joined her in sitting in the corner.

'Why aren't you dancing?' Carolyn asked.

'I can't find anyone worth dancing with.' Rosie did not mind if Jimmy had decided to stay at home, just wished that he had told her sooner.

'Alf's watching you.' Carolyn nodded across the room to where Alf Bolitho was dancing with the girl from the dress shop.

Rosie shrugged moodily, 'Let him, I don't care.'

'Who *did* you want to be here?' Carolyn asked.

Rosie shrugged again.

'Come on, Rose.' Her sister elbowed her in the ribs with a smirk. 'I know you're courting someone, we all do – well, maybe not Da, but still. Clearly he ent here and you've got teasy cos of it!'

'I'm not teasy!' Rosie insisted. 'You're the one sulking in the corner.'

'Yeah well, I don't like dances, do I.' Carolyn sunk further into her chair.

'Why are you here then?'

'Cos she made me.' Carolyn nodded to Inez who was still serving tea, although a little less enthusiastically than before. 'She's only here cos she thinks Mrs Howard's grandson is going to show up.'

'Poor Inez,' Rosie said quietly. 'She just wants Charlie back, doesn't she?'

'We all do. But I think she's trying to convince herself that Ralph *is* Charlie…and he just ain't.'

After a moment, Rosie stood up. She did not want to be like her sisters, both miserable at dances, so decided to do something about it. 'I'm going to go and get a dance off Alf,' she announced and began walking across the room.

Alf was no longer with the girl and was now talking to his

101

twin brother Walt. They were identical, with the same short sandy hair and wide brown faces, although Rosie had been able to tell them apart since school.

'Hello, Alf.' She gave him the most charming of her smiles. 'D'you fancy a dance?' 'Course,' Alf replied, 'Now?'

'Why not?' Just as Rosie took his hand, however, she saw someone racing across the room.

Jimmy knew that he was late, but he had fallen asleep in the afternoon and had only just woken up. His head was still pounding, and had not been helped after a day spent with his father. As he reached Rosie, he smoothed down his shirt.

'Hello.' He sounded breathless and Rosie suppressed a smile. 'It's not too late to ask for a dance, is it?'

Rosie glanced at Alf, who was watching Jimmy cautiously.

'I'm sorry,' she said and released his hand, taking Jimmy's instead.

Throughout their dance, Rosie kept asking Jimmy if he was alright.

'I'm fine,' Jimmy kept insisting. 'I promise! I don't feel ill at all!'

'I'm just worried, I don't want you collapsing at my feet and dying!'

'I won't.' Jimmy laughed. Suddenly an idea came into his head and he bent in close to her ear.

'Let me show you how well I really am,' he whispered.

Carolyn was growing bored. Her siblings were all busy and she was alone, sitting in the corner. She knew that this would happen. No one ever asked her to dance, not that she would want to dance with any of the men anyway. It was embarrassing, nonetheless, to be the forgotten one. People always commented on how beautiful Rosie was; 'Like a Pre-Raphaelite painting' she remembered hearing Mrs Howard comment once. 'A very pretty girl' they would call Inez, and Fred was known as the 'handsome son'.

The words that she had always heard people use to describe her were 'wild' or 'strong-willed' and 'bright'. 'A pussy willow', her nana used to call her. Sometimes, however, just sometimes, Carolyn wanted to be the beautiful one, the person that somebody loved. She was different to her siblings, she had always known it but as they grew up it became only more apparent to her. She did not fit in and often found herself floating out of her body and watching a situation as though she was at the pictures. What was she doing at a dance with people like this?

Carolyn suddenly felt the desire to be alone. No one would even notice that she was gone. She stood up, bundling the alien skirt of her dress around her and crossed the hall. Behind the long red curtain at the back of the hall were three doors, used for storage and office space. Carolyn turned the handle of one. It was unlocked but shut, so she threw her weight into it and the door opened. As she stepped inside, however, she froze. There, in front of her, entangled in each other's arms, were Rosie and Jimmy. They both stopped what they were doing and stared at Carolyn in shock.

'Carrie!' Rosie's voice came out a little squeal and Carolyn backed away, mortified by what she had just witnessed.

'I didn't see a thing.'

'Don't tell anyone.' Rosie smoothed her skirt down as she

hurried to Carolyn and caught her hand. 'Carrie, please! Don't tell anyone!' Carolyn pulled free from Rosie and walked out of the room, then out of the hall. She just wanted to go home.

Rosie corrected her dress and shook back her hair as she and Jimmy left the room. She looked around in panic, but the room was now just a blur of faces. 'Where is she?'

'Would she tell anyone?' Jimmy asked quietly. 'Rosie, would she tell anyone?'

'I don't know,' Rosie said. 'She might do.'

'We need to stop her.'

Edward watched the two of them whispering from his table. As soon as he had seen Jimmy and Rosie dancing around the room he had lost his enthusiasm. He did not mind watching from the sidelines, however, as he saw things that no one else did. Like the two of them disappearing behind the curtain and Carolyn running out of the room in a panic. It looked like he was no longer the only one in on their secret.

'Why don't you just ask him to dance?' Kerenza slumped onto her elbows, sprawling across the table. She was bored. Edward had told her that he wanted to rest, but was now refusing to dance at all.

'What?' Edward felt the heat rising in his face.

'Well I assume that it's Jimmy you've been staring at all night,' Kerenza replied sarcastically, 'Cos it couldn't possibly be Rosie Tregidden, could it? Look, I know that she's prettier than me, but I deserve some respect surely? As soon as she started dancing, you couldn't take your eyes off her.'

'I'm sorry,' Edward said, his eyes still on Jimmy.

'You're still doing it!'

At that point Fred and Madge joined them at the table. They had not stopped dancing all night.

'It's fun, ent it?' Madge said breathlessly, and Kerenza grunted in reply.

'Ev'rything alright?' Madge asked her friend as Kerenza stood up.

'Your brother would rather dance with Rosie Tregidden, so I'm going to find someone else.' She then barged past Edward and stormed away. It was not long before she found Walt Bolitho, however, and the two were soon happily arm in arm.

'You ent been eyeing my sister up, have you?' Fred asked with a smirk, but Edward was not listening. All of a sudden he was on his feet and Fred turned to see Jimmy locked in an argument with Alf.

'You took her from me!' Alf cried.

'She don't wanna dance with you,' Jimmy insisted, 'So go away!'

'Let her speak, Worthing!'

'Jimmy's right, Alf.' Rosie sighed. 'Alright? I'm sorry.'

'You promised me a dance!' Alf insisted.

Fred, Edward and Madge then appeared, all of them trying to split the argument up.

'Alf, calm down,' Fred begged as Edward held Jimmy back. Jimmy pushed him away and gave Alf a shove.

'Leave us alone!' he shouted. Alf went to shove him back. He was a lot bigger than Jimmy, though, so Fred caught hold of him. Alf pushed Fred out the way, sending him crashing back into the tables. With a sudden loud bang, everything went black for Fred.

When he opened his eyes, he found Inez crouched down beside him.

'Freddie?' Her voice was soft and quiet. 'It's all OK.'

Fred looked around to see that everyone was watching him. He was wet with sweat and ached from shaking. His throat felt ragged, like he had been shouting. Madge had hold of Rosie, both of them had been crying, while Jimmy, Edward and Alf were watching him in shock. The music had ceased and even across the room Kerenza and Walt were watching.

'It's OK.' Inez carefully helped him to his feet and watched him cautiously. 'Ev'rything's OK, I'm here. You're safe. Let's get you home.'

'I'll come with you—' Rosie began.

'No,' Inez said. 'Look after Madge, she looks traumatised, bless her.'

'I'm sorry,' Fred said, though had no idea if this was to Inez, Madge or everyone in the room.

'You have nothing to be sorry for.' Inez gave him a reassuring smile and led him from the room.

Rosie and Edward walked Madge to a chair and she sat down. 'What was that?' she sobbed. 'He was screaming!'

Kerenza came over and crouched down at her knees. 'What happened? He was fine when I left the table?'

'Alf pushed him.' Jimmy said.

'Not that hard.' Alf looked terrified. 'I swear!'

'It weren't you.' Rosie said quietly.

'OK, ev'rybody, the drama's over.' Mrs Green came scurrying along, clapping her podgy hands together. 'Could we have some music again, please?' Rosie did not feel like dancing any more, so Jimmy offered to walk her home. As they reached the door, however, a man bumped into her. 'Sorry.' Her vision was blurred from the tears and exhaustion.

'Rosie?'

The voice was vaguely familiar and Rosie realised that she was talking to Ralph Howard. 'It is Rosie, isn't it?'

'Yes.' Rosie smiled weakly, 'Sorry, this is Jimmy. He works for my father. This is Ralph, Mrs Howard's grandson.'

'Alright?' Jimmy shook his hand with a smile.

'Is your sister around somewhere?' Ralph asked.

'Inez?' No, no, sorry you missed her.'

'Oh.'

'Sorry, I know I seem really out of it, it's just not a brilliant time. I'm sorry.'

'Not at all.' Ralph gave both Rosie and Jimmy a cheery smile as they walked out into the night. He looked at the crowd in front of him. There were dozens of faces, and he did not know a single one.

Chapter 20

Neither Inez nor Fred said anything for a long time as they made their way along the country lane back to Beacon Farm. Despite it now being dark, they both knew the way so well that they could probably walk it blindfolded – which the density of the night gave the feeling of.

'Freddie…' Inez began.

'Don't.'

'But, Fred—'

'I don't want to talk about it.' Fred plunged his hands deeper into his black trouser pockets.

'Maybe you don't, but I think you have to,' Inez said. 'This ent right, what's happening to you. I want to help, but I don't know how when you ain't telling me what's going on.'

'Nothing is. When Alf pushed me I hit my head, must have knocked me out or something.'

'You weren't knocked out, Fred,' Inez said quietly. 'You were quite conscious, just…not there.'

Fred glanced at her. He was not sure what she meant. As far as he was concerned, he had blacked out.

'You were screaming,' his sister explained. 'I didn't even see the fight. All I saw was you screaming and flailing about on the floor. It took both me and Jimmy to calm you down. I've seen you have these attacks before, but nothing as bad as that.'

Fred could feel his eyes prickling and looked away into the night. 'I humiliated myself,' he finally managed to choke out. 'Madge was looking at me like I were the Devil... Ev'ryone was.'

'No they weren't.' Inez tried to hold onto her brother's hand, but he would not let her.

'Don't tell anyone about it,' Fred did not even realise that he was crying. 'Please, Inez, please! You have to promise!'

'I can't, Mum and Da need to know.'

'They don't!' Fred was wailing now. 'Inez, I'll get on my knees! I will! See!'

He collapsed to his knees, but Inez caught him by his elbows. 'Fred, get up,' she said quietly, trying to force him to stand again.

'Please, Inez! For me! Just for me! I'm your brother!'

'That's why I have to tell them.' Inez gently wiped Fred's tears away with her thumb.

George and Helen had not been expecting any of their children back from the dance so soon, so were rather surprised to hear the kitchen door open and for Carolyn to come walking in. They had been trying to listen to the wireless while Frank explained, very loudly, the fantastic deal that a friend of his could do them on a flock of goslings. Carolyn's arrival was a much-craved distraction for Helen who had just about had enough of Frank's shady deals.

'You're back early! Good dance, was it?'

'Oh, you know.' Carolyn threw herself down onto the sofa

beside George. 'Sat in the corner and watched everyone else dance.'

'Did no one ask you?' Frank asked and Carolyn began to laugh.

'Oh yes, a whole queue of boys were begging me to let them take me for a spin around the floor!'

'Maybe if you asked them?' Helen suggested.

'I'd be turned down on the spot! I'm hardly Rosie, am I?'

'Rosie asks boys for dances?' Frank asked. 'Well, I din't expect that, thought they'd all love to be seen with her on their arm.'

'Hey,' George said. 'She's too young to be dancing with boys.'

'She's eighteen.' Helen rolled her eyes, 'I was only a year older than her when we married.'

'But she's my little girl.'

At this, Carolyn scoffed.

'She is! As are you. I hope she weren't dancing with anyone inappropriate.'

Carolyn involuntarily rolled her eyes; if only he knew. 'I think she was dancing with Jimmy most the time.'

George grunted in reply.

'Jimmy's no trouble.' Helen sighed.

'Look at his father, though,' George said. 'Jimmy's turning out like him; lazy, lying to me. Just like Samuel, eh, Father?'

Frank dropped his eyes from them all. 'S'pose,' he muttered. 'I'm goin' bed anyway.'

'Do you want a hand?' Helen asked as Frank made his way to the stairs.

'No!' he grumbled, swatting her away.

'You'll find someone.' Helen gave Carolyn a reassuring smile. 'Somewhere out there, there's a boy waiting just for you.'

'Well I ent found him yet,' Carolyn said, 'I wouldn't touch any of the boys 'round here with a bargepole anyway.'

'What about one of the Bolitho brothers?' Helen asked. 'They ent courting no one, not according to their mother last time I spoke to her.'

'I know things about those two boys that'd make Poll Bolitho's hair drop out,' George grunted. 'I hear things those boys talk about in the field when they think I ain't around. Those twins get it from their father; Henry's all well and good while he's serving drinks, but it's the things he gets up to after hours that no one knows.'

'And no one cares about,' Helen put in. 'You've become a right ol' gossip, George Tregidden.'

'All I'm saying is that the apple don't fall far from the tree – or apples in their case. And I'm afraid to say the same things happening to ol' Jimmy.'

At this Helen flared up, startling Carolyn.

'Jimmy is nothing like that disgusting father of his, and don't you dare go saying anything so horrible ever again! Alright?'

George nodded. 'Just so long as our daughters do nothing but dance with him.'

The tension was broken by the second arrival in the house and Inez and Fred's voices sounded in the kitchen. Inez was using her motherly voice while Fred was mumbling in reply.

'They're back early as well,' Helen craned her neck around to peer into the kitchen. As soon as she saw them both, her stomach dropped. Something had happened at the dance.

'Ev'rything OK?' she asked, walking into the kitchen.

Inez was hanging her coat up and glanced at Fred, who was sitting at the table, his head in his hands.

'What's going on?' Helen's eyes darted from her daughter

111

to her son. Fred looked over his shoulder at Inez, who closed her eyes.

'Fred, I have to tell her,' she sighed before stepping towards her mother. 'Fred had another bad turn. It was the worst one I've ever seen.'

'Oh, Freddie!' Helen sat down in the chair beside him.

'Please just leave me alone.' Fred dodged the arm that she attempted to place around him. 'I told her not to tell you because I knew you'd worry.'

'Of course I'd worry, you're my son, Fred.'

Fred shut his eyes tightly and clenched his jaw, pulling away from her again. 'Don't!'

'What's happened?' Carolyn came into the room.

'Fred had another bad turn.' Inez said.

'Cheers, Inez!' Fred cried. 'Broadcast it to the world, why don't you!'

'What am I meant to say? That you're fine? Because you ent! You screamed the bleddy village hall down!'

'OK, Inez,' Helen said loudly. 'No need for that language.'

Fred stood up, knocking his chair back. 'I'm goin' bed,' he mumbled before marching out of the kitchen. As he reached the living room, he saw George still sitting on the sofa, watching him from the dim glow of the lamp. Fred only glanced at his father for a second before running up the stairs, but still caught his expression. Disappointment.

Chapter 21

'He's refusing to talk to me.' Helen made her way back down the stairs slowly. She had followed Fred to his room, but he lay down on his bed and stared at the wall, refusing to say a word.

She found George standing in the living room, while Carolyn and Inez sat on the sofa. 'Tell me exactly what happened,' he ordered.

'I don't rightly know,' Inez said. 'There was some sorta fight and Fred got pushed and he knocked a table over or something. All I know is that I suddenly heard all this screaming – like proper horrifying screaming, turned and it were him.'

George began pacing back and forth across the room, toward the back door and then over to the fireplace. All the while he glared at the floor. 'There must've been something else, Fred ain't like that, he ain't!'

'George.' Helen just wanted to keep everybody calm, there would be no use in shouting and arguing. 'Fred's not been right since he's come home.'

'He's fine.' George surrendered himself to Frank's armchair. 'Our boy is fine.'

'He ent, Da,' Carolyn said quietly. 'He's not right.'

'Oh, course you'd pipe up now,' George grumbled. 'You sniff

a chance to get some work on the farm and pounce.'

'That ent true!'

'You think that if Fred's too poorly to work then I'll give his job to you.'

'I don't care about that!' Carolyn cried. 'All I care about is my brother!'

'George, don't go taking it out on Carolyn,' Helen said.

'His first turn happened after she stole the tractor,' George insisted. 'She upset him!'

'Dad!' Inez placed her arm around Carolyn, who had started to cry.

'I saw it all last time 'round!' George insisted. 'Shellshock, they called it, gets sparked by things. Well, Fred was upset by that argument.'

'Da, he's been struggling since he returned,' Inez said. 'You saw his face when he first came home.'

'I saw a lad who was exhausted, not screaming and blacking out and who knows what else.'

'Then you're saying that we need to get him help?' Helen said. 'Proper, professional help?'

'No!' George almost shouted this word and then retreated. 'No,' he repeated this more quietly. 'We need to…we can help him ourselves, OK? All of us. We can help him get back to normal.'

He stared at his family in desperation. He needed them to help him. They had to help him. He could not fail Fred, not like all those who had been failed the last time. Slowly, Helen looked at him. 'You saw this the last time?'

George nodded.

'So you're certain you know what it is that Fred needs?'

Again, George nodded.

114

'OK,' Helen said. 'OK.'

'Surely he can't keep on working as hard as he does?' Inez asked. 'At least at the moment.'

'I'll see what I can do.' George replied.

'I know what you're going to say,' Carolyn began, 'But I could always…'

George scowled at her. 'This ent about your petty little fight against me. You can do an afternoon each week, Fred can have that off.'

'How does that help anyone?'

'Take it or leave it, m'bird, your choice.'

At this, Carolyn shot to her feet. 'Why do you treat me like this? None of the others get treated like this.' George did not say anything and she shook her head in despair before thundering off up the stairs.

'I'll go after her—' Helen said.

'No, I will.' Inez stood up and smoothed down her dress. 'You ain't the most sensitive of people at times, Da.'

Inez found Carolyn in her bedroom. She was already in a pair of Fred's old pyjamas and sat at the mirror removing the minimal makeup that she had allowed Inez to apply just before they left for the dance. This used to be the guest room, for whenever the relatives came to stay. Until a few years ago the two had shared a room and, because of that, Inez felt a special connection to Carolyn. They were the eldest two, with only just over a year between them. They had been in each other's lives for ever and Inez felt like she understood her sister in a way that nobody else in the world did. The dress that she had lent her was tossed carelessly over a chair by the door and Inez picked it up, folding it carefully to smooth out any creases.

'I dunno why I bother,' Carolyn said. 'Ev'rything I ever say or do is wrong.'

'It ent.' Inez perched on the edge of the bed. 'He's just under a lot of pressure at the moment, what with Fred and Grandad.'

'Inez, this ain't new.' Carolyn stood up and made her way over to the bed. She pulled the cover back and climbed under it, lying down on her side. Inez knew what she meant. Since they were children, Carolyn had always been different. She was not like her or Rosie, more like Fred, enjoying the things that he and their father did. George thought this was cute when they were little, allowing Carolyn to help plant crops and sit in the tractor as he drove through the village. As they all got older, however, he had started trying to make Carolyn conform more. Inez lay down on the bed beside her sister.

'We've all been saying that there's something wrong with Fred, but what if there's something wrong with me?' Carolyn asked.

'There's nothing wrong with you,' Inez said, 'I promise you, Carrie.'

'I know that people in the village think I'm weird, even when I was little I knew.'

'What, running round and beating up boys twice your size?' Inez smiled and Carolyn let out a laugh.

'I can't believe Mrs Howard remembers that.' She rolled over to face her sister.

'She don't think you're weird,' Inez said. 'She was saying to me that she's proud of you for fighting for your job.'

'Really?'

'Maybe you're right to make a stand.'

116

'Did you get to see Ralph?'

Inez's face closed up a little again as she shook her head.

'What is it with the two of you?' Carolyn asked, 'When I saw you together you got along really well, but whenever you talk about him you don't have a good word to say.'

'That's what it's like with him,' Inez rolled onto her back, 'I don't know what it is. He is quite possibly one of the most rude and annoying people that I have ever met, but then sometimes we get along really well and I feel like we could be good friends.'

'Does he remind you of Charlie?' Carolyn asked.

'No,' Inez said. 'Yes. I don't know. Sometimes.'

'He's not Charlie,' Carolyn said. 'You know that, don't you?'

'Of course.'

'Do you miss him?'

'Of course.' Inez sounded further away. 'Being with Mrs Howard helped me before, but now that Ralph's there, I don't know. It makes it harder. He don't understand the way anything works.'

'Maybe he wants to learn?' Carolyn asked, 'Maybe he wants to fit in but doesn't know how?'

'Maybe...' Inez wanted to like Ralph a lot, but it seemed that every time they took one step forward, they took two steps back. She felt as though everything was slipping through her fingers; her parents, her siblings, the Howards. As she lay on her sister's bed, she made a vow to herself. Inez would make it her goal to put the village back together.

Chapter 22

When Rosie first opened her eyes, she was unsure of where she was. The bed was harder than her own and creaked whenever she moved. As her conscience returned to the land of the living, she remembered. She had been very upset by the events of the night before, playing the terrifying sight of Fred screaming over and over in her mind. As Jimmy walked her back, she decided that she could not go home, not tonight, and begged Jimmy to take her back to his house. He had been reluctant, pointing out that her parents would wonder where she was. Rosie had insisted that they would assume that she was staying at Kerenza's and, eventually, Jimmy agreed.

As Rosie sat up in Jimmy's empty bed, she looked around. Where was he?

Laurel Cottage was very small, much smaller than the farmhouse that Rosie had grown up in. She always felt like an intruder while there, like it could never be her home. She often wondered where she and Jimmy would live if they ever married. She could not imagine living with her husband in her childhood home, but then she could not imagine living in a place like this either – especially not alongside Samuel. It was not something that she needed to think about too much however, for Rosie knew that they were both a long way off marriage.

Outside of Jimmy's bedroom was a tiny two-foot square at the top of the steep and dangerously shallow wooden stairs. To her left was a door that was partially open. Inside Rosie could see Samuel lying in his bed fast asleep, his crooked nose twitching as he grunted and murmured. Rosie, not wanting to wake him, crept down the stairs as silently as she could, clinging to the banister to hold her balance.

Rosie found Jimmy in the kitchen cooking something on the filthy stove. As she watched him pottering around the kitchen, absorbed in his own world, she smiled to herself; what she felt for Jimmy ran much deeper than just a childish crush.

'That smells nice,' she said and Jimmy turned to her, giving her a smile.

'It's just the last few bits I could find in the cupboard.'

Rosie turned to see that three plates had been laid out on the counter.

'Oh, I think your dad's still asleep.'

'I know.' Jimmy began dishing up the breakfast. 'I'm gonna take it to him in bed. Don't think he'll be getting up today.' Rosie had known Samuel to suffer from hangovers, but never to be bed-stricken by them before. He usually dealt with them by getting some more alcohol from the shop, hair-of-the-dog style.

'Is he hungover?'

'Prob'ly,' Jimmy glanced at Rosie before hastily turning back to the plates. 'But that ent why. He always spends today in bed. It's Mother's birthday.'

'Oh god,' Rosie groaned. 'Jimmy, you should have said. I'm

119

so sorry.'

'S'alright,' Jimmy replied, 'Only another day of the year, enit.'

'Are you OK, though?'

Jimmy's mother died when he was very young, leaving him with Samuel. And despite never speaking about her, Rosie had always noticed a small smile creep across Jimmy's lips whenever anyone mentioned Imelda Worthing, almost as if their memories of her were his as well.

'Course.' Jimmy nodded.

'Mum always says what a lovely person she was,' Rosie was hoping to see that smile appear. It did not.

'I'm just gonna take this up to my old man,' Jimmy picked up one of the plates as he walked out of the kitchen. 'You start without me.'

Rosie watched as he left and then took the two remaining plates to the table in the middle of the room. It was piled high with things, so she made two spaces and sat down. Despite Jimmy's obvious attempts to talk quietly, Rosie could still hear him through the paper-thin walls as he tried to hush Samuel's drunken sobs. Her appetite vanished as she listened to the heart-breaking wails. She could not believe how badly a community could treat such a sad and lonely man.

The air was cold, summer had definitely now left. Carolyn was wearing her striped jumper that Helen had knitted two Christmases ago over her dungarees – the first time she had worn a jumper since March. She had not seen her father nor Fred all morning, though she did not mind. George seemed to think that it was some kind of honour to allow her to work one afternoon a week, yet Carolyn just found it insulting. Her father was so adamant to not have her work that he refused to allow Fred even a whole day off.

She was choosing to rise above it, however. Her fighting did not seem to be having an effect, so she decided to try a new tactic. It all began with her offer to go blackberry-picking that morning.

The blackberry-picking was usually a task for Rosie, although she was not yet back from Kerenza's, so Carolyn decided to take the opportunity. She had not fully realised it before, but blackberry-picking seemed to be the task that she was built for. She was tall and her limbs so long that she had no trouble reaching into the brambles and plucking the plump, juicy purple berries from their branches. It was a peaceful job and gave her time to think, though she was not alone. Jessop was keeping her company by running back and forth down the lane and circling her feet.

Every now and then, Carolyn would pop a blackberry into her own mouth, and toss another to Jessop, who would spend the next couple of minutes frantically searching for it in the lane. Jessop had always been her favourite of the farm's animals. Rosie and Fred's had been the horses, whom they groomed and rode for hours; while Inez liked the dozens of cats that seemed to multiply every year, all descendants of their Nana Lizzie's two infamous childhood moggies Thumbelina and Rumplestilskin. The two had given birth to so many litters of kittens that no one was quite sure the exact amount. Some had been sold and given away, but the majority had all moved to Beacon Farm when Lizzie married Frank. It was widely estimated that the Tregiddens' were currently the owners of twenty-three cats and Inez knew each one by name and sight. For Carolyn, however, no animal could beat the scruffy mutt that was Jessop. Other dogs had come and gone over the years; Albert, Trusty, Selma and Rita, to name a few, but for Carolyn none of them came into comparison to Jessop – her boy.

The hedge that she was picking from boarded the field that everyone was working in today, something that Carolyn was already aware of regardless of the loud sounds of shouting and machinery coming from the other side of the bushes and trees. As she rounded the corner and reached the bottom of the field, she heard their voices. She knew that they would be there, which is why she had offered to pick the blackberries here. Her father may think that she never listened to a word he said, but that was not true at all. She had been listening very carefully last night when he mentioned the Bolitho twins' secret chats.

'Jessop, sssh!' she pointed a commanding finger at the dog, who was wagging his tail and pawing at her for more blackberries. The hedge was spacious down at this end of the field so Carolyn found that she was able to crawl inside. The brambles and leaves pulled her hair and caught her jumper as she tried to make her way through as noiselessly as she was able. Jessop had tried to follow, but she made sure he stayed away.

Crawling over the tangle of branches, Carolyn found that she was able to see them. Alf and Walt were digging next to one another barely six feet away.

'Are you sure?' Walt asked, 'I thought Dad said—'

'Yes.' Alf replied in a hoarse voice. 'He heard this morning that the plan's changed. Wednesday night, alright?'

'Is it gonna be worth it?'

'Should be, always good on Skilly, ent it?'

'S'pose.'

Carolyn felt something barge into her and fell forward. Both Walt and Alf turned.

As they studied the hedge, Carolyn held her breath, but they fortunately turned away. 'Alright, let's get back,' Alf said. 'Mr Tregidden will see we're missing.'

As they trudged back up the field, Carolyn turned to see that Jessop had followed her and was trying to take the blackberries from her bowl.

'Ge'off yeh git tuss.' Carolyn pushed him away and climbed from the hedge. Her hair had fallen from the scarf and was hanging in blonde straggles in her eyes, and her jumper was beginning to unravel, but Carolyn did not care. She might finally have found a way to make everything turn out right.

Chapter 23

When autumn came, so did the Harvest Festival, a celebration that the Tregiddens' always revelled in, for most of the produce that the village gave thanks for came from Beacon Farm.

This was the first proper Harvest Festival in six years and Helen was determined to make it triumphant. George and Fred were busy with the final crops up at the farm and Carolyn had mysteriously disappeared. Helen decided to pay a visit to the church to make sure that everything was in order for the service and encouraged Inez and Rosie to tag along.

'I won't be able to stay for long,' Rosie said, 'I've got a few things I need to do this afternoon.'

'The harvest is all about what we do as a family,' her mother insisted. 'It makes sense for my daughters to be in on the organising of the celebrations. Besides, you still haven't told me why you decided to stay at the Roskelleys' house rather than come home on the night of the dance.' Rosie began spieling off some long-winded excuse, but Inez was not listening. She had with her a posy of flowers collected from the hedgerow early this morning and had plans to split it in two. Half of the flowers would be laid on Nana Lizzie's grave, while the other she would place on the war memorial.

Charlie's body had never been recovered from the sea, so this memorial was the closest thing that she had to mourn over for him. She would have liked to go alone, but her mother had decided to use this as an excuse to make sure that Reverend Jelbert knew exactly what she had planned for the celebration – and to make sure that Mrs Pascoe wasn't sticking her nose in where it was not wanted.

As they reached the church, Helen headed straight inside, while Rosie took Inez's arm.

'Shall we go and visit Nana?' she suggested. 'Lay the flowers?' The Tregiddens' were an ancient family in the village, so much so that there were a cluster of graves that bore their names only, reaching back through the centuries. Over the years this corner had become the one dedicated to the Tregiddens. It had the best view in the cemetery, on top of the hill and overlooking the entirety of Mount's Bay.

'There are worse places to end up,' Rosie said, running her hand over a moss-covered grave belonging to *Branok Tregidden*, who died in 1759.

'Let's hope it's a long time before either of us ends up here though,' Inez pointed out and Rosie smiled. Inez used to spend hours in this graveyard as a child. While the rest of the village and her family would congregate around the church, eager for Reverend Jelbert's attention, she would come to this area of the graveyard and speak to the Tregiddens buried here. She always loved imagining what they were like, how they looked and the things that they had seen. Her childhood favourite was always *Jenetza Tregidden*, whom Inez had decided was a runaway princess who married a farmer. Even now she felt strangely at home here, surrounded by the people who all came before her, as well as those she loved.

125

The newest Tregidden grave belonged to Lizzie. The sisters stood beside one another as they silently read the inscription on the headstone:

In Loving Memory of
Elizabeth Rebecca Tregidden
(nee Polgreen)

A loving wife to Francis and Mother to
Robert and George
As well as her many cats

~

A wonderful member of the community

'I miss her,' Rosie said.

'So do I.' Inez smiled. Sectioning off some of the flowers, she placed them at the foot of the headstone.

Next to Lizzie's grave was another. This one was smaller and simple, an arch with a small engraving. Inez never liked seeing this grave, it made her feel uncomfortable and she found that she was unable to keep her eyes on it for too long.

'Are you going to put some flowers there?' Rosie asked and Inez did not reply. She had intended for the remaining flowers to be Charlie's, but now she was here she felt guilty for not leaving any at all.

'He wouldn't know.'

'Neither would Nana,' Rosie pointed out. 'Or Charlie.'

Inez looked at the flowers in her hand and split them again. A few of them she lay down at the foot of the grave:

In Loving Memory of
Thomas Tregidden
5th April – 12th June 1924
(Aged 2 Months)

~

Taken far too soon

'Love you, big brother.' Rosie ran her hand carefully over the headstone.

'Come on,' Inez said briskly, turning on her heels, 'We'd better get going.'

'What was he like?' Rosie asked as she hurried after her sister. No one ever mentioned Thomas, her mysterious baby older brother.

'He was, you know, a baby,' Inez said, 'Just a baby.'

'I never got to meet him—'

'Neither did I really, like I said, he was just a baby.'

She refused to say anything more until they reached the gavelled path again. 'You head back to the church,' Inez said, 'I'm going to the memorial.'

Rosie nodded and ran off back down the path as Inez watched her go. It was not an easy job being the eldest; she had seen each of her siblings arrive, each of them grow up, each of them turning from babies to children to now they were adults. All except for Thomas.

The war memorial was very big and striking, standing in the middle of the path. On it was a plaque listing all the boys from the parish who had perished in the first war. The tally from this time around was still incomplete, although Inez knew that Charlie's name was there. It had been almost a year now since his death, so he was now part of it. As she walked towards the structure, she saw two people coming out from behind it, a young man and an elderly lady.

Mrs Howard was stooped, her knuckles white as she clutched her walking stick, while Ralph supported her on the uneven gravel.

'Hello, my dear!' Mrs Howard beamed, waving her free hand at Inez, who smiled back.

'Hello, you two,' Inez said and nodded to the flowers in Ralph's hands. 'Great minds think alike.'

'Are those for Charlie?' Mrs Howard asked.

'Yes.'

'We saw you over in your family's part and I was telling Ralph all about it, how there ent been a Tregidden not buried here in centuries. There's your wonderful nana, and your grandad's parents and brothers – oh, and of course little Tommy...'

'Granny,' Ralph said, catching Inez's eye. 'Maybe Inez doesn't want to dredge up all of her dead relatives?'

'No it's fine,' Inez smiled. 'I would have had more flowers for Charlie, but Rosie convinced me to leave some for Thomas.'

'Quite right too.' The old lady nodded. 'Shall we lay them together?'

Ralph released his granny's arm and she took hold of Inez's instead. The three then walked around to the side of the memorial that the sun was still on. The temporary plaque, about midway down, read:

Charles Howard

Mrs Howard reached back and Ralph handed her the flowers. Inez waited for her to move before lying her own flowers down in sync. 'Bless you, my brave little soldier.' Mrs Howard kissed her hand and pressed it against the granite slab.

Inez turned back to look at Ralph, who appeared to be bearing a pained expression on his face. 'Are you OK?' she asked.

'Yes,' Ralph replied hastily, 'Of course. I'm fine.'

The three turned and began walking back, Mrs Howard between Inez and Ralph, clinging onto their arms.

'Where were you the other night then?' Ralph asked casually. 'I popped by the dance but you weren't there? Nor Carolyn. I saw Rosie, but she was leaving too.'

'You came?' There was a note of surprise in Inez's voice, as she cleared her throat. 'Oh, there was a little bit of a problem with my brother, I had to take him home.'

'Weren't causing trouble, was he?' Mrs Howard asked.

'No, it's a bit complicated. I'm sorry, I didn't think that you were gonna come.'

'No it's my fault,' Ralph insisted. 'I was late. I was doing some work and lost track of the time. That's the trouble with working from home in a peaceful village like this.'

'There's something going on at the Winter Gardens next week,' Inez said. 'I'm not sure what, I heard someone talking about it the other day. I can find out and we could go to that if you fancied it?'

'I would love to,' Ralph said, 'But I'm back in London next week.'

'I thought you were here permanently?'

'I am, but they need me back up there for a week or so to help with work on a case.'

Inez nodded and gave him a careless shrug. 'Oh, OK. Pr'aps another time?'

'Definitely.'

As they reached the church, Inez released Mrs Howard's arm. 'Well, my mother and Rosie are inside so I'd better go and find them.'

'Thank you for thinking of Charlie, my dear,' Mrs Howard beamed, 'You're always such a thoughtful girl.'

Inez smiled to herself as the Howards' began making their way down the path. She began heading towards the church, but heard the sound of gravel crunch. Turning, Inez was surprised to see Ralph dashing back to her.

'Dinner!'

'Sorry?' Inez frowned.

Ralph smiled bashfully. 'Would you like to have dinner before I go? Or lunch? I don't leave until Friday morning.'

'OK.'

'Yes?'

'Yes.' Inez laughed. 'I have a day off on Thursday?'

'Thursday? Brilliant! We can sort out the finer details nearer the time?'

'Of course.'

'Brilliant,' Ralph said again. 'So dinner – or lunch – on Thursday, perfect!'

'Only if you call it tea,' Inez teased.

'Tea or lunch on Thursday.'

'Perfect.' The two fell into a slightly awkward silence again, until Ralph flashed her a smile. It was a smile unlike any he had given her before, yet something about it seemed remarkably familiar...

She watched as Ralph hurried back to Mrs Howard and the two began ambling away again. They made a funny pair, him so tall and she so short. Ralph stooped down to talk, while

Mrs Howard craned up. Sometimes Inez would see flashes of *him*, Charlie, and forget that he was gone. It was Charlie's height, Charlie's walk, Charlie's smile.

But then she always had to remember the truth. This was not Charlie Howard, he was someone completely different, he was Ralph Howard.

Chapter 24

On Wednesday night, Carolyn Tregidden wrapped up in the warmest clothes that she owned – everything woollen that Helen had knitted for her over years, complete with the hat given to her by Nana Lizzie the Christmas before she passed away.

After she was certain that everyone was asleep, she crept downstairs as quietly as she was able and left the house.

The autumn night was bitterly cold and stung her face and bare hands as she crossed the yard. Her bicycle was kept in the shed nearest the house. It was old and cronky, but served her well. She had found it abandoned in the street as a youngster and decided to fix it up herself, much to her family's concern. Until then the siblings had shared one bike between them, though at the time it was usually hogged by Fred, who went off on long bike rides with all of his friends leaving his sisters stranded at home.

This was *her* bike, however, something that no one could take away from her. A couple of years ago some men had come around looking for metal that the army could melt down and her father had suggested her bike. Carolyn, however, had cycled it down the road and tossed it in the hedge, claiming to have given it away to one of Kerenza's younger sisters.

The bike had grown rusty while waiting for her to ride it again, but after a little bit of loving it was just as good as before. Tonight, as she climbed on the back of the bike, she felt like a child again, off on an adventure. She had no idea what was in store for tonight, but knew that it would be as exciting as ever.

She did not have a light for her bicycle, so instead clamped a torch between her teeth. It was not comfortable at all, but Carolyn did not mind. She enjoyed cycling at night more than any other time of day. She had only realised how much she enjoyed it during the war, when the only time she could take it for a ride was in the middle of the night when no one would be around to catch her. It was different to riding the horses; it felt smoother and more free, almost as if she was a bird of prey gliding through the air. The four of them had all been taught how to ride in the same way. George took them to the hill at the top of the farm, sat them on the back of the bike and pushed. After many cuts and bruises and tears, each of them became very proficient riders. Rosie was the one who rode the least, choosing to stick to her horses rather than a piece of metal with wheels.

She rode down through Penzance, cringing every time she hit an uneven stone and sent it clacking away into the night. There were still some lights on, but most of the buildings were dark with the only light coming from her torch and the orange glow of the streetlights. She ground to a halt and took the torch from her mouth, placing it back in the bag slung over her shoulder. There was no need for it now, not until she had left the town. Although, as she began to near the seafront, the light began to fade again and Carolyn found that she could not see the sea, only a black void, though could tell that it must have been choppy, due to the echoing crashes of the waves. There was not far to go now.

Carolyn began to daydream as she peddled alongside the promenade. This was such a peaceful ride that it gave her time to think. By this time tomorrow she would have proved everyone wrong. She was so much more than George Tregidden's daughter, she was his equal. Tonight she would discover the shady business that the Bolitho family were involved in and then tomorrow she would expose them. It was perfect.

She was so caught up in her daydream that she only noticed the car coming out from the docks at the last minute and swerved to miss it. Her bike toppled over, sending her skidding across the road. The car did not stop and hastily drove away, leaving Carolyn alone. Slowly she sat up. Her head had narrowly missed the lamppost, yet her hands and knees had not been so lucky. From the dim streetlight, she could see that both of her palms were bleeding and her thick trousers had torn, exposing her thermal underwear. Though what Carolyn was more concerned about was the state of her bike! The front wheel had been bent and the handlebars made a gruff clunking sound every time that they moved. She knew that she would be able to mend it, but was not sure how much more it could take tonight. It was broken, yet she still needed it to carry her all through Newlyn.

The trip through Newlyn took a lot longer than she would have liked. It was fine until she reached Paul Hill, which was so steep that her bike decided that it had had enough. Not wanting to mistreat it any more than she had to, Carolyn decided to take the rest of her trip on foot and left her precious bike hidden under a sheet at the fish market.

Finally she reached her destination. Skilly was a small cove in between Newlyn and Mousehole. As a child Carolyn had been very jealous, for the Roskelley sisters would always boast about how their family owned Skilly. It was not until Carolyn was older that she came to the realisation that 'Roskelley' and 'Roskilly' were two completely different names and still felt a certain sense of frustration for ever allowing herself to believe them.

Climbing down the steep overgrown path to the beach, Carolyn paused. She could already hear voices and hastily turned her torch off. She recognised all of the voices immediately, every single one of them. They were all regulars in The White Lion and amongst them she heard the distinctly gruff voice of Henry Bolitho. 'Ge'ere!' he hissed to them all. Carolyn peered out from the trees to see the men congregating around him, each of them illuminated by the dim lamp in his hand. Standing beside him on either side were Alf and Walt, both with their hands behind their identically straight backs.

'Right,' Henry said, 'They're gonna be 'ere any moment, ev'rythin' ready??'

The men grunted in reply.

'Good.'

Barely a minute later, Carolyn saw a light bobbing in the distance. It was a boat coming towards them.

'Right then, boys,' Henry said. 'Let's get to it.' As soon as the boat reached the shallows, the men waded out to it, removing crates and putting them into another boat that Carolyn only just noticed poking out from behind some rocks.

'Smuggling...' she breathed, instantly scolding herself for

saying this out loud.

'I thought I saw something.' Tony Jenkins looked straight up at her and Carolyn drew back into the path, tucking her knees up to her chin as to not be seen.

'Don't see nothing.' This voice came from Tony's son Dennis and Carolyn held her breath.

'Go and check, boy,' she heard Henry say and in a moment heard Alf clambering up the rocks towards her. Carolyn climbed back further into the trees, until she lost her footing and fell backward through to the other side. There was a couple of feet drop from the path down onto the rocks below and Carolyn fell flat onto her back. Though she could not have made too much sound, for Alf clearly did not notice and carried on up the path to the road. Carolyn lay there, desperately trying to force air back into her lungs; it felt as if someone was standing on her chest, crushing her. She saw movement just above her head and turned to see both of the boats rowing away. The delivery boat headed back out to sea, while the second boat scaled the rocks, looking like it was heading back to Newlyn or Penzance, with Tony Jenkins rowing. Carolyn listened silently as the group of men trooped back up the path to the road and when they were eventually gone, she attempted to sit. Her back was killing her and she could still not breathe properly. Finally she managed to get a wheezing gasp in and out and let out a pained splutter. Carolyn's eyes were streaming from the pain her night of sleuthing had endured, but she did not care. She finally had some power and tomorrow she would take her life back.

Chapter 25

Fred was exhausted – more exhausted than he usually was. Every day this week George had woken him at the crack of dawn and taken him for a long run around the fields.

'This is what I did when I got back,' George would always insist as he rode Maxwell, one of the stallions, along beside the struggling Fred. 'Running cleared my mind, got me back into the swing of things!'

Fred would begin his days seething with pain and exhaustion as the dew-covered grass whipped his bare legs.

'Can we stop?' he would cry as they neared the top of the hill where the Tregiddens would have summer picnics.

'Up and over and then you can!' George would call back, 'This is all for you, m'boy!'

On the fourth morning, Thursday, Fred was certain that he could not take anymore – not on his own anyway, so suggested to Jimmy that he join them, desperately hoping that Jimmy's presence might deter George from being so militant.

The morning began exactly the same; George opened his bedroom door and instructed him to dress while it was still dark outside. Then George mounted Maxwell and Fred began to run across the yard.

As they reached the bottom of the lane, however, the two met Jimmy coming along from the village.

'Alright, Worthing?' George asked, 'Din't expect to see you out this early?'

'Thought I'd go for a run, you know.' Jimmy shot a scathing look at Fred, who smiled guiltily back.

'Join us if you want?' he said, 'Going up the fields we are. S'alright ent it, Da?'

'If yeh want.' George motioned for Maxwell to start again. 'We don't stop though.'

'Great,' Jimmy said through gritted teeth. As George began to trot away, Jimmy whispered into Fred's ear, 'You owe me one.'

Fred found that the run was easier with someone else running along beside him, and someone who did not shout as much as George – although that is not to say that George's bossing ceased at all.

'Worthing, you're slacking!' he kept on yelling from up on Maxwell's back.

'How d'you expect me to run through this bleddy grass?' Jimmy shouted back. 'He's spraying freezing mud up at me!'

'I can'elp it,' Fred said, 'S'not my fault it rained last night!'

'Stop complaining, you big Jessie!' George said. 'You've been through worse.'

'I think I'd take being back in the French café over this, wouldn't you, Freddie?' Jimmy grunted.

Fred kept silent. He had no energy to talk, nor will. He just wanted to get this over and done with – which was how he dealt with everything these days. Life was just a series of jobs to get through.

By the time they returned to the farmyard, the rest of the workers had already arrived and were all milling around waiting for George to give his commands. As soon as they saw them, Fred and Jimmy's running slowed down to more of a stagger. George, however, galloped into the yard and ground to an immediate halt, glaring at all of the workers. 'What are you all doing just standing round here?'

'Waiting for you, Mr Tregidden,' Alf said. 'Din't know what we should be doing.'

'You know full well what you should be doing!' Sitting on top of a restless stallion seemed to give George a sense of higher superiority than he usually conveyed, for Fred had never seen his father so short-tempered with the workers. 'It's the Harvest Festival in less than two weeks and I need all of the final crops gathered before then – don't roll your eyes at me, Edward Pascoe, your sister did a fine job of it I seem to remember last year, so I expect your work to be sublime. Got it?'

Edward grunted in reply.

'Good,' George said and clapped his hands together. 'We an't got all day!'

He then pulled at Maxwell's reins and galloped away to the stables.

'Where have you been?' Edward walked over to Fred and Jimmy, who were still trying to catch their breaths. 'Someone said they reckoned Tregidden had given you your marching orders, Jim.'

'Ent got a reason to, 'as he?' Jimmy asked, slight panic lacing in his voice. Edward glanced at Fred and appeared to suppress a smile. 'No, course he ain't.'

Fred looked at his friends. 'Is ev'rything alright?'

139

'Course.' Edward said.

Fred slowly nodded. 'Right, I'm gonna go and get changed, tell Da I'll be there in a sec.'

Jimmy watched as Fred disappeared into the farmhouse and turned to Edward. 'Who knows?' he suddenly asked. 'How many people know about me and Rosie? Have you told anyone?'

'No!' Edward insisted, 'Course I ent! I wouldn't do that to you. But a few people noticed you spending the entire dance together.'

'But that was…' Jimmy began to argue.

'To be fair, mate, even I thought you were laying it on a bit thick. If you don't want people to know then maybe don't spend a whole dance with her in your arms.'

He turned to walk away but Jimmy caught Edward's arm. 'Ed,' he said and Edward turned back. Jimmy glanced over his shoulder to make sure no one was listening to them. 'I'm sorry for blaming you. I should've known you wouldn't do anything like that.'

'You really like her, don't you?' Edward felt his heart plummet when he saw Jimmy's smile.

'I really do,' he grinned and let out a long sigh. 'Right, I'd better go and find some clothes somewhere, can't really work all day dressed like this, can I?'

As Jimmy walked away, he gave Edward a friendly slap on the back. Edward watched Jimmy crossing the yard in his running clothes, his scent lingering. He had never been more envious of anyone or anything as he was of Rosie Tregidden.

He turned around and found himself face to face with Carolyn, who collided with him. 'Sorry!' she said hastily, before seeing the look on Edward's face. 'Edward? Are you alright?' 'I'm fine,' he said and walked away. He had looked so sad about something, almost like he might burst into tears. Still, Carolyn barely gave him a second thought; she had bigger fish to fry. Having spent most of the night deciding what to do about her newfound knowledge with the goings-on down at Skilly, she had finally chosen to target one of the twins, and settled on Walt, whom she perceived as the easiest target.

'Walt!' she called, running towards the barn where she found him and Ivor Sleeman setting up the tractor. 'Walt?' She entered the barn with a smile. 'Can I have a quick word?'

'What about?'

Carolyn purposely caused her cheeks to blush and swept her hair out of the way.

'It's a bit embarrassing.' She glanced at Ivor, who appeared to be pretending not to listen. She nodded towards the door and Walt frowned.

'I'll be back in a sec,' he told Ivor and followed Carolyn outside.

Once Carolyn was sure they were out of earshot, she turned to him, folding her long arms in front of her. 'It's just…well… you see…I'm not sure where to begin.'

'It's alright.' Walt seemed genuinely concerned. 'You can talk to me, Carolyn, we're friends.'

Carolyn smiled at this, feeling slightly guilty about what she was about to do. 'The thing is… I heard your mother talking the other day and she was telling someone – I think it was Mrs Roskelley – that her and your father are struggling a bit, with the pub I mean.'

Walt frowned. 'They ain't said anything to me or Alf?'

'I know,' Carolyn said. 'But that's just it! She don't want to worry either of you. She knows how much you both enjoy working here, but she don't know how much longer her and your father are going to be able to run the pub, just the two of them, see?'

'Right…' Walt said slowly. 'And when did you hear her say all this?'

'Oh.' Carolyn scratched the side of her head, pretending to recall a date. 'A few days ago. In town I think.'

'You know that they work with my auntie and uncle, don't you? All four'a 'em taking turns.'

Carolyn had forgotten that. She had not been into The White Lion for a while and the past few times it had always been Poll and Henry behind the bar.

'Oh.' She had spent a long time planning her story, in the hope that she might be able to persuade Walt to hand in his notice rather than resort to point blank blackmail. But it looked like she had no other option.

'What's all this about, Carolyn?'

Carolyn ran her tongue over her teeth and inhaled. 'I didn't want it to come to this, but you might as well know, I saw you last night.'

'What?' Walt forced a confused laugh.

'I saw you and Alf and your father with a load of others, collecting goods from a rowing boat down Skilly. And by the looks of things they were illegal goods. And what's more, it looked as though you Bolithos were running it all.'

The colour had drained from Walt's face and he stared at her, barely flinching. 'What are you going to do?'

'Nothing,' Carolyn said. 'If you hand in your notice, that is. If you resign from the farm and go and work for your family or something, I'll forget that I saw anything.'

'How do I know I can trust you?' Walt was very clearly

beginning to panic.

'Cos I'm a Tregidden,' Carolyn said, 'And we never go back on our word.'

Chapter 26

At twelve o'clock, every day, Helen laid on a spread for all of the workers across Beacon Farm. Every day was different, sometimes sandwiches, sometimes pasties. Rosie also helped out. She had been hopefully awaiting a job to come up in Polglaze's Dress Shop, but as of yet nothing had surfaced. While Inez worked in the bookshop, and Carolyn in the tearooms, Rosie had remained at home, helping to take care of her grandfather as well as assisting Helen in laying on the daily spread. Rosie enjoyed serving lunch, for she and Jimmy treated it like a game. She would ignore him, purposefully giving her attention to all of the others instead. Jimmy would then try his hardest not to pine; it was the unspoken rule of the game.

At ten to twelve, Rosie always delivered Frank his lunch on a tray in the living room.

'Here you go, Grandad.' She placed the tray down on the coffee table with her usual smile. 'You got sandwiches made with the last of the ham from the Angove farm.'

Frank looked at the tray begrudgingly as Rosie poured some tea from the pot into a cup for him.

'What's that look for?' She asked this despite already knowing the answer. The same answer that he gave every day.

''S'not fair me getting stuck in 'ere.' Frank took the teacup in his quivering hands. 'I'm a farmer!'

'It's more comfy in here though.' Rosie carefully took the cup from him before he spilled it.

'I ain't a baby! I should be running this place, just like my father ran it before me! I never took his farm away.'

'Da's only trying to help, you ain't well enough to work out there, you know that.'

'What d'you know?' Frank grumbled bitterly.

Rosie knew that whilst he was in this mood there was no getting through to him, so she walked back to the kitchen.

'Enjoy your sandwiches.'

Her mood soon lifted however, for, in a matter of moments, the kitchen was full of hungry farmhands all waiting for herself and Helen to serve the food.

'What is it today, Mrs Tregidden?' Alf asked, 'Something tasty I hope!'

'Ent it always?' Helen teased and handed Rosie a tray of sandwiches. Jimmy was sitting in the corner, beside Fred, so Rosie purposefully took the tray to the other side of the table. 'Here you are, Alf,' she said, placing the tray down directly in front of him. As she stepped back, she caught Jimmy's eye but walked away. Jimmy let out a snort-like laugh, which only she and a few others noticed. She felt privileged, however, that she was the only one who knew what had made him laugh.

As she returned to the table she realised that Edward must have heard the laugh as well, for he was now scowling at his sandwiches. *Bless him*, she thought, and carried the teapot over to his end of the table.

'Here you go, Ed.' She smiled as she topped up his mug. As she finished, she noticed that no one was looking and took the opportunity to place a light kiss on Edward's cheek. He jumped in shock, raising his fingers to his cheek, while Jimmy stared at her from across the table. Rosie gave him a shrug and continued topping up the rest of the cups, while Jimmy rolled his eyes and laughed to himself.

She returned to the counter where she found Helen watching her carefully.

'I don't know what's going on between you and Edward, but maybe kissing him in front of you father and brother ent the best idea,' her mother said quietly.

'Oh!' Rosie laughed. 'No, it was just a joke!'

Before she could say anymore, however, Inez entered the room. She was wearing her new red coat and a rather smart dress that Rosie had only ever seen her wear on special occasions. There was something different about her and Rosie only realised that it was her hair when she began walking towards her sister. Inez appeared to have done something different to her, usually very simple, caramel hair – and appeared to have borrowed some of Rosie's own products as well.

'Is Grandad alright?' Inez asked as she reached her. No matter how much she changed her hair, Inez would still always have that mothering concern etched into her face. 'He seems like he's in one of his sulks.'

'Oh he is,' Rosie said impatiently. 'Something about wanting to sit out here and that Da stole the farm from him, blah-blah-blah. Anyway, you look nice, have you done something different with your hair?'

'Oh yeah.' Inez lightly bounced the bottom of her curls with her hand. 'D'you like it?'

'Where you off to?'

'Just the pub.' Her sister refused to meet her eye, 'Me and Ralph are meeting there for lunch.'

Finally Inez looked at her and Rosie gave her a grin.

'Are you?'

'Stop looking at me like that, we're just friends!'

'I never said you weren't! Have a nice time though.'

'Thank you.' Inez walked out of the house, leaving a waft of sweet-smelling perfume behind.

Once lunch was finished, and the farmers were getting back to work, Walt went in search of his boss. He found George in one of the sheds, searching through old engine parts. He stepped inside and anxiously cleared his throat.

'Mr Tregidden? Can I have a word, please?'

George stumbled back over a particularly rusted piece as he wiped his oily hand down his front. 'Course! Ev'rything alright, Walt?'

Walt took a while to reply, rubbing his hands back and forth as he attempted to conjure up the words. 'Yeah, yeah, it's just… well…I wanted to give you my notice.'

George stared at him in shock. 'Your notice?'

The Bolitho twins were two of his best workers and he had been banking on keeping them all through the winter. 'But why? I thought you were happy here?'

'I am,' Walt said. 'It's just Mother and Father need some help in the pub, and I feel like I should give 'em a hand.'

'But I thought your uncle and aunt worked there as well?'

'Things are a bit complicated at the moment, they really need my help.'

'Well, are they OK?' It was true, George had not seen Henry

or Poll for a while.

'Yeah.' Walt was practically trembling. 'Yeah, they're fine. Look, I can work up until the Harvest Festival, but then I'm gonna have to leave.'

'What about your brother?' George asked.

'I think he's gonna stay, but, um, don't say anything to him about it, OK?'

George watched Walt carefully for a moment or two.

'Walt? Tell me what's really going on.'

'Nothing.'

'Walt, tell me what's going on.'

Chapter 27

Ralph was already sitting at a table when Inez arrived. 'I'm so sorry I'm late!' she gasped as he stood to greet her. 'You haven't been waiting too long, have you?'

'Not at all.' Ralph kissed her cheek in a friendly manner. 'I'm typically early for most things anyway.'

Inez pulled out her chair and sat down. 'So am I usually.' She did not want to admit that her reason for taking so long was because she could not get the hang of the style she was trying to copy from Rosie's magazine, so instead said, 'My family always seem to slow things down.'

'It must be nice growing up with a big family around you?'

'I s'pose I'm just used to it, we've always lived together in that house; my grandparents, parents and siblings.'

'I'm still trying to get a hold on the whole family thing,' Ralph said as Inez smiled.

'I feel like we prob'ly know more about each other through your granny than from actually spending time together.'

'That's most likely true,' Ralph agreed. 'Granny does love to gossip. Tell me then, what exactly do you know about me?'

'Let's order first and then we'll compare the rumours that she's spread about us.'

The White Lion had a very limited menu, with only a few dishes that Inez knew were edible. Most days, Poll was the only cook and had a tendency to become overwhelmed when too many orders of various dishes were placed. Once she had subtly explained this to Ralph and he gave their orders to Henry, he returned to the table with an eager look.

'Go on then, I'm intrigued to know what my dear old granny has told you about me.'

'Let me see.' Inez took a mouthful of sherry as she thought. 'I know that you're the elusive Richard's son. That you grew up in London because that's where Richard ran away to and that you're some hotshot lawyer.'

'Less of the hotshot, but the rest is pretty accurate. My father went to university in London and loved it there so much that he didn't ever feel the inclination to return home.'

'So Mrs Howard told me.' Inez felt strange having heard all of the Howard family stories without ever having spent much time with Ralph.

'Yes…' Ralph said quietly, 'Granny has a lot to say about my father. I don't think he ever quite matched my loyal Uncle Michael.'

'I s'pose that's the case when you lose someone young,' Inez said, 'They become these kind of immortal angels that you idolise.'

'You're talking like you have experience of that.'

'I s'pose I do.' Inez sat back and swilled the remains of her drink around her glass. 'Ev'ryone here loved Charlie and I s'pose he'll always be this hero from now on.'

She felt rather peculiar talking about Charlie while having lunch with his cousin.

'I've got that impression,' Ralph said. 'You see, London's

different. There are so many people that no one ever really notices you. You could walk around all day without anyone ever speaking to you. Here, though, it seems like everyone knows everybody.'

'I s'pose we do,' Inez said. 'We've all grown up here, as have our parents and as have theirs. I think your granny was the only person to move here in a long time.'

'So she's not a local?' Ralph asked and Inez let out a laugh.

'Believe me, Mrs Howard is the most local person I know! I don't think there's a single rumour that she hasn't heard – or started.'

Ralph smiled to himself. 'You know, this is the most amount of time that I've spent with her – I know how awful a grandson that makes me sound, but it's true. She used to come to us for Christmas and we would come down on occasion, but I feel I have only gotten to know her now.'

This sounded strange to Inez. For her, Mrs Howard had almost been like a second grandmother. She would buy her and her siblings Christmas presents and had babysat all of them on one occasion or another. She remembered Mrs Howard once telling her that she could not take her eyes off her when she played Mary in the Nativity, despite Charlie having played Joseph.

It was only at this moment that Inez realised something; she was far closer to Mrs Howard than Ralph had ever been. She knew Mrs Howard better than anyone while Ralph was still discovering who his own grandmother was.

'She loves you very much,' Inez said and Ralph gave her a weak smile.

'You don't have to pretend. She's grateful for having me around, but, put it this way, you've known her your whole

151

life, yet when I arrived you did not have the foggiest idea who I was. Neither she nor Charlie had ever mentioned me, had they?'

Inez swallowed another awkward mouthful. 'I knew about your father and I assumed that he had children.'

'Had a child,' Ralph corrected. 'Just me. All Granny had were Charlie and I, yet we still never came down to visit her. I understand her not thinking of me like Charlie. She raised him while I was just the boy in London who sent her a letter every now and then.'

'She loves you!' Inez insisted, 'That day I came 'round for tea. All she could talk about was how proud she was of you and how clever you were and ev'rything that you'd ever done.' She reached forward, placing her hand on Ralph's. 'And now's the perfect opportunity to make up for all that lost time between you both.'

'I'm sorry.' Ralph frowned as he shook his head, 'Bringing the mood down, let's talk about something else.'

At that moment, however, the two were distracted by the pub door bursting open and Henry Bolitho grunting, 'Out.'

Inez turned to see Samuel Worthing standing at the bar. It had been a while since she had last seen him, and he looked worse than ever before. His skin was now the same shade of grey as his lank and greasy hair as he rocked back and forth on his feet at the bar.

'I jusswanna drink,' he slurred and Henry shook his head.

'Not in here you're not.'

'This is a pub!' Samuel slammed his hand down on the bar. 'My local!'

'Which you're barred from,' Henry said. 'Leave now while I'm still civil with you.'

'You ain't civil with me!' Samuel stumbled around in a circle, pointing at every single person around, 'None'a'you are civil with me!'

Inez and Ralph both glanced away, neither of them wanting to get involved.

'Samuel,' Henry's voice was calm but very stern. 'Leave this pub, now. We don't want you in here.'

At this Samuel's face crumbled and he began to tear up. 'What 'appened to community spirit? I were one of youse lot, I grew up 'ere! Why are me and my boy not welcome anymore? I'm a grieving widower!'

'I think poor old Imelda had a lucky escape,' one of the locals called out.

Ralph turned to Inez in shock. 'Surely he can't speak to him like that?'

'Ev'ryone does,' Inez said in a very matter-of-fact manner. 'Ev'ry village has its outcast. He's ours.'

'But why?'

'If you don't leave now, I'll ban your son as well,' Henry said, 'Don't like him very much anyway. Heck, I'll ban ev'ry person in the country that bears the name Worthing if you ain't careful!'

'Worthing?' Ralph asked suddenly.

'Get out, Samuel!' another regular cried, grabbing him by his collar and dragging him wailing out of the door.

'Samuel Worthing?' Ralph gasped.

'Sorry?' Inez frowned.

All of a sudden, Ralph leapt up.

'What's wrong?' Inez asked.

'I'm really sorry, but I'm going to have to go!' Ralph sprinted across the pub.

'Ralph?' Inez called as he hurried out of the door. She flopped down in her seat in defeat and drained the rest of her sherry.

Outside, Ralph looked around. There he was, stumbling down the street. Finally he was able to put a face to the name. That was the infamous Samuel Worthing.

Chapter 28

'Fred?' Helen asked, walking out of the back door. She had been walking down the stairs when she spotted him just standing in the garden, staring at the fields. 'Freddie?' Her son still did not respond. He just stayed completely still, staring at nothing. The sun was setting and had bathed everything in a deep glow of orange and purple. Helen gradually reached out, placing her hand on his shoulder. At this Fred jumped, tearing himself away from her.

'Fred!' she gasped, 'Oh god, Freddie, I'm sorry. I didn't mean to startle you.'

Fred's face was practically grey and glistening with sweat. His breathing was erratic, just as it had been the night after the dance. But this was different. Fred was awake, but…not quite there.

'Freddie?' Helen reached forward, placing her hand on his arm. 'It's Mum.'

Slowly, Fred began to nod. 'Mum,' he replied quietly. 'I'm sorry.'

'It's OK.' Helen drew him into a tight hug and rested her chin on his head. 'Ev'rything's OK.'

'Come. Here. Now.' The voice made Carolyn jump and she turned to see her father standing in the doorway of the farmhouse. She knew exactly what this was going to be about, so made sure to take as long as she was able to cross the yard.

As she entered the kitchen she found George standing in the middle of it, with his thick arms folded across his chest. 'Is ev'rything OK?' she asked innocently and George let out a loud laugh.

'*OK*? Christ, girl, course it ent! I had a conversation with Walt Bolitho earlier.'

'That must have been nice,' Carolyn said as she sat down at the table, resting her chin in her slender hands. 'Walt's a lovely boy, ent he? Nicer than Alf, I think anyway. What was your conversation about?'

'You know full well. He handed in his notice.'

'I'm *shocked*!' Carolyn sat back with her hand springing to her chest. 'Did he give a reason?'

'Oh yes,' George said. 'Some rubbish about his parents needing help with the pub.'

Carolyn let out a long sigh. 'It is a busy place—'

George slammed his hand onto the table and Carolyn leapt back. 'THE NERVE OF YOU!' he roared.

'Don't talk to me like that!' Carolyn cried, 'Just because one of the boys decided to quit! Why d'you always blame me for ev'rything? Maybe Henry and Poll just need help?'

'You scheming cow!' George shouted as Helen came rushing in.

'What's going on?'

'This little madam has taken it upon herself to fire *my* staff!' George spat as Carolyn glared at him.

'How d'you know it was me?'

156

'I got the truth out of him in the end; he told me you blackmailed him.'

'Carolyn,' Helen groaned.

'But did he tell you why? Did he tell you what I caught him and his family doing?'

'Yes he did, but he needn't have bothered because *I knew*.'

Carolyn retreated in shock. How could her father be aware of the operation down at Skilly?

'George,' Helen said. 'Be very careful.'

'What?' Carolyn frowned. 'You knew that the Bolithos were smugglers and didn't bother telling anyone?'

'You think the whole world's black and white, don't you?' George snapped. 'Hasn't what we've all been through the past few years taught you anything?'

'Both of you calm down,' Helen begged. 'Fred's through there an—'

'What we do here,' George interrupted. 'What we've been doing here. People would say that's illegal.'

'What d'you mean?'

'Keeping back eggs and crops, giving them to the people who really need them. The people who can't live off the measly rations the government seems to think they'd be able to. We helped 'em, didn't we?'

Carolyn nodded.

'Well what's so different about what Henry Bolitho and his boys do? I'll admit, when I first heard about it I was shocked. But then your grandad explained it prop'ly to me. They're importing goods to sell cheaply to the people who can't afford nothing else. And what you did was jeopardise it for them. You and your stupid vendetta against me.'

'George…' Helen said, 'Carrie knows what she did was silly.'

'People rely on 'em, like they do on us. Imagine what a mess Janey Roskelley would be in if it weren't for people like us and the Bolithos?'

'Maybe she wouldn't be in a mess if you hadn't fired her daughter?' Carolyn grumbled.

'Kerenza's job was temp'ry!' George cried, 'And she accepted that! All of them girls did, all 'cept you!'

'George, calm down!' Helen begged.

George shook his head and rubbed his face as he let out a groan. 'Carrie, what is wrong with you?'

'I don't know,' her voice came out a very small squeak.

George shook his head and turned away as Carolyn cleared her throat.

'Is Walt staying then?'

'No,' George said. 'He decided that he don't want to work here anymore.'

'Then.' Carolyn took a deep breath, 'Maybe I could have his job?'

George turned to face her, a strange smile on his face. 'There is no way on earth,' he growled, 'that I would ever employ you after all the stunts you've pulled.'

'What about my afternoons?'

'Fred can have 'em back.'

'No, George—' Helen began.

'I hate you!' Carolyn yelled and ran from the house.

'George, Fred can't have his hours back.' Helen said.

'I need some air.' George walked towards the front door.

'But, George—'

'I won't be long.'

'GEORGE TREGIDDEN, LISTEN TO ME!'

George spun around to face his wife, shocked at her

outburst.

'Frederick cannot have all those hours back, he ent well.'

'Nonsense, he's fine. Complains when he's running, but then I s'pose I do push him a bit. Tell you what though, he's a better runner than Jimmy Worthing.'

'Then stop pushing him!' Helen begged. 'George, please! Admit that you don't know what you're doing with him, he's ill.'

'He's not!' George swatted her comment away like an irritating fly. 'Our boy is fine.'

'He was standing in the garden in a trance for crying out loud! He needs help. We need to take him to the doctor's because, from what I can see, he's getting worse instead of better.'

'No,' George said. 'No, I'm putting my foot down on this. Fred don't need a doctor.'

'Why are you so against it?'

'Because you weren't there!' George cried. 'OK? You weren't there, Helen. You didn't hear the stories and see the men who went to see the doctor.'

Chapter 29

After leaving Inez at the pub, Ralph had gone for a walk. It had not occurred to him that he had acted rudely towards her, for his mind was too occupied with other, more pressing, thoughts. He had wandered through the streets and found himself somewhere up in the fields. He had not known how he had gotten there, nor how to return back to his home. He did not mind, however, for it gave him all the time in the world to think. To think about Samuel Worthing. The sun was getting lower and had bathed the entire landscape in a rich, warm glow. Over the hills, Ralph could see the sea sparkling and rippling like liquid gold. There was nowhere else like this, nowhere else so serene. In many ways this landscape unnerved him for he was not used to it. He had grown up in the city, surrounded by big buildings and constant noise and traffic. Upon his initial arrival he had worried constantly about how to fit in. He was different to all these people, that was for sure. And he worried about being able to fit in with them. But then he had found a deep love for everything that the Cornish coast had to offer; the fields, the sea, the people. Ralph had begun to entertain the thought of living here for ever. But that was until this afternoon. Until he finally laid his eyes upon Samuel Worthing.

As he made his way through the long dead grass of the particular field that he had found himself within, Ralph spotted somebody lying down. This person was a young man, who was tall with a dark-haired head that was resting on his arms, which he had folded beneath his chin. Ralph had wondered initially if he was hurt, but, as he neared, realised that this boy was watching something.

'Are you alright?' he asked and the boy jumped. 'Sorry.' Ralph smiled, 'I didn't mean to startle you.'

'S'alright.' The boy got to his feet hastily. He brushed his shirt and trousers down and swept his hair back into place.

'I'm Ralph,' Ralph found himself saying, before immediately cringing. 'Sorry, I just thought I would introduce myself so that you didn't think I was some strange man watching you.' He outstretched his hand with a weak laugh and the boy took it.

'Edward.' He gave the hand a small shake.

'Were you looking at something, Edward?' Ralph asked. 'A field mouse or snake perhaps?'

Since being here, he had not made the most of enjoying what the countryside had to offer, so knelt down in the grass.

'I weren't looking at nothing.' Edward said hastily.

As Ralph peered down the field, he spotted a young couple sitting in the middle of it. They were talking and laughing, enjoying each other's company. Edward had been watching them.

As Ralph concentrated, he realised that he knew the girl. 'Is that Rosie Tregidden?'

Edward glanced at him, startled. 'You know her?'

'A little. Let me guess, you have a thing for her but she's chosen someone else?'

'No—'

'It's alright.' Ralph turned to him with a smile. 'I won't tell her. I think I've met the boy that she's with as well… Jimmy, isn't it?'

Edward nodded. 'Jimmy Worthing.'

'Worthing?' Ralph turned back to the couple in shock. *Another Worthing?*

'Yeah.' Edward said. All of a sudden, Ralph was on his feet.

'Are you OK?' Edward asked.

Ralph slowly nodded. 'Tell you what. Maybe don't go peeping on people, alright?'

He turned and walked away back through the field. Leaving a bewildered Edward behind.

As he reached the bottom of the field, Ralph spied Rosie coming out of the gate. Looking up, he spotted the silhouette of Jimmy walking the other way. 'Rosie?' he called, sprinting after her.

'Oh,' Rosie said. 'Hello, what are you doing out here?'

'Just going for a stroll.'

'How was your lunch with Inez?'

'Really nice.' Ralph suddenly remembered that he had walked out before their food had even been served. 'Who was that you were with? Jimmy from the dance?'

'Yes…' Rosie slowly replied. 'But we were just talking!'

'OK,' Ralph said, 'Just…be careful of him.'

What makes you say that?' Rosie began to laugh, 'You don't even know Jimmy.'

'I know, but he's a boy, isn't he? And you're only young.'

Rosie rolled her eyes. 'You sound like my da.'

'Sorry.' Ralph glanced over his shoulder again, there was no sign of either boy. 'Let me walk you home.'

'It's fine, it's only up there.'

'Please, just for my peace of mind.'

'D'you want to protect me from Jimmy, by any chance?' Rosie asked, as they made their way up Beacon Hill.

'You never know,' Ralph said. 'I'm only looking out for you, Rosie.'

If Jimmy Worthing was as dangerous as his father, then Ralph wanted to keep him as far away from Inez's little sister as possible. And then there was that Edward fellow who had been spying on her through the grass. Ralph felt a sense of protection around Rosie whom he felt did not quite realise the full power of her beauty. He insisted on walking her right to the front door where she let herself in.

'Well,' she said. 'Thank you for walking me back. But you really don't have to worry about me. I've grown up in this village, I know I'm not in any danger.'

'I just wanted to make sure you got home safely.'

'Thank you.' Rosie stepped up onto her toes and planted a kiss on Ralph's cheek. 'Goodnight.'

And with that, she walked into the kitchen, where Ralph spotted Inez. She gave him a look of shock and shot up from the table. 'What're you doing here?'

'I was just walking Rosie back,' Ralph said. 'I caught a boy spying on her.'

Inez glanced over her shoulder to make sure her parents weren't listening. 'Who?' she asked, walking towards him.

'A boy named Edward?'

'Edward Pascoe? His family are devout church-goers, I couldn't imagine him doing something like spying.'

'I haven't told Rosie what I saw,' Ralph said. 'I didn't want to worry her.'

'OK.' Inez nodded. 'Well thank you for telling me.'

As she went to close the door, Ralph said. 'Inez, I'm sorry about earlier, running off like that.'

'It's OK.'

'No, it isn't,' Ralph said. 'It was seeing Samuel Worthing. It's just, you see – oh, it's complicated. I will tell you about it though, when I get back from London.'

'OK.'

'When we go to the Winter Gardens?' Ralph suggested, hopefully.

Inez watched him for a moment as she attempted to read his always carefully guarded face. 'What d'you want, Ralph? You ask me out and then run away halfway through the date, then come and ask me out again?'

'Who's that at the door?' George's voice came from further inside the house.

'No one,' Inez called back.

George then appeared in the kitchen and walked to the door.

'Who's this then?'

'This is Ralph Howard,' said Inez. 'Ralph, this is my father.'

'It's nice to meet you, Mr Tregidden.' Ralph shook George's outstretched hand, surprised by how firm the farmer's grip was.

'Charlie's cousin are you, then?'

'Yes,' Ralph said. 'I am.' He then let out a sigh. 'Well, I'd better be getting back. I'll see you soon, Inez?'

Inez gave him a very weak smile and closed the door.

By the time that Ralph reached his home, the darkness was setting in. He opened the door and found his granny sitting in her armchair. 'Hello, my love,' she said. 'You been gone a while, have a nice time with Inez, did you?'

Ralph silently undid his coat and hung it up in the hall, before walking back into the room.

'Ralph?' Mrs Howard frowned.

'I met someone today, someone whose name I have heard time and time again.'

'Who was that?' Mrs Howard asked.

Ralph lowered himself onto the sofa. 'Samuel Worthing.'

Mrs Howard twitched at the name. 'What d'you know about that man?' she asked.

'Only that you tried to hire my father to take him to court,' Ralph said. 'He still has all of the letters that you sent him, I read them during my training. I used him as a case study. He's the man who killed Uncle Michael and Aunt Olive, isn't he?'

Chapter 30

Inez found her family gathered together in the sitting room. The wireless was playing quietly in the corner as George and Frank both drifted off to sleep in their chairs. Helen was tucked in one corner of the sofa knitting what looked like some sort of jumper or cardigan made from deep-red wool. Her face always contorted tightly whenever she knitted, and she was never able to concentrate on anything else.

On the floor Fred and Carolyn sat playing a game of rummy. They were talking quietly, laughing every now and then at something the other one had said. Inez enjoyed watching Fred smile; it had become such a rarity.

Rosie was sitting beside Helen, perched on the edge of the sofa as she looked in the small round mirror that she had brought down from her room and methodically brushed her long blonde hair. Rosie's hair was her pride and joy and she always made sure to brush it one hundred times, three times a day, a ritual she had learnt from her Nana Lizzie. As a child Rosie had been swamped with waist-long ringlets, which Inez had always thought looked beautiful.

'I remember tying your hair in rags for you,' she smiled, perching on the edge of Frank's armchair. 'When you were little.'

'I used to like you doing it,' Rosie said. 'You used to tell me stories. The ones from Nana's fairy-tale book. You memorised them all, didn't you?'

'Most of them, your favourite was Rapunzel.'

'I always said I would grow my hair like hers – I definitely preferred you tying my rags to the few times Mum let Carolyn, I'm surprised I had any hair left at all!'

'Hey,' Carolyn cried up from the floor. 'You used to wriggle, I only ever held you down!'

'Pinned me down more like!' Rosie laughed.

Inez thought about what Ralph had told her, that Edward Pascoe had been spying on Rosie. She worried about her siblings, as oldest sisters often do, but worried about Rosie the most. Fred was a typical farmer's son, taking no nonsense from anyone – until recently that is; and Carolyn had shown all throughout her life that she knew how to take care of herself. Rosie, however, was different. When she was a little child Inez always viewed her like a porcelain doll, with her mass of blonde waist-length ringlets and pretty dresses; she'd always had a feeling in the pit of her stomach that something would go wrong, that someone might hurt her little Rosie one day.

As she grew up, Rosie's purity never faltered. She was still the sweet-tempered girl that Inez had played with as a child. There was something about Rosie, a quality that she possessed that her siblings lacked. An unwavering kindness towards almost anyone. She could shout and argue just as good as the rest of them, but never over selfish things. The thing that Rosie cared about the most was everyone else. This was not only a quality of Rosie but also a fault, for she could not always see people for what they truly were. Inez saw the way that boys looked at her sister as they walked through Penzance on Saturday mornings. The way that their eyes would linger and they would whisper to one another. But Rosie never appeared to notice.

This scared Inez for she knew what these boys were like and had had her fair share of them whispering about her in the street. She had just never thought of Edward Pascoe as being one of them. He had always seemed so quiet and gentle; a proper Christian boy to fit in with his family. Clearly not everyone was as they seemed.

'How did your lunch with Ralph go?' Fred looked up from his cards.

'Oh.' Inez shook her head with a sigh, 'Fine…until Samuel Worthing showed up, that is.'

Carolyn let out a dramatic groan. 'Ugh! I feel ill just looking at him.'

'That's not very nice,' Rosie said. 'He is Jimmy's dad at the end of the day.'

'Jimmy's very different to his father, though,' Inez pointed out.

'I feel sorry for him,' Rosie said quietly, running the brush through her hair again. 'I think he seems sad.'

'Sad?' Fred let out a laugh of disbelief, 'Don't you remember the bruises Jimmy used to come into school with?'

'It's not like Da never hit you when you deserved it.'

From within his dozing, George grunted.

'I ain't like that bleddy tuss Worthing.'

'No, I know, I'm just saying…'

'Rosie,' Helen said. 'That's enough. Samuel Worthing is an animal and I won't have his name mentioned under this roof.'

168

'But why? What did he do that was so bad?'

'I'm goin' bed.' Frank rocked forward and stood up.

'Rosie, give your grandad a hand,' George said, but Carolyn leapt to her feet instead.

'I will.' She refused to look her father in the eye. 'Come on, Grandad.'

'I can do it!'

'I know.' She took Frank's arm, regardless, and helped him up the stairs.

'What did Mr Worthing do to ruin your lunch?' Fred asked, 'other than being there.'

'Fred.' Helen sighed.

'Oh, the usual,' Inez took her grandfather's seat and settled back. 'He wanted Henry to serve him and then started crying when he refused, so someone threw him out.'

'See,' Rosie said quietly, 'He's sad.'

Meanwhile, down at Myrtle House, both Mrs Howard and Ralph were sitting in the dim light from the lamp standing beside Mrs Howard's armchair. Every one of their conversations since Ralph's arrival had been cheerful and frivolous. This was the first time that Ralph had seen his grandmother so serious.

'I studied the case,' he explained, 'I used the letters that you and my father sent to each other about Uncle Michael's death. You were trying to take Samuel Worthing to court because you were convinced that he was the man driving.'

'I *knew* it were him,' Mrs Howard insisted. 'He was driving the tractor that ploughed into my Michael and Olive! It's common knowledge that he was the man driving.'

'Then why did nothing come of the case? Why was he not prosecuted for dangerous driving?'

Mrs Howard closed her eyes and held her shaking hands up, as if in defence. 'I don't like talking about this. It upsets me to remember.'

'I'm sorry.' Ralph reached out and took his grandmother's hands. 'I'm just trying to understand. The man I met today appeared to be shunned by the entire village. But if it was because of what he did then why didn't he get prosecuted?'

'Cos he lied,' Mrs Howard growled. 'He told 'em that my Michael was the cause of the crash! 'Parently he and Olive were driving too fast and that he couldn't stop in time cos the tractor was old.' Her face flushed red with fury. 'I knew he was lying.'

'How?'

'Because Samuel Worthing has always been drunk from dawn till dusk!' Mrs Howard thumped her fist on the arm of her floral chair. 'I watched him grow up. You know, he and Michael were friends, they grew up together and worked up at the farm. Michael used to tell me what he was like, getting drunk all the time at work and what not. I know that he was drunk when he drove the tractor that day, I just know it.'

Ralph slowly sat back, processing this information. 'Did Charlie know?'

'No.' Mrs Howard shook her head as she dabbed her eyes on her handkerchief. 'I let him believe it were a stranger in the village who did it.'

'Why?' Ralph asked, 'By the looks of it the whole village blames Samuel Worthing?'

'Because right after the incident, Samuel's wife had a baby,' Mrs Howard explained, 'And I didn't want Charlie hating

Jimmy when he was the only innocent one in all this.'

Ralph sat quietly, lost in his own thoughts. His uncle's killer had not paid for his crimes. And his son was now courting Rosie Tregidden.

Chapter 31

The next morning, Fred found himself waking up naturally. It felt strange for once not to have his father waking him up to run. As he sat up, however, Fred felt the uneasy feeling that something was wrong. Why was everything so quiet? The piercing daylight was peeking through his curtains and a quick glance at his clock assured him that it was gone ten. This was the longest he had slept in a long time.

Walking through the farmhouse felt strange. What was usually a buzzing, clustered place was now silent and deserted. As he walked along the landing, he glanced into every room for some sign of life. Each of his sisters' rooms seemed perfectly preserved, like a museum dedicated to the Tregidden girls. Fred found that even his grandfather's room was empty and, upon descending the stairs to the living room, Fred found his armchair vacant as well.

It reminded Fred of the *Mary Celeste*. He remembered first reading about it in a book that he had as a child, spending hours in bed at night pouring over the pages and the mysteries of the universe.

In the kitchen, Fred finally found a sign of life, for his parents were sitting at the table. As he entered the room, they turned, Helen jumping up and giving him a smile.

'Good morning! Would you like a cup of tea?' Fred slowly crossed the room and sat down as Helen presented him with a cup of steaming tea. George seemed very quiet, although this was not particularly unusual at the moment, for he always seemed to fall silent whenever Fred was around.

'Where is ev'ryone?' Fred asked.

'The girls are mucking out the horses,' Helen said. 'And your grandad's gone out with Dick Jenkins on a "spot of business" apparently.'

Fred glanced at his parents. ''S'not like you two to be sitting in the house all day.'

'Well, we actually wanted to talk to you.'

At this, Fred straightened his back. They might want to talk to him, but he certainly did not want to talk to them.

'Go on then.'

Helen glanced at George, who let out a loud sigh. 'Look, we know that you're not very well.'

'I'm fine.'

'No you ain't.'

'I am!'

'Freddie,' Helen said. 'You haven't been right since you returned.'

'That's because I was fighting in a war!' Fred cried. 'I'm hardly going to be thrilled about ev'rything I've seen, am I?'

'But that's not it,' Helen said. 'It seems as though you're getting worse. Almost like you're shutting down.'

'You're wrong,' Fred said. 'I'm getting better!'

'There are some days when you don't utter a single word, not to anyone. We're just worried about you. You're our son.'

Fred sat back and rolled his eyes. 'You think I can't run the

173

farm, don't you?'

'That has nothing to do with it,' George said.

'Course it does, it's all you bleddy think about! It's not even meant to be my job to run the farm, Thomas should have taken that role, but lucky him died as a baby!' As he said this, he glanced at his mother. She looked as though he had just staked her in the heart.

'Fred,' George said sternly, 'We want you to get better for *you*. Not for me or your mother or the farm. For you.'

'Then why did you say to pretend that I was fine? Why did you tell me to hide it?'

'Cos I thought I could mend you.'

'Cos you're ashamed of me?'

'Cos I'm scared!' George cried. 'When I fought in the Great War I saw the treatment that they gave soldiers like you.'

'George, don't,' Helen said quietly.

'The treatments made 'em worse! Some'a them…they ain't right even now. Some'a them are dead.'

'George, you're scaring him.' Helen said.

'He should be scared!' George insisted. 'Helen, he needs to know what might be in store for him.'

'What did they do?' Fred asked. 'To the soldiers, what did they do?'

George sat back, rubbing his rough chin in his equally rough palm. 'Some'a them were locked up by themselves for days and days. Others had what the doctors called "electric shock therapy". They were all called cowards and yelled at until they broke. And then…well…some'a them, the really bad cases… they were lobotomised.'

Fred drew back.

'But that ent going to happen to you.' Helen clasped his

hand in her own. 'OK? Not all of it was bad, was it, George?'

Her husband did not reply.

'George!'

'At the end of the day, most of the lads got worse,' George said loudly. 'Alright? That's why I wanted to do it myself, that's why I didn't want my son going to the doctor.'

'But now?' Fred asked.

George shook his head in despair. 'I don't know what else I'm meant to do.'

Fred pushed his chair back and slowly stood up.

'Freddie, sit back down,' Helen said. 'We'll figure this out.'

But Fred was not listening. He walked across the kitchen to the door and left the house.

'Fred!' Helen called after him, her heart breaking.

Fred felt as though he was dreaming as he walked across the yard and away from the farm, continuing down Beacon Lane. He kept on walking, unaware of anything but the path in front of him. Even the occasional 'good morning' from passer-bys were met with a wall of silence. Why did this have to happen to him? Why could he not be like Jimmy or Edward, shaken by events but, on the whole, fine? Why did they not play the events over and over again? Jimmy told him that Edward had tried to kiss him while out there; that was not normal. Yet he now seemed fine. The whole world was getting back to how it had been before, every cog slotting back into place, but it was as though he no longer fitted. Fred was outdated and no longer designed for this world. When he thought about the time before the war, it seemed like a different life. Like he was someone else entirely. He no longer felt like the boy who ran through the fields and wound his teachers up with his double act with Jimmy. He felt like a stranger in the place he had spent his entire life.

Finally, a voice penetrated his thick veil of paranoia.

'Fred? Are you OK?' He turned to see Madge walking down the path from the vicarage.

To her, Fred looked like a wild animal caught in the sight of a hunter. He was pale and wide-eyed.

'Fred?' She slowly stepped towards him and took one of his shaking hands, holding it tightly. 'Let's find you somewhere to sit.'

Before he knew it, Fred found himself sitting beside Madge at the bus stop. His entire mind was a scrambled blur.

'You were at the vicarage?' he said slowly, trying to organise his thoughts.

'Yeah,' Madge said. 'I was helping Mrs Jelbert with her plans for the Sunday School's Harvest Festival.' She gave Fred a look of sympathy. 'Fred, you don't look well.'

'Ev'ryone keeps saying that.' Fred gritted his teeth, 'They wanna send me to the doctor.'

'Maybe that's for the best?' Madge suggested and Fred drew away from her. 'I'm sorry – do you not want to?'

Fred shook his head.

'Why?'

'Cos of what they do,' Fred said. 'They lock you up alone and cut your brain away.'

Madge frowned. 'For shellshock?'

Fred nodded.

'Who told you that?'

'Da.'

'Fred, I don't think they do, not anymore.'

'He said.'

'But that was the first time round.' Madge took his hand again and ran her thumb over his palm soothingly. 'Fred, I have a cousin who had shellshock this time round.'

Fred looked at her, startled. 'Did he go to the doctor?'

Madge nodded. 'It was while he was fighting. I don't know the ins and outs of it, but, whatever they did, he's so much better now.'

Slowly Fred nodded as Madge tightened her hold on his hand a little. 'Fred, I promise you that no one will hurt you. I know your family would never put you in danger and neither would I, OK?'

Fred looked at Madge properly, eyes brimming with tears. 'I just want to be normal, I want to be *your* Fred again.'

He wanted things to be like they were before, when he would lead the perfect Madge astray. The two would go for night-time swims and kiss behind the church. He longed for those days so much.

'You'll always be my Fred.' Madge wiped a tear from his cheek. 'And I will always be your Madge. Freddie, I am not going anywhere, I promise you.'

Chapter 32

Jimmy wrapped Rosie tighter in his jumper as she gazed out to sea. It was one of those days that was so grey and misty that you were unable to see the horizon at all. All that was in front of them was a wall of white, like they were stuck on a deserted island alone. They could no longer see St Michael's Mount just off from Marazion, let alone The Lizard Point, which usually jutted far out towards the horizon. The two had taken to escaping to the harbour during Jimmy's visits home. There they would share chips and kisses, certain that no one would catch them. Even now it felt like their own safe haven.

'On days like this I like to imagine it's just us,' Rosie rested her head against Jimmy's shoulder. 'That the rest of the world don't exist with its wars and politics.'

'I think the village is just as complicated.'

'No, I mean *just us*,' Rosie sat back up to look at him. 'No one else to interfere or judge. Not your father or my family.'

'I wish that as well.' Jimmy forced a smile. 'I don't want people shunning you like they have me an' my old man.'

'I thought people were getting better, but maybe not. Did I tell you what Ralph said to me the other day?'

'Who's Ralph?'

'Howard. You met him at the dance, Mrs Howard's grand-son?'

'Oh yeah,' Jimmy took another chip. He vaguely remembered him. 'What did he say?'

Rosie rolled her eyes. 'For me to be "careful" around you; he saw us together. I'm sure he meant well, but he don't even know you!'

Jimmy let out a small laugh. 'It's fine, I've had it my whole life, you know that. People hear the name Worthing and assume the worst.' Rosie was beginning to grow cold, so decided to change the subject. 'Are you going to the Harvest Festival?'

'I doubt it.' Jimmy was not much of a church-goer, never had been. Even as a child he could never understand why God had taken someone as lovely as his mother and left him with someone like his father. At school when they would stand to sing hymns, Jimmy merely mouthed along to them and made sure to never say 'Amen' when the headmaster had finished reeling off a prayer. He could not remember the last time he had even set foot inside a church and was sure that this did nothing to help his popularity with the locals, but, quite frankly, did not care. His relationship with God was his and his alone. He saw men sobbing and praying all the time during the war, but could not bring himself to join them. This was a manmade disaster and no almighty being in the sky was going to help them through it.

'Oh please,' Rosie begged, 'Madge has roped me and Renza into singing a song.'

'It ent really my scene.'

'You work on the farm and the Harvest Festival is about celebrating ev'rything that's been cultivated over the year.'

'Yeah, and thanking some imaginary man in the sky,' Jimmy said, 'When really we should be thanking people like your father!'

'How do you know he's imaginary?' Rosie asked.

Jimmy shrugged, 'I don't feel him, not anymore, I don't think I ever have.'

The Harvest Festival was one of Helen's favourite dates in the Christian calendar and she always loved to become involved with the goings-on at the church, although for the past few years Hilda Pascoe had always insisted on joining in as well and what had once been a simple arrangement between Helen and Reverend and Mrs Jelbert had now turned into a committee which Hilda had apparently put herself at the head of. On the day of the festival, Helen was not happy. Hardly any of her ideas had been included in the service, despite her being the wife of a farmer. George had tried to cheer her up, pointing out that she had had a lot on her plate recently with Fred and trying to convince him to see a doctor. Their son had been fiercely refusing, barely even allowing them to mention the word 'doctor'.

Her concern for her son did not outweigh her envy of the service however, as she sat seething on her pew when the reverend began to speak. At the foot of the pulpit was a huge basket overflowing with local produce, all gathered from the neighbouring farms, including Beacon. Helen was not happy. 'They're all in the wrong order!' she hissed into George's ear, 'I specifically told 'em to put the pumpkins at the bottom! But oh no, of course Hilda knew best! I mean look at it, the whole basket looks like it's gonna tip up any second!'

'Ssh.' George whispered, Helen was not exactly talking quietly and Hilda and Victor kept looking at them from over at their pew.

'Top heavy,' Helen said, 'That's what it is.'

Reverend Jelbert either had not heard, or chosen not to take any notice of her talking and had begun the service regardless.

They began by all standing to sing 'All things bright and beautiful', another choice that Helen was not best pleased about. 'I told 'em to pick something a bit different,' she grumbled, 'It's always the same old hymns, ent it?'

'What would you have suggested?' George asked. 'Bit a Glenn Miller? Or that Vera Lynn?'

At this Helen began to laugh, clamping her handkerchief to her mouth in an attempt to muffle it.

Inez was sitting a couple of rows behind them with Frank wedged between herself and Fred.

'What are they laughing about?' she wondered aloud.

'Dunno,' Fred replied. 'But I don't think Mrs Pascoe's very happy about it.'

The Pascoe family were sitting on the other side of the church – at least Mr Pascoe, Mrs Pascoe and Edward were. Madge and Matty were down at the front with the Sunday school children, along with Rosie. Every now and then Fred and Inez heard their parents whisper something and laugh, which was always met with the same icy glare from Mrs Pascoe. She was a very sensible woman with tidy hair and straight, sharp features. Inez had never liked her for she had once heard her calling the Tregiddens 'dirty' when she was a young child. It was true that when they were growing up, Inez and her siblings were usually a little grubby, with grass stains on their socks and mud under their fingernails, yet she took offence to this remark; Helen had bathed them every day so there was no way they could have been dirty. She suspected that this comment merely came from the fact that the Tregidden's were not quite so straight laced as Hilda Pascoe's own children – though judging by what Ralph had caught Edward doing, it was clear that he was dirtier than any of them.

After one of Reverend Jelbert's sermons, the Sunday school was called up to perform their song. At the very last minute a few members had dropped out, so Madge had to step in. She assisted Mrs Jelbert in running the weekly classes so had taken on the role of finding some replacement singers, finally managing to recruit Rosie and Kerenza. The three of them gathered the children together at the altar and stood in an orderly fashion, with Rosie and Kerenza exchanging glances of despair.

Mrs Jelbert started playing a tune on the piano and the group began to sing. At first they were slow, each of them coming in at the wrong time as Madge winced and cringed her way through the first few lines. Kerenza had an amused smile glazed across her face as though she found the whole situation hysterical; a trio of eighteen and nineteen year olds all trying to blend in with an out-of-tune group of children.

Carolyn was watching the whole ordeal from one of the very back rows. It had taken a lot of convincing to get her to the church for it was never her favourite place to be. Now that she was here, however, it was not too bad. She had been expecting the same old dreary spiel, thanking the Lord for a fruitful season, but thanks to her parents' audible commentary of the entire service and now this entertaining spectacle, she was thoroughly enjoying herself.

She vaguely noticed someone sit behind her and glanced around to see Jimmy there. 'Hello, I didn't expect to see you here.'

'Thought I'd come to see what all the fuss was about.' Jimmy rested his elbows on the back of Carolyn's pew.

'You ain't missed much, only my mother and Mrs Pascoe firing shots at each other across the church, and now…this…whatever this is.'

'She's always been a good singer, an't she?' Jimmy smiled to himself.

Rosie was the only person singing who was remotely in tune with the piano. Kerenza appeared to have given up and was standing there grinning while Madge looked as though she wanted to cry and was purposefully avoiding her parents' eyeline.

Rosie, however, was still singing, almost as if no one else was around. Not the children, not the reverend, just her. This was one of those moments, Jimmy thought. The moments when it was just the two of them.

Chapter 33

Once the Sunday school had finished their extraordinarily long song, Reverend Jelbert requested that some of the local farmers come up to say a few words.

George glanced at Helen begrudgingly as she enthusiastically elbowed him. This was one of her ideas that did make it to the final cut!

George made it up to the pulpit at the same time as Murphy Granger, the eldest of a trio of bachelor brothers who owned Galowva Dairy, the farm on the other side of the village.

'Alright, Murph?'

Murphy nodded as they each waited for the other to begin. George, who was reluctant to give public speeches if he had not first had a drink, nodded to Murphy, who merely returned the nod. George finally let out a long sigh and stepped forward slowly, hearing a small tut from somewhere conveniently near the Pascoes.

'Thank you, vicar,' he said, glancing out at the sea of familiar faces. In the middle of them all Helen sat beaming, while a few rows back, his father was scowling at him.

'So!' George clapped his hands together. 'The Harvest Festival! Always a good day innit? It's the day we farmers all get to celebrate ev'rything that we've done throughout the year! See, when we stick 'em potatoes in the ground, none of us know if anything's gonna grow. Not until the harvest. So we all hope and wish that the weather's nice and don't rain too much, but that it ain't too dry neither. And then when all'a that's done, wow, you got a potato!'

George grinned desperately out at his audience, hoping for some sort of reaction. Instead, all he received was a deafening silence. He turned to Murphy, a pleading look in his eyes. 'I'm sure you've got a bit to say as well, an't you, Murph?'

'No,' Murphy crossed his arms with a smile on his face. 'No, you keep talking, George, you're the one who has a harvest. As you said, you "got a potato". I just milk cows.'

George nodded and turned back to the people in front of him. He could feel himself breaking into a sweat.

'I could do better than that tuss,' Frank grumbled as Inez and Fred fought to hold him down in his seat. 'I could! I should be up there you know. Beacon Farm's still *my* farm! Not his!'

'Grandad, calm down!' Inez begged.

'Just stay sitting!' Fred hissed.

George racked his brain, desperately trying to think of something else to say as well. 'Yeah,' he kept on saying, 'Yeah, the harvest…The harvest ent actually today at all. It were a few weeks ago, the main one, and I'm sure we'll still be digging things for months more. It's a funny thing, ent it? I wonder who chose to have the harvest festival now?'

'It's to thank the Lord for a bountiful season,' the reverend said.

George hastily nodded. 'That's right, well done, vicar.' He looked up at the ceiling and suddenly called, 'Thank you!'

Turning back to everyone else, George motioned to them,

'Go on, thank you!'

Slowly they all joined in, shouting their thanks to the church ceiling.

Carolyn and Jimmy were sitting in the back, doubled over in laughter while the Pascoes glared at George fiercely.

'Right!' George announced, confidence kicking in now his speech was over. 'We got a whole loada last year's blackberry wine back at the farm, for anyone who wants to come back and continue thanking the Lord for a boun'iful season!'

That afternoon, Beacon Farm was buzzing with people, from farmers to families to old folk who wanted to make a day of it. George always loved to host; it made him come alive. There was something magical about a whole group of people enjoying themselves, especially these days. This harvest felt incredible; the crops had thrived and everyone had returned home.

'Hello!' George beamed as he reached Victor and Hilda Pascoe. 'Fancy a little glass? My Rosie handpicked all the blackberries and Inez did all the fermentation herself!'

'No thank you,' Victor said.

'We came to speak to you and Mrs Tregidden actually,' Hilda added.

'Come on, Hilda,' George said, 'You've known us long enough, it's George and Helen!'

'Is Mrs Tregidden around?' Hilda asked. George glanced over his shoulder.

'Somewhere, but she's enjoying herself, she's been under a lot of pressure recently.'

'Still I don't believe that warrants for how the two of you

behaved today,' Hilda said, 'Fancy purposefully disrupting the reverend's service just because you can't have your own way.'

'More your service by the sounds of it,' George said, rather matter of factly. 'You know how important the Harvest Festival is to my Helen. She lets you volunteer with helping with all the other special ones, Christmas and Easter and what, but the Harvest is *ours* and you ignored all her ideas.'

'Because, frankly, they were ridiculous! She wanted us to not sing 'All Things Bright And Beautiful' and wanted the Sunday school to put on a play about farmers.'

'What's wrong with that?' George asked, 'It's farmers who put food on your table.'

'You are merely the Lord's vessels and the Harvest Festival should be about thanking him for allowing you the privilege to grow produce. You get thanked all year through the money that you receive.'

'What money?' George began to laugh at the mere idea. 'Any money I receive gets swallowed up by this place! It's all one long cycle. You think you know what God says to you? Well I think I know what he says to me an' all. He says, "Well done, Georgie boy, you keep doing what you're doing, an' ignore them Pascoes, they've got it wrong." You think that you're so much better than us, calling my children dirty.'

Hilda's eyes widened in horror.

'That's right.' George nodded. 'My Inez has always had a good pair of ears ever since she was a little 'un.'

'I weren't talking about your children back then,' Hilda hissed. 'I was talking about you.'

George frowned.

'Just remember, George,' Victor said, 'We know the truth.'

Inez was in the kitchen with Frank, still trying her hardest to calm him down.

'He's taken all this from me! Ev'ry little bit! It should all be mine!'

'Grandad,' Inez groaned, this conversation was becoming a daily occurrence. 'Da hasn't taken anything, he's helping you out! Why can't you see that we all only want what's best for you?'

'Oh sorry,' came a voice and Inez turned to see Ralph and Mrs Howard standing in the doorway. 'Not interrupting, are we?'

'Ralph? No, no, of course not! Come in.'

'It was getting a bit windy out there, wasn't it, Granny?' Ralph pulled out a chair at the table for his grandmother.

'I thought you were in London?' Inez asked.

'I came back earlier than I was expecting.'

'Grandad, this is Ralph.' Inez turned to her grandfather with a smile.

'My Richard's boy,' Mrs Howard added.

'He looks like his grandfather,' Frank nodded, eyeing Ralph up and down. 'That James were never as good-looking as me.'

'Grandad!' Inez groaned, 'He don't mean it,' she added.

'I do!' Frank insisted and gave Mrs Howard a wink. 'I'm sure you'd say the same, eh, Hetty?'

'You do say some awful things, Frank Tregidden!' Mrs Howard laughed. 'I loved my James like you loved your Lizzie.'

'Course, still, we're free and single now, ent we?'

'Stop it,' Mrs Howard warned.

'I've always liked that purple coat you wear.' Frank gave her wink. 'Plum, is it?'

'Frank!'

'Grandad!'

'Excuse me,' Ralph said sternly. 'That's my grandmother you're talking to. She has already told you to stop, so I think you should listen to her.'

'Ralph,' Mrs Howard pulled at his sleeve and he turned to her. 'Don't talk to Frank like that.'

'But, Granny—'

'It were a joke,' Frank said.

'They always flirt with each other,' Inez explained, 'It's just their sense of humour.'

Ralph's face began turning a deep shade of red and he cleared his throat before holding a hand out to Frank. 'I'm very sorry.'

''S'alright,' Frank swatted him away. 'Not ev'ryone gets my jokes, I understand. Mind you, your Charlie always knew how to egg me on!'

'Would you like a drink?' Inez hastily decided to change the subject.

'I s'pose my father hasn't offered you any blackberry wine yet?'

'I'm OK thanks,' Ralph said, 'I'm just going to…' Before he had finished his sentence however, he had already walked from the kitchen and back out into the bustling yard. Once again he was on the outside, oblivious to the in-jokes and going-ons of the village. He decided to enter the nearest barn due to the desire to be alone. Once inside, however, he found that there was one other person there already. 'Oh, sorry.'

At the back of the shed, a boy was sitting on a bale of hay. He had the same face as Inez, though his was possibly even more anxious than hers.

'It's alright.' The boy held up the bottle that was sitting at

189

his side. 'Fancy some wine?'

'Thank you. It's Fred, isn't it?'

Fred nodded. 'Are you Ralph?'

'Yes, how did you know?'

'Lucky guess, Inez talks about you all the time.'

Ralph smiled to himself and crossed the barn towards him. 'What are you doing in here, Fred?'

'I wanted to disappear for a while.' Fred sighed.

Ralph slowly nodded. 'So do I.'

Chapter 34

'He's nice,' Fred said as he walked back through the kitchen. The party was over and all of the guests were long gone. 'That Ralph, I mean.'

'When did you meet him?' Inez looked up from the tea that she was making. Four cups and saucers were laid out on the tray as well as the fat teapot that she was filling up with boiling water.

'Earlier, I had a conversation with him – a long conversation, in fact.'

'About me?' Inez asked and Fred smirked back.

'Wouldn't you like to know.'

From the cupboard he took another teacup and joined his parents and grandad at the table.

'I din't like him,' Frank grumbled, shaking his head.

'You don't like anyone.'

'The way he spoke to me in my own house, on my own farm!'

'He made a mistake,' Inez said. 'And he apologised.'

'Was still rude to me,' Frank muttered.

'Here you go.' Inez walked over with the tea and set it down in front of them.

'What's wrong with you?' she added to her father, who

looked at her confused.

'Me?'

'You've been quiet all evening.'

'And you disappeared halfway through the afternoon,' Helen pointed out.

''ad a bit too much to drink, that's all.'

'You were all cheerful in church,' Fred grinned. 'We could hear the two of you laughing.'

'And we could hear that old man moaning.' George grunted at Frank.

'That's cos you've stolen my farm!' Frank thumped his fist on the table, making the entire china set jump.

'OK, OK, OK!' Helen said loudly. 'I've had enough of you two being at each other's throats; you're family, father and son, no one's stolen anything, you're both cogs in the same machine.'

'Where's Carrie and Rosie?' Fred decided to change the subject, but not to the one that he knew he needed to speak about.

'Not sure,' Helen said. 'I saw Carolyn here and there this afternoon, but Rosie completely vanished.'

'Vanished?' Inez asked suddenly. 'What d'you mean?'

'I don't think I've seen her since church.' Helen began pouring the tea.

'And you don't think that's worrying?' Inez leapt up from her seat. All she could think about was Edward Pascoe. 'We need to go and find her!'

'Inez?' George frowned.

'Da! Why aren't you worried?' Inez asked. 'Your daughter is missing!'

'Is ev'rything alright?'

Inez turned to see Carolyn and Rosie standing in the doorway.

'Where have you been?' Inez marched across the room and embraced Rosie in a tight hug.

'With…the girls.'

Inez stepped back and looked at her sister carefully. 'Are you OK?'

Rosie began to laugh. 'Inez, I'm fine, what's wrong?'

'Nothing.' Inez attempted to sound as breezy as she was able.

'Come and have a sit down with us,' Helen said. 'Your father's had too much to drink.'

'Don't mind if I do.' Carolyn sat down at the table and gulped back the tea from Inez's cup. Rosie crossed over to the other side of the table and sat down, planting a kiss on Frank's head as she did.

'You sounded beautiful in church,' her grandfather said, squeezing her hand in his.

'Thank you, bit embarrassing, weren't it? Madge didn't tell us what it was gonna be like.'

'I don't understand why you needed to sing anyway.' Fred frowned, 'I counted the children and all the local ones were there.'

'There were tons more last year,' Helen said, 'But they've all gone now.'

'Where?'

'Home,' replied Carolyn. 'They were evacuees.'

'They left just before you returned,' Inez said, 'I told you all about Molly – the little girl who stayed here along with Cousin Florence – in my letters.'

'Oh yeah,' Fred said quietly. Why did he not remember

any of Inez's letters? Why did he not remember any of their letters? If he concentrated hard enough, he found that he was able to remember the ones from Madge, and those from his mother as well. But even then the details escaped him.

'I think about Molly a lot,' said Rosie. 'Wonder how she's doing?'

'I gave her our address,' Helen replied. 'She hasn't written yet.'

'Spect she's getting on with her life in the city,' George said. 'It's like the last six years never really happened, like it were all a dream.'

A nightmare, Fred thought.

George then announced that his head was hurting too much and decided that he was going to bed. He was then joined by his family one by one as they all disappeared upstairs also, until just Rosie was left. She had had a wonderful afternoon and was delighted that Jimmy had eventually decided to show up to hear her sing. After church they went for a walk along the cliffs, somewhere it would just be the two of them. Despite initially being concerned that Carolyn knew about them, Rosie was now relieved that her sister was in on her little secret. Carolyn had had every chance to expose them but had still chosen not to; in fact, she had even kept people away so that she and Jimmy could have some time to themselves on occasion. As she crossed the landing to her bedroom, Rosie felt somebody grab her arm and drag her into the bathroom.

'Carrie…' she began as Carolyn closed the door.

'I'm sorry, Rose, but I can't keep lying for you.'

'What d'you mean?'

'You made me act as a lookout so that you could run off with Jimmy this afternoon!' Carolyn hissed. 'They all hate me enough as it is at the moment, and I know that Inez suspects that something's going on. Why don't you just tell them?'

'Because I'll be banned from seeing him,' Rosie insisted. 'Carrie, please! I've begged you before and I'll beg you again if I have to! Please don't tell anyone!'

'What d'you mean, they'll ban you from seeing him? You're eighteen, an adult, Mum and Da can't stop you.'

'But they'll hate me! Everyone hates the Worthings.'

'But you ent a Worthing, you're a Tregidden.'

'Please!'

Carolyn had never seen Rosie so desperate before. She may not have been best pleased that her little sister had fallen for Jimmy Worthing, but she was not about to step on her happiness either.

'I won't tell anyone,' Carolyn finally said, 'But I won't be your accomplice anymore either. From now on, I'm keeping out of your drama.' She turned and walked from the bathroom, leaving her sister alone.

Rosie felt a strange sensation forming within the pit of her stomach. She could feel that her house of cards was on its way to tumbling down.

Chapter 35

I t was so quiet that Fred could hear his own heart beating in his chest. He felt as though it was slowly making its way up his throat and into his mouth and worried that he was about to cough it up onto the floor of Dr Drake's waiting room. There was one noise; a clock on the other wall whose deafening ticks echoed in Fred's ears along with his heartbeat. It was Ralph who had finally convinced him to go. That conversation the two of them had had in the barn on the day of the Harvest Festival had changed Fred's view of the world. Ralph seemed intelligent and experienced. He knew about things that Fred's parents could not even begin to comprehend. Somehow during the conversation, Fred had explained how he felt. It was strange, but it felt easier telling a stranger than someone that he knew and loved. Ralph did not know the old him, he had no preconceptions about who Fred Tregidden was and because of this Fred took his advice to heart. He had no agenda, not like his father or mother or Madge.

The very next morning Fred had booked an appointment to see Dr Drake. He did not tell his parents for a day or so, but when he finally did, Helen insisted on joining him. 'I can explain your symptoms to him,' she had said, 'the things that you might not even realise ain't normal.'

Fred jolted as his mother's small hand squeezed his knee and he tried to calm his racing heart.

'This is the best thing.' She whispered this, despite them being the only ones in the room.

Fred merely nodded, afraid that if he opened his mouth then his heart might actually escape.

'Frederick Tregidden?' The detached voice came from around the corner and Fred felt his heart race again. All that he could hear were the madness-inducing sounds of his heart and the clock. His mother stood up and held a hand out to him. Fred stared at her for a moment, utterly confused, before rising to his feet of his own accord and blindly heading towards the voice.

Dr Drake was a little older than George, and Fred had grown up with him as the family doctor. Despite that, on this particular occasion, Fred felt like Dr Drake was an utter stranger. Everyone was – including his mother.

'So then, Fred.' Dr Drake smiled as he took a seat on the other side of his desk, 'What can I do for you today?'

Fred found that he was unable to look up from the ground; he could not make eye contact with Dr Drake as hard as he tried. Instead he felt the tightening of his skin as he perspired more than ever before. His throat was dry yet every other inch of him felt soaked.

'Freddie hasn't been feeling well,' Helen took the seat beside Fred, placing her hand protectively on his knee. 'Since he returned home from – well – you know.'

'Ah.' Dr Drake nodded, 'I see. D'you think you could explain to me exactly how you've been feeling, Fred?'

Fred shook his head.

'OK, well how about you explain to me why you've decided to come here now. You've been back for a few months, haven't you? So why choose to come and see me now?'

'I can't.' Fred whispered.

'You can't tell me?'

'Go on, darling,' Helen nudged her son gently, 'You can tell Dr Drake, he just wants to help you, that's all.'

'No.' Fred sat back, rubbing his face in his hands, feeling his damp hair stick up. 'I can't. I'm here, because *I can't*. I can't do anything anymore.'

'What d'you mean?' Dr Drake asked. 'That you can't do anything anymore?'

'He's been blacking out,' Helen explained, 'Forgetting what he's doing, having…episodes I think you call them?'

'OK,' Dr Drake wrote this down in his notepad. 'So, tell me, Fred, did you experience this while you were away fighting or since returning home?'

Fred shrugged.

'What about telling me where you went? The countries that you went to?'

'You went to lots, didn't you?' Helen said. 'Let's see, you went to France, Germany, Poland…'

Fred was not listening. His mind had gone blank once again. When he opened his eyes he saw his mother and Dr Drake watching him closely. How long had they been watching him? 'OK…' Dr Drake looked concerned. Before he could conclude his sentence, however, Fred was on his feet.

'Freddie?'

'No,' he mumbled and headed to the door. 'No, I can't –

sorry. I'm sorry.'

'Freddie!' Helen called as he ran from the room.

Fred thought that the fresh air might have helped him, but that was not the case. He did not even realise that he was moving – not at first. It was only when he finally looked up from the road that he realised he had walked from the doctor's surgery and back into the village. People were looking, he knew they were. They were all looking at him and laughing. They wanted to cause him harm, he just knew it!

There was only one person who Fred was certain could help. Only one person Fred knew was safe. Before he knew it, he found himself knocking on his door.

Ralph's automatic smile transformed into a concerned frown as soon as he saw him. 'Fred? What's wrong?'

'I need your help.' Fred had not realised that he was crying until now. 'Ralph, you are the only one I can talk to!'

'OK.' Ralph placed a hand on Fred's shoulder and guided him into the house.

'You just wait here.' Ralph released Fred once they were in the safety of the hall and poked his head into the living room.

'Is that Little Fred?' Fred heard Mrs Howard ask, 'How are you, darling?'

Fred took a shaky step into the living room and saw Mrs Howard in her armchair. He had not been inside Myrtle House since he was a little child and Mrs Howard would babysit for them, it had not changed in the slightest though. There was the same old coffee table with the chip missing from when Charlie fell into it; the same floral curtains and lampshade; even the same expensive-looking mirror above the mantelpiece. As Fred caught sight of himself in the mirror it startled him. His face was red and blotchy and under his swollen eyes were dark bags. He was shaking and his sweat-soaked brown hair was hanging down in tangled streaks. He reminded himself of the monster from that film that Charlie and Inez had taken him and Jimmy to see when they were only ten. Fred had not slept for weeks afterwards, but that monster seemed like a clown compared to the things that kept him awake nowadays.

'Fred?' Mrs Howard said, 'I asked how you were?'

Fred looked at her, he could not find any words.

'I just asked Fred to pop around,' Ralph said, 'I needed to ask him about something. We'll just be in the kitchen if you need anything.'

'You men and your secrets.' Mrs Howard laughed to herself. Fred remained staring at her until Ralph placed an arm around his shoulders and walked him into the kitchen.

'Take a seat, Fred,' he said, and Fred collapsed into one of the three wooden chairs at the table.

Ralph sat in his seat more slowly. 'What's happened? Did you go to see the doctor?'

'They ain't gonna help me,' Fred replied, 'I know they ain't! They can't! Ev'rybody thinks that I'm mad!'

'I don't,' Ralph said and Fred looked at him carefully. Why was he here? Why did he trust him? Who even was Ralph Howard?

'Did you fight?' he finally asked and Ralph shook his head.

'Don't get me wrong, I wanted to,' he hastily explained. 'But they had me dealing with food logistics and prisoners of war – the paperwork, mainly. My father was so ashamed. You know he's barely spoken to me since?'

'Why?'

'Because he wanted his son to fight – and I wanted to fight as well – that's why I feel so awful when I see men like you. Everything that you've been through, everything that you've seen, I got off lightly.'

'So did I,' Fred said, 'I'm not dead, not like your Charlie.'

'You have to live with it,' Ralph pointed out. 'You have to relive everything over and over, Charlie doesn't.'

Fred closed his eyes and breathed in deeply. He had not told anyone about his experiences. 'One day,' he found himself saying, 'We were in Paris and were scoping out a deserted street. Ev'ryone had gone, all the shops and houses and cafés, all of them were empty. And…we were looking in the café – there were five of us, Jim was with me, and suddenly there was this noise. This rumbling that got louder and louder, and we looked out the window and saw them. They were there marching down the road in front of us. Nazis. And we hid behind these big bags of flour and heard guns firing at a different place. They came into the café and were looking round, in all of the cupboards and rooms and they were taking things and talking and joking with each other. I've never been so scared before in my life. I dream, ev'ry night, that they don't leave, that they move the bags and find us all there. I never stop thinking about those people in the café across the road, the ones that they did find.'

Ralph sat silently as he listened to Fred's story. 'I'm so sorry,' he said, 'That must have been petrifying.'

Fred laughed slightly, 'That weren't even the worst thing. That's just the one I can talk about.'

'Why do you think that the doctor can't help you?' Ralph asked.

'Because of what my da said. He told me what they do; they torture and lobotomise and I don't think I can deal with anything else like that. I just wanna sleep, I want to sleep for ever.'

'Fred, there are other means of dealing with this,' Ralph said. 'Your father fought the first time around, but that was thirty years ago. The world of medicine and treatment has changed a great deal since then.'

'They want me to go though!' Fred insisted. 'Mum and Da are always whispering about things and even Jimmy and Edward don't talk to me anymore! No one tells me the truth!'

Ralph frowned. 'I can't talk for Jimmy and Edward, but I am certain that your family only wants what's best for you.'

'What d'you mean?' Fred grew tense. 'What have Edward and Jimmy said?'

'Nothing.' Ralph reached out, trying to calm him down, 'Fred, don't worry, I'm your friend, I want to help you.'

'Sometimes…' Fred said quietly, 'Sometimes I'm jealous of Charlie.'

Ralph slowly nodded. He felt terrible for admitting that he often did too. The boy that everyone loved. The hero of the village.

'You said that you want to sleep?' Ralph asked and Fred nodded. 'Why don't you go upstairs and have a lie down? I need to do something quickly, but then I promise that I will try and help you.'

Fred's eyes widened. 'You won't tell my parents where I am?' he asked and Ralph shook his head. It was not Fred's parents he was going to fetch.

Chapter 36

Inez had always loved the smell of new books. From the still fresh ink to the crisp, unturned pages, to the brown paper that they were wrapped in; all of it practically made her mouth water as she opened each new box. This was where she was at her happiest, in the cosy shop surrounded by unlimited portals to other worlds. Just by opening a cover she could become anyone that she wanted to be. She was certain that this was why she was filled with the warm feeling of love – not because Ralph had just entered the shop.

It was not that the warm feeling faded as such, more that it was masked. Masked by an intense concern as she saw the panic-stricken look on his face.

'Thank God you're here,' he said, dashing through the shelves to her.

'Is ev'rything OK?' Inez left the big box of Du Maurier as she headed towards him.

'It's Fred,' Ralph said breathlessly, 'There's something seriously wrong with Fred.'

The walk back to the village from Penzance was not a long one, yet it seemed to take for ever today, despite the majority of it being dominated by Ralph's panicked and frankly incoherent explanation of his encounter with Fred.

'I have never seen anyone like that before, he seemed so… paranoid, so untrusting of everyone.'

'Ev'ryone but you?' Inez asked and Ralph nodded.

'He begged me not to tell your parents so the first person that I thought of was you.'

'You've prob'ly done the right thing,' Inez said. 'My parents would only panic.'

She knew that her mother was taking Fred to see the doctor that morning so was shocked to hear about the state that he was in now. Earlier he had seemed so willing, eager even, to see Dr Drake.

As they entered the house, Ralph glanced into the living room, before saying in a hushed voice. 'He's in my bedroom – the door on the left. I haven't told Granny that he's unwell, I don't want to worry her, or for her to make things worse.'

'OK.' Inez began running up the stairs, before pausing and turning back to him. 'Thank you.'

Ralph watched her go before entering the living room. Mrs Howard looked up from her book with a smile. 'Did you pick his brains well and good?'

Ralph frowned. 'Sorry?'

'Fred,' Mrs Howard said, 'Did he give you the advice that you needed?'

'Oh.' Ralph glanced over his shoulder. 'Yes, don't worry, he did.'

Inez followed Ralph's instructions and entered the room on the left. This had been known as the guest bedroom for as long as she had been coming to the Howards' house. She had once stayed in this room when she was young. On the night that Tommy died. She only remembered things very fleetingly, having been woken up by her mother's frantic cries for help being the first. Carolyn, in the bed across from her, had started crying from the noise of their parents and grandparents running about trying their best to help, but Inez had sat there silently, listening as the ordeal unfolded. She distinctly remembered the orange strip of light that had leaked in under the door from the landing outside and every now and then an elongated shadow appearing along with the frantic padding of feet.

Then Nana Lizzie had come in. Her round face, which was usually so rosy and kind, looked strangely contorted and shiny. What Inez remembered most clearly, however, was her hair. She had only ever seen her nana's grey hair tied up and out of the way as she fussed with her cats and chickens and granddaughters. But that night it was long and wispy, like the illustration of the witch in the book that Inez had been reading. For the first and only time in her life, Inez was scared by Nana Lizzie, even as she smiled.

'Come here, Carolyn,' Nana Lizzie had said, her voice did not sound right either, cracking and squawking. She had climbed onto Carolyn's bed and cuddled her in close.

'Come here, Inez, sweetheart.' She had extended an arm to Inez, who had simply stared back warily.

Then she had told them the news. That they were going on a little adventure to Mrs Howards' house and the next thing that Inez could remember was being tucked up in Mrs Howards' spare room by Nana Lizzie and Mrs Howard. Carolyn was cuddled in close next to her, her blonde curls tickling her ears.

'I love you both very much, my little princesses,' Nana Lizzie had said and kissed both of their foreheads.

Inez had heard her crying from behind the closed door and Mrs Howard comforting her.

'Hetty, he's gone!'

'These things just happen, Bets.'

Despite not being told the news of Tommy's death until the following day, as Inez lay in the strange bed with her sister, she knew that she would never be seeing her brother again.

Inez braced herself as she opened the door, with memories of that blank room still etched into her mind. It was a pleasant surprise however, to see that the room had changed. It was no longer bare and empty, but looked lived in.

Ralph's clothes were all hung up neatly in the wardrobe, of which the doors seemed to have disappeared revealing his various suits and shirts and jackets. In the middle of the room Ralph's bed stood, the very same bed that Inez had lain in all those years ago, and now on which her other brother lay, his head against the pillow, seemingly sound asleep.

On the bedside table three photographs were standing. One was of Ralph and his parents when he was a young child, all serious-faced and sensible. Beside this one, a photograph of Ralph and his granny at his graduation from law school; Mrs Howard looked so proud as she beamed up at him. Inez remembered this day, for she remembered Charlie inviting her around, saying that his granny had gone to London for his cousin's graduation. Inez had stayed for tea and nothing more.

The third photograph stunned Inez, for it was one that she had seen many times before. It was of a naval soldier taken just before he went to sea, a proud grin on his face and a hat that made his ears look bigger than they were. He looked like a boy playing dress up, Inez always thought whenever she looked at the identical photo on her bedside table. For her to have this photo was normal, but for Ralph it seemed rather peculiar.

Why did he have a photograph of his cousin beside his bed? Before she had a chance to question this anymore, however, Fred began to stir.

'Freddie?' she said and crouched down beside him. Immediately Fred drew back, startled.

'Don't send me away!' he begged, 'Don't! Please!'

'Fred,' Inez stroked his dark brown hair as she soothed him. 'I'm not going to send you anywhere. It's me, Inez.'

Fred's eyes widened with recognition. 'Inez? Is that you?'

'Yes, Freddie, it's me.'

Fred buried into her arms and began to whimper.

'I'm scared they're gonna hurt me, you won't let them hurt me, will you?'

'Course not,' Inez kissed his forehead as Fred lay back down. Ralph had explained to her how her brother had been, acting erratic and delusional. 'I promise you, Freddie, I'm not going to let anything bad happen to you again.'

Chapter 37

After a long time, Fred finally agreed to leave Myrtle House and allowed Inez to take him back home to Beacon farm.

It became clear that they could not keep Mrs Howard in the dark for much longer, so Ralph decided to explain to her what had been going on.

'That poor boy,' the old woman sighed as Ralph concluded his story. She hung her head and shook it. 'I remember when Michael came home from the Great War,' she said, before letting out a small laugh. 'Seems strange, don't it? That was always the Great War, but it was nothing compared to this last one, I wonder what we'll all call it in the years to come?'

'I don't know,' Ralph said quietly. 'You were going to say something about Uncle Michael though, about when he came home?'

'Yes, he was taken to hospital while he was away and treated for shellshock, don't think it did him any good though. Why, I remember when he came home, I had never seen a person look so ghost-like. He was twenty years old and looked like an old man, but they said he was well enough to fight, and so he did.'

Ralph shook his head in disbelief, he could not believe how

these men had been treated.

'He used to cry ev'ry single night,' Mrs Howard continued, 'I could hear him. Your father had left home by then so it was just the two of us, I never knew what I was supposed to do.'

'But he got better?'

'In many ways yes, but never completely. It was Olive that helped him. When he met her, it brought him out of his shell and when they were together I could see him again. My Michael.'

The two sat quietly for a moment before Ralph conjured up the courage to ask, 'What about my father? How was he when he returned?'

At this Mrs Howard glanced away, suddenly finding interest in a stain on the mantelpiece.

'What you have to understand about your father, Ralph, is that he has always been a very private person, even as a boy. When the war happened he was already living in London and was married. He never told his old mother anything.'

'He was furious with me,' Ralph said, 'When I told him that I wasn't fighting.'

'But that was your work.'

'I know that, but he didn't see it that way. He thought I was a coward and that I didn't care about the country, but I did!'

'Of course you did.' Mrs Howard reached across and enclosed a shaky hand around Ralph's.

'But then I see boys like Fred Tregidden and it makes me feel ashamed for not doing my bit.'

'But you did do your bit!'

'But I didn't suffer, I wasn't tormented like they all were. You know – and I know this sounds awful – I think men like Charlie had a lucky escape; they don't have to live everyday remembering the horrors.'

'Neither do you,' Mrs Howard replied indignantly, releasing Ralph's hand as he cringed.

'I don't mean me, I mean the likes of Fred!'

'More boys than Fred Tregidden went to war,' Mrs Howard said bluntly. 'There's the Pascoes' boy, those Bolitho twins, even James Worthing, to name just a few.'

'That was the other thing.' Ralph knew that he was turning the subject onto an even riskier one. 'I remember you told me that the reason why you never pushed charges against Samuel Worthing was because of his son. Well, what if I told you that his son was bad news as well?'

'James?' Mrs Howard let out a laugh, 'Don't be silly. He might be a bit cheeky sometimes – 'specially when he was a boy, but that don't make him bad news.'

'He seems to have this strange obsession with Rosie, you know, the youngest Tregidden daughter. When Fred was here earlier and I mentioned Jimmy, he seemed terrified of him.'

'You're mistaken, Ralph. Jimmy and Fred have been the best of friends since they were tiny children. Now, I'm going to make some tea, would you like any?' She hauled herself from her chair, her stooped back cracking and popping.

'But, Granny, I'm just telling you what I heard,' Ralph said. 'I don't want Jimmy doing what his father did!'

'What d'you mean?' Mrs Howard scoffed. 'Like father, like son?'

'I-I suppose.'

'Well maybe you should stop worrying about people you don't even know and start worrying about yourself!' his granny snapped, glaring at him.

Ralph fell silent immediately.

Mrs Howard turned and began to shuffle out of the room.

'What do you mean?' Ralph asked, following her. 'Granny?'

'I mean, the longer I spend with you, the more I worry that you're like your father!' Mrs Howard threw over her shoulder, 'Cold and selfish, dealing with things like a bull in a china shop, and always sticking your nose where it's not wanted and never sticking it where it is!'

Ralph remained completely stunned by this sudden outburst. 'I don't understand?'

'What I mean is, your father ran away from here as quick as he could just cos he thought he was better than us, more clever than us. Did he ever write? Never. Did he ever come home? Only when he had to. And now here you are like his little shadow. You never took the slightest bit of interest in me until Charlie died.'

'That's not true—'

'What d'you want from me, Ralph? Did your father send you for my money? Because I can assure you that I don't have any!'

'Granny, when have I ever mentioned your money?' Ralph asked. 'I'm here because you're on your own! I'm here because I love you.'

'But did you love me before you became my only grandchild?' Mrs Howard asked.

'Of course,' Ralph insisted. 'It isn't my fault that my father never let me see you!'

'You're a grown man, Ralph,' Mrs Howard snapped. 'And yet still you hide behind Daddy. It seems to me that you've turned up to try and replace Charlie. Getting involved in ev'ryone's business, getting close to the Tregiddens. Even courting Inez, for crying out loud! You will never be able to replace Charlie, because my Charlie was special! He was so, so special and—'

She held her hand up to her mouth to stifle her sobs. 'He was all that I had left!'

Ralph wanted to comfort her, wanted to reassure her that she still had him, but did not know how. He was terrified of being accused of stealing Charlie's identity again. He had not thought of it like that. When he made his snap decision to move to Cornwall it was all based on the guilt he felt whenever he thought of his granny alone at home. But maybe he was wrong. His granny had lots of people; she had Inez, she had Frank, she had the entire village and Charlie was just one of those people. Maybe Ralph was just a fool for thinking that she needed him too? Maybe this had all just been a nice holiday, but now it was time to go home.

Mrs Howard pulled out a chair at the kitchen table and sat down in it as she sobbed.

'I'll be out of your hair soon,' Ralph said. 'I'll go back to London. I'm sure that they'll take me back in the office, I haven't been gone for long. If that's what you want, Granny?'

Mrs Howard did not reply. Slowly, Ralph nodded and turned away.

'I've locked him in his room,' Helen said. 'So that he can't run away again.' She placed the key to Fred's bedroom door on the kitchen table and threw herself into a chair.

'What good's that going to do?' Inez asked. 'From what Ralph told me, Fred's terrified of being locked up, whether that's by enemies or doctors.'

'But we're his family,' George said.

'I don't want to lay the blame on anyone.' Inez stood up

and began pacing around the kitchen. 'But Fred's got worse since…'

'Since I tried to help him,' George grumbled, 'Sorry, but I ent an expert, am I?'

'Course not,' Helen said. 'Which is why I said he should have gone to the doctor straight away.'

'I thought I knew what was best, but clearly I was wrong. It ent easy juggling so many plates!'

'Spinning plates,' Inez quietly corrected.

'Whatever,' George grumbled. 'Maybe I could have taken more time with Fred, done things differently, but I've been trying to keep this farm afloat – which ent easy, I might add, when I've got my father criticising me day and night and my daughter trying to sabotage my livelihood.'

'This ent Carrie's fault, so don't put the blame on her,' Helen said.

'She's not exactly made things easy, has she? We're all here trying to help Fred while she's stealing my tractors and firing my staff!'

Inez groaned. 'She did that once.'

'I'm sick of her!' George cried. 'My only son's gone mad and I'm too busy running around and cleaning up the mess that she creates!'

'Maybe it's my fault?' Inez said. 'I told her it was a good idea to make a stand.'

'No, it's all her own doing,' George replied. 'She's never been one to do as she's told.'

'Fred and Carolyn are two very different issues,' Helen said calmly. 'We need to deal with them one at a time.'

'Which is more important?' George asked sarcastically. 'Our son who's on self-destruct mode, or our daughter who's about to detonate?'

Little did any of them realise that, just behind the kitchen door, Carolyn was lurking and listening to every word. They were sick of her? Well she was sick of them as well.

Chapter 38

I t may have looked like it was all little Matty Pascoe's fault, but he had only been looking for somewhere to keep his drawings – and, after all, secrets always have a way of coming out eventually.

Hilda was having one of those days where she had too much to do and no time to do any of it, which is why she became so frantic when, upon entering the living room, she found a pile of letters scattered on the floor and Matty filling the box that they had once occupied with copious amounts of drawings involving the biblical scenes that he had been creating.

'What are you doing?' Hilda cried, 'You know we have the reverend and his wife coming for tea this afternoon!'

Matty retreated immediately. 'You told me to organise my drawings for Mrs Jelbert to look through. I thought I'd put them in a box in order, but this was the only box I could find.'

'But it was full!' Hilda said. As she began gathering up the letters, all of which were delicately handwritten, she happened to skim over a line or two.

'Matthew,' she squawked, straightening up again sharply, 'Where did you get these from?'

'In the box.'

'But where was the box?' Hilda hastily clutched the letters

to herself before her innocent son could read them. Matty shrugged and turned his attention back to his drawings. 'Have you read them, Matthew?' Hilda asked. 'Any of them?'

'I just wanted the box,' Matty said quietly.

Without another word, Hilda folded the letters up and walked into the kitchen where she threw them onto the table and stared at them in disbelief. How could someone under her roof write this filth?

Just as she was contemplating it, the culprit came walking in.

Madge had been up in St Just for the day with Kerenza and was surprised to see the look on her mother's face upon entering the house again.

'Mum? Is ev'rything OK?'

'You tell me,' Hilda growled. 'I just found Matthew reading through your *disgusting* letters!'

Madge frowned. 'What letters?' She had barely gotten through the door.

'You know exactly what I'm talking about, Margaret! The letters that you've been writing to James Worthing!'

'Jimmy?' Madge exclaimed. 'Mum, you have to believe me. I have never written a letter to Jimmy in my life! 'Specially not the kind you seem to be insinuating.'

'James Worthing of all people as well?' Hilda cried. 'What about Frederick? When the two of you first began courting you know I wasn't so happy, but over time he has proved that he is devoted to you and now I discover that all the while you've been writing letters to someone else!'

'But I haven't been,' Madge insisted. 'If I had been writing to Jimmy then surely I would have sent them.'

Hilda's face turned white. 'He's possessed you with the very same Devil that resides within him!'

'Mum.' Madge began to laugh, this was ridiculous. 'I promise you that I am not possessed and neither's Jimmy; he's good as gold when you get to know him.'

'Like you have, you mean?' Hilda gathered the letters up and marched over to the sink.

'Mum, what are you doing?'

'Burning them to get rid of the evil on these pages!' Hilda dumped them in the basin and began searching around for matches.

'You're being paranoid about nothing!' Madge insisted.

'Then who wrote those letters?' Hilda cried.

'What's going on?'

Madge turned to see Edward in the kitchen doorway.

'Nothing,' Hilda said as her hand stumbled across a box of matches up on top of the kitchen cabinet.

'She's accusing me of having a sordid affair with Jimmy,' Madge said. This was not exactly a rare occasion in the Pascoe household, for both of their parents could often be found flying off the handle over the most random of events.

'Why does she think that?' Edward could feel a prickle of sweat begin at his spine.

'I found letters,' Hilda cried. 'Filthy letters that she hid inside a box!'

'I didn't hide them,' Madge insisted. 'Because I didn't write them!'

'Well someone did!' Hilda's eyes were wide and manic with fury. '"I long to feel your body against mine, our hearts beating as one",' she quoted and struck a match. 'When Frederick finds out that his girlfriend is a jezebel! When your father finds out his daughter's a slut!'

217

The flame hovered teasingly over the crumpled pile of letters below.

'I didn't write them!' Madge cried.

'I did,' Edward said. Both Madge and his mother turned to him.

'You?' Madge frowned.

'It can't have been,' Hilda said. 'These are letters of love and lust.'

'And I love Jimmy.'

Hilda then made a noise, a very strange noise like a strangled cry as she clasped at her chest and dropped the match into the basin, allowing the sink to fill with flames. 'I always feared the Devil would infect my family and I feared the Worthings would be the cause, but never my boy, never my poor poor boy.'

'Ed?' Madge's gaze had not left him.

Edward stared at the leaping flames as they licked the edges of the worktop and began to die back. 'I never sent them, I wrote all the things I wanted to say but never sent them.'

'But – Jimmy and Rosie?' Madge frowned.

'They're keeping it a secret. Jimmy doesn't know what he wants.'

'He's infecting us all!' Hilda's knees buckled and she slid down onto the floor, her head resting against the kitchen cupboards. 'Ev'ry family in the village! The Tregiddens let the Devil in long ago, as did the Roskelleys – that's why God chose to take Bernard. But it all began with the Worthings. Samuel Worthing brought the Devil to the village!'

But Edward did not necessarily believe his mother. If what she said was true and Jimmy was the product of the Devil, then why did Edward love him so much?

Chapter 39

Inez wanted to thank Ralph. She wanted to thank him for a lot of things, not only for the way he handled Fred, but for the way he had been with her as well. After losing Charlie, Inez wondered if she would ever feel happy again. And while she still missed Charlie dearly, Ralph helped her feel a little lighter every day. They may have had their ups and downs and rowed, but that seemed to all be part of it. It felt as though she had known Ralph Howard for ever.

Even Myrtle House looked brighter, with the garden pruned and tidy and paintwork perfect once again – all Ralph's handywork.

As Inez entered the house, however, she found that the atmosphere was less than bright.

'Hello?' she called, surprised to find the door unlocked yet no sound of conversation between granny and grandson. Inez moved through the hall and glanced into the living room. It was deserted, including Mrs Howard's armchair.

'Hello?' Slowly she made her way through to the kitchen. 'Mrs Howard? Ralph? It's just me.'

Upon entering the kitchen, she found Mrs Howard sitting at the table, her chin resting in her hands as she stared vacantly at a now-stone-cold cup of tea.

'Mrs Howard?' This time Inez used a softer voice. The old woman leapt out of her skin as she turned to face her.

'Oh, it's just you, dear. Sorry, I was miles away. Would you like a cup of tea?'

'I'm OK, thank you, is ev'rything alright?'

'Course.' Mrs Howard vigorously nodded her head and took a swig of freezing tea, which she fought back from spitting out again.

'I've, um, I've brought you something.' Inez began rummaging about in her bag and removed her gifts. 'It's just a little something to say thank you for yesterday with Fred. It's, um, some of last year's blackberry wine – one of the few bottles that wasn't drunk at the Harvest Festival anyway. Oh, and this is just some blackberry jam that I made last week.'

She placed the bottle and jar on the table and smiled at Mrs Howard, hoping that the old woman might smile back. She didn't.

'Where's Ralph?'

'Upstairs.' Mrs Howard's voice was slow and melancholic. 'He's packing.'

'Packing? For London?'

Mrs Howard nodded.

'Well I'm sure it's only for a few days, ent it? He'll be back in no time.'

'No,' Mrs Howard said. 'He's going back to London again. To live.'

Inez couldn't breathe. It was as though Mrs Howard's words had hit her in the stomach, knocking all of the air from her lungs. 'You must be mistaken, he's prob'ly just working on a case, ent he?'

Mrs Howard's pale eyes seemed even more watery than

usual. 'We both said things yesterday, things that I don't think either of us will ever be able to take back, so Ralph is leaving.'

No. No, surely she had got it wrong. Ralph would not just leave like this. Inez found herself standing and walking hastily out of the room before sprinting up the stairs. Sure enough, Ralph's bedroom was slowly turning back into the blank room that she remembered from her childhood. He stood at his bed, methodically folding his clothes and laying them into a suitcase.

'Ralph?' Inez was in a daze as she entered the room. 'When your granny said – I thought she had to be wrong. Why are you going?'

'Because this was a mistake.'

'What was?'

'Coming here.' Ralph slammed the case closed and moved onto a second. 'Thinking that I could just slot in, that I would be able to make a life for myself here; a life that wasn't tainted.'

'Tainted?' Inez took the jumper that he was folding from him so that he had no choice but to look at her. 'Tainted by what?'

Ralph smiled weakly. 'You know.'

'I don't! Tainted by what?'

'My cousin!' Ralph cried. 'All Granny sees when she looks at me is that I'm not him.'

'She don't, Ralph, she loves you.'

'Do you know what she said to me last night?' Ralph was not going to cry, he refused to allow himself. 'She accused me of using her for her money. She said that I'm only here because Charlie isn't and I want to make sure I get my share.'

'I'm sure she didn't mean it,' Inez said, 'We all miss Charlie so much.'

'I know you do, but I'm not him, I'm Ralph.'

'I know that.'

Ralph looked at Inez doubtfully. 'Do you?'

'What d'you mean?' Inez allowed him to take the jumper from her.

'I just mean that I worry that everyone in this village views me as a substitute for Charlie,' Ralph said. 'But I'm not him! I can't be him, and I certainly won't compete with a ghost.'

'So what? You're just going to up and leave? Leave your granny? Leave Fred? Ralph, my brother is *so* poorly and you are the only person that he trusts!'

'I'm sorry, Inez,' Ralph said. 'But I can't live my life based around people I don't even know.'

Inez watched as he resumed filling his case and shook her head in disbelief.

'I thought I knew you; after all these weeks I thought I'd finally found out who you were. But it turns out my very first opinion of you was correct after all. You're a selfish, stubborn man who thinks he's above all of us little Cornish folk just because you're from London. Well, listen to me carefully, Ralph Howard, you are so much more naive than any of us.'

She turned and stormed back across the room.

'Inez—' Ralph began.

'Have a safe trip back!' Inez spat as she hurried away.

'Inez!' Ralph threw his clothes down and ran after her.

Mrs Howard watched as Inez hastily descended the stairs with Ralph running after her. Without so much as a word to her, Inez fled the house, slamming the door behind her. Ralph turned to his grandmother in despair. Once again he had ruined everything.

Chapter 40

Carolyn had not been home. She did not want to see any of them, her so-called family. How could they blame her for what was happening to Fred? But that was always the case. Anything that ever happened could always, and would always, somehow be traced back to her, even if she was not there. It was not exactly a shock though, more the confirmation that she had been waiting for; that she was her parents' least favourite.

She was not the blue-eyed boy like Fred, nor the dutiful daughter like Inez. Rosie took the role as family sweetheart, so what did that leave her? The troublesome one. The problem child. Carolyn never meant to cause trouble, it just so happened that things never went her way. She was never completely happy nor satisfied, so would try to find a way to create her own happiness, but then everyone always got cross with her because of it.

She often thought about giving up, surrendering herself to the life that her parents wished she would take. Find a random man and settle, like Inez with Charlie and now Ralph, and Rosie with Jimmy. But whenever these thoughts crossed her mind, Carolyn grew angry with herself. Why should she conform just to please everyone else when all she really wanted was happiness and fulfilment. Both of which she had yet to find.

She had spent the night sleeping in the stable with Delilah and her foals and was now trudging along the cliff tops and planning where to sleep tonight.

If it had been the middle of the summer then she may have just slept on the beach, but the nights were much too cold and wet for that now. She did not want to resort to asking to sleep on a friend's sofa, but knew that if she spent another night somewhere on the farm then she would be easily found. She lost her train of thought, however, when she spotted a figure standing out on the edge of the cliff.

Edward Pascoe was motionless as he stared down at the grey, choppy sea below him and imagined plummeting in.

'Edward?' Carolyn slowly approached him. There was very clearly something not right. 'Are you OK?'

Edward still did not look at her, just remained staring at the water below.

'They say I'll go to Hell if I don't let them help me,' he said. 'But I don't need help.'

'Who says that?'

'They don't like that I'm different, that I don't fit in with them.'

Slowly, Carolyn nodded. 'They don't like me for that either.'

'But to me they're strange,' Edward said. 'I'm normal. I live and love the way that I do. Why do I have to change?'

'You don't,' Carolyn carefully reached out, wanting to take a hold of Edward, but not wanting to scare him either. 'You don't have to change yourself for anyone, Edward, just so long as you're happy.'

'But I'm not.' Edward began to sob and his knees buckled. Carolyn lurched forward and grabbed hold of him before he toppled over the edge of the cliff. The two then fell back onto the safety of the grass bank. 'Ed!' she gasped, her hands still clinging to his arm.

'How d'you make them see that you're normal?' Edward wiped his eyes in his sleeve. Carolyn had no answer; that was still a question that she was trying to work out.

'He told me that he loved me.' Edward closed his eyes, remembering that scenario. 'He held onto my hand and said, "I love you, Ed", but now he's chosen her.'

Carolyn finally understood. She had never been close to Edward Pascoe, but now felt that they might be more similar than she had thought. Nobody understood them.

'How do I carry on, Carolyn?' Edward asked.

Carolyn thought about her reply for a moment.

'You try and move on,' she finally said. 'You take yourself out of the situation and try to survive.'

Back in the village, Ralph carried his cases down the stairs and into the hall, his granny watching him from the living room door.

'Well,' he said, 'That's me.'

They embraced for a moment and kissed the other's cheek.

'Thank you for having me, it's been a nice *holiday*, but it's time I went back to my life.'

Mrs Howard nodded. 'It's been a pleasure, my dear, now you have a safe trip back.'

'Thank you.' Ralph picked up his cases and walked to the

door. Glancing over his shoulder he said, 'I have always loved you, Granny, I was just never allowed to love you as much as Charlie did.'

He then stepped out of Myrtle House and closed the door behind him.

The village seemed so strange, the place that had nearly become his home. It could have been, Ralph thought, if he had lived another life. As he walked along, not a single person said hello. They were still strangers after all this time – and that was not entirely their fault, Ralph knew that. Maybe he could have tried harder to be himself and not the person he thought that they wanted, perhaps he could have made more effort? There was one person he recognised though, leaning against the wall, smoking a cigarette. Carolyn always looked confident, so at ease, even as she gave him a confused smile. 'Are you off somewhere?' she asked as Ralph crossed over to her.

'Back to London.'

'Does Inez know?'

'Me and your sister have said our goodbyes.' Ralph avoided looking her in the eye.

'What about your granny?'

'I think she can manage more than people think; besides, she has all of you, and I'm sure I'll pop back every now and then.'

Carolyn took a drag on her cigarette and looked at him.

'It's a shame it didn't work out, you being here, I thought we could have turned you into a right country bumpkin.'

Ralph laughed at this. 'I'm going to miss you Carolyn, all of you Tregiddens.'

Carolyn rolled her eyes. 'I wouldn't miss them.'

Once again, Ralph laughed. 'Goodbye, Carolyn.'

'Bye.' She watched him go and took another drag on the cigarette. Inez always told her what a nasty habit it was for a lady, but Carolyn did not care. She was not a lady; she was Carolyn Tregidden and that's all she would ever be. Suddenly a thought struck her and she decided to take her own advice. She needed to take herself out of the situation.

'Ralph!' she suddenly called, 'Wait!'

Chapter 41

'**G**EORGE! GEORGE!'

The tractor had begun to struggle halfway down the field, so George had recruited Alf to help him. He was tinkering with the fuses while Alf sat up on top, gently revving the engine in the hope of getting it going.

'GEORGE! GEORGE!'

'Here we go!' George slapped the side of the vehicle and grinned. 'Try it again!' Once again Alf revved the engine and the tractor appeared to splutter to life.

'Come on, you beauty! There's still life in you yet! Gently does it, Alf, gently does it!'

'GEORGE! GEORGE!'

It was Alf who saw her first and hastily pointed to the overgrown lane reaching towards the field.

'Mr Tregidden!'

George followed his gaze across the field where he saw his wife running towards them. Her greying-blonde hair was billowing behind her as she tore through the ploughed earth wailing.

'GEORGE! GEORGE!'

'Wait here,' George instructed Alf as he ran towards her. 'Hel? What's wrong?'

'George!' Helen sobbed as she reached him, clinging onto his hands to steady herself. 'She's gone!'

'What d'yeh mean? Who's gone?'

'Carrie!' Helen cried. 'Carolyn's run away!'

To whom this may concern, (AKA The Treigiddens)

They had all gathered around the kitchen to read it – even Frank had left his armchair to join in on the latest family fiasco. Helen, despite having already read the letter when she found it on the kitchen table, could not stop sobbing and was being consoled by George as he tried to concentrate on his daughter's scrawl.

I was not originally going to write a letter and allow this to be a glorious surprise, but then I imagined you all running around melodramatically and crying your little hearts out that your darling Carrie hasn't come down for her tea and decided that it might be pushing things too far.

The reason for my mysterious disappearance is because I am not at home – though a quick check in my room would have determined that. I'm not in the village either, in fact I'm not even in Cornwall anymore!

'What does she mean "not in Cornwall?" George asked, 'Where else could she be?'

'Does she even know anyone outside of Cornwall?' Rosie

asked. 'Besides Uncle Robert?'

'And I very much doubt he would take her,' Fred said, 'Not after last time he came to visit.'

'Shush,' Inez said, 'I'm trying to read it.'

A handsome knight came to my rescue and whisked me off to a faraway kingdom, just like a story in Nana's book. Obviously that is not really the case, although I know that you all think that I need a handsome prince to come and save the day. In all seriousness I was tossed a lifeline and decided to take it. Well, actually I clung to it until they dragged me out of this pit.

No prizes for guessing who they were, hey, Inez? I heard that you weren't exactly nice to him so I thought he might want some friendly company.

'Ralph took her?' Inez knew that things had ended badly between them, but how could he do this to her? To her family?

Anyway, the fact is I need a break. From what? I hear you ask, well to put it bluntly, you lot. It's not normal for one family to all live in the same house for ever, so I've decided to do an Uncle Robert and run for the city so that I can spread my wings and stop being George Tregidden's troublesome daughter.

'She heard you,' Helen sobbed. 'The other night, she heard what you said!'

'What *we* said,' George corrected.

I know that I am odd. You know that I am odd. I don't think that there is a single person who doesn't know that I am odd, and I don't fit in the village – I don't think I ever have.

So hopefully now I will be able to reach my full potential as Queen of London – I'd make a good queen.

'She should be 'ere!' Frank cried, ''Ere with us! 'Er family!'

Just remember that I love each of you in your own little way, but when you're together you drag me down.

Oh, and don't worry, Da, this isn't because of you blaming me for Fred being ill, that was just the tip of the iceberg.

'You said what?' Fred turned to his father in disbelief.

George's face was flushed and shining with sweat.

'It weren't like that,' he insisted. 'She – Carolyn – she must have mis'eard.'

I might write soon, but I won't be coming home.

Lots of Love,

Carolyn

(Though I might change my name, as I've always hated it.)

X X X

'I don't blame her for going.' Rosie stepped away from the table and her family. 'No one's been very nice to her, not for

231

a long time.'

Fred pulled a chair out and slowly fell into it. 'You blamed her for *me*? Why?'

'Like I said, she mis'eard,' George said.

'Stop lying!' Inez cried, 'Just tell the truth for once! Me, you and Mum were all saying horrid things about her and she heard us!'

'We need to get her back!' Helen paced around the room as she scraped her hair from her face. 'We need to go after her and tell her that we're sorry, that we love her!'

'Helen.' Frank caught hold of her, 'London's a big place and we don't know where she is.'

'I just want my little girl back!' Helen began to sob and Frank held her like a child.

'I know,' he soothed, 'But Carolyn ent a little girl anymore, she can make her own decisions.'

George then turned to Inez. 'Your friend took her, maybe she'll still be with him in London?'

'I-I don't know where he is.' It was true, Inez had barely asked Ralph about London at all. Maybe if she had taken more interest, maybe if she had not tried to mould him into Charlie, then he would not have left, and Carolyn would still be here too.

'Why did you blame her for me?' Fred thumped his fist on the table in anger.

George glanced at Helen. Inez was right; he needed to start being honest.

'I said that she was taking up too much of my time and that's why I couldn't help you.'

Fred began to rock back and forth on his chair. This was his fault. Why could he not be normal? Why could he not just be the boy he was before?

Rosie felt terrible; she had begged and convinced Carolyn to keep her secret without realising how much her sister was dealing with herself. She thought that they understood each other; why had she not seen how sad Carolyn was?

She turned and hastily left the house, walking outside.

She knew that the workers' eyes were all on her as she hurried across the yard and Jimmy was the last person that she wanted to see right now.

'Rose?' he asked, walking towards her, 'Is ev'rything alright? I saw your mother earlier, an—'

'Not now, Jimmy.' Rosie wiped her eyes.

'Rosie?' He caught her arm gently. 'What's happened?'

'Leave me alone, Jimmy!' Rosie snapped and pushed him away. Jimmy stumbled back, catching his hand on a rake. Rosie turned and began sprinting towards the barns.

'What was that about?' Edward asked, coming up behind Jimmy.

'I dunno.' Jimmy watched in confusion as Rosie disappeared. He noticed a vague stinging in his hand and looked down to see puncture wounds in his palm.

'Hey.' Edward took his hand gently and examined it. 'Come with me, let's sort that out.'

He placed his hand on Jimmy's back and guided him back across the yard. If Rosie did not want him, then he certainly did.

Chapter 42

'Here you go,' Edward carefully dabbed Jimmy's palm with a cloth. 'It looks worse than it is.'

'I don't understand,' Jimmy said. 'Something must have happened; you saw Mrs Tregidden earlier as well as I did, and now for Rosie…' He stood up from the upturned crate. 'I need to go and make sure they're all OK.'

'Wait,' Edward begged. 'Maybe they'll want to be left alone? Pr'aps Old Man Tregidden's died or something? They'll prob'ly want to grieve as a family?'

Jimmy looked out of the shed door and up towards the farmhouse.

'Maybe…'

Glancing back at Edward, he saw his friend rolling up his sleeve and dabbing disinfectant on his own wounds running along his forearm. They looked like burns. 'Ed, what's that?'

'Nothing.' Edward hastily pulled his sleeve down.

'Edward.' Jimmy walked to him and gently lifted his sleeve up, exposing the burns again.

'It's nothing,' Edward repeated. 'I caught it on the tractor when it was still hot.'

'They look like match burns.' Jimmy had seen enough of them during his life from when his father fell asleep smoking a cigarette. Edward turned away from him.

'I said it were nothing.'

'Ed…' Jimmy asked quietly. 'Who burnt you?'

Edward turned back to him, his eyes wet. 'Mother said she were burning the Devil outta me.'

'The Devil?' Jimmy took Edward's arm and carefully studied the burns. They were meticulous and detailed, not random like his father's. Mrs Pascoe had intended for Edward to be hurt. 'Why did she think that you had the Devil in you?'

His eyes met Edward's; who stared at him blankly.

'I don't know, she just…has strange thoughts sometimes.'

'Ed.' Jimmy placed his hand on his friend's arm. 'I'm sorry.'

At Jimmy's touch, Edward felt alive, like nothing could ever hurt him again.

Rosie hated everything about this. A few short weeks ago she had been so happy. She had Jimmy home, she had her brother home, but now her family was falling apart. If she had not been so self-centred then maybe none of this would have happened? Maybe if she had been a little more like Inez, less of a child, then none of this would have happened. She kept her relationship with Jimmy a secret as a way to keep the two of them safe from everyone else's prejudices, but now those very same secrets and opinions were tearing her family apart. Carolyn was right about one thing; Rosie was eighteen, an adult, why should she still be scared of what her parents thought? Why should she not just tell them about Jimmy? At that moment she decided that she would tell them – just not yet. She would wait for the dust to settle from the latest drama before kicking up some more.

As she pulled at the loose ends of straw coming from the bale that she was sitting on, Rosie looked up to see Jimmy in the doorway. He had a wary look about him, one that she had only seen him bear when around his father. She immediately felt the twisted guilt in her stomach when casting her mind back to how she had acted.

'I'm sorry,' she said, and spotted the bandage on his hand. 'Your hand! Are you OK?'

'I'm fine.' Jimmy cautiously stepped into the barn. 'Are you?'

'Carrie's gone.' Rosie fought back the tears that were attempting to escape. They were not tears of sadness, however, but frustration. Frustration at herself and her sister – all of her family, in fact.

'What d'you mean?' Jimmy joined her on the bale.

'She's run away to London with Ralph.'

Jimmy was shocked. Out of all of the Tregiddens, the last one that he would have expected to leave the farm was Carolyn. She was practically part of the fields.

'We didn't know,' Rosie explained. 'I think Inez knew that Ralph was leaving, but then Mum found a letter on the kitchen table and...oh god.' She buried her face in her hands and rubbed her eyes.

'Hey.' Jimmy placed his hand on her knee gently. 'Don't cry.'

'I'm crying cos I'm angry! I'm so bleddy angry! God, Jim, you should've read the letter, she was so upset; she hates every single one of us.'

'That's not true, Carolyn loves you all so much.'

'Then why did she go? Why did she go and not tell me?'

'Come here.' Jimmy kissed the top of Rosie's head as he held her close. 'Carolyn's a big girl, Rose, she knows how to look after herself.'

'I just want my sister back! I feel so guilty, making her keep our secret.'

'You didn't force her to do anything.'

'But I did! I've not been partic'ly nice to her, and on top of what she heard Da saying…'

'What did he say?' Jimmy asked.

Rosie was about to tell him everything, about Fred, about her parents, but then decided that it was not her story to tell. Besides, by the sounds of things, even she did not know the full truth about what had been going on with them. The only person she had was Jimmy. He was hers entirely.

'I love you.' She ran her hand over his stubbled cheek, 'Even though you need to shave.'

'And I love you, Rosie Tregidden.' Jimmy smiled. 'I always have and I always will.'

'Can we pretend that it's just us again?' Rosie asked. 'And ev'rything outside this barn has melted away?'

'For as long as you want,' Jimmy said and wrapped his arms around her.

'Edward?' The voice made Edward jump and he hastily pulled his sleeve back down, hiding the burns, which did not appear to be getting better.

'Yes, Mr Tregidden?' He turned to find his boss marching towards him.

'You ain't seen my Rosie about, have you?'

George did not look happy. Whatever news the Tregiddens had received was most definitely bad, Edward thought. He then thought about Rosie, running to the barn in tears, and then about Jimmy following her.

'No,' he said, scratching the burn. 'No I haven't, sorry.'

''S'alright.' George said, and, without another word, the farmer began to walk away towards the lane.

'Is ev'rything OK?' Edward called after him and George stopped before turning back. 'Sorry,' Edward said, 'It's just I saw Mrs Tregidden was upset about something earlier.'

'Oh.' George shook his head. 'Yeah, no, just Carolyn being… Well, Carolyn.'

'Right.' Edward nodded slowly. He watched as George walked away and scratched at his burns. Those damn burns. The burns that he got for telling the truth.

The truth.

'Actually,' Edward called. 'I think I did see Rosie not that long ago.'

George turned to him. 'Where?'

'I think she went into one of the barns.'

Chapter 43

'I still don't understand,' Frank said, 'Why did George blame Carolyn for Fred being ill? He's fine, ent he?'

He, Helen and Inez all looked across to Fred, who was staring into space catatonically.

'Grandad…' Inez realised that he had been kept in the dark throughout all of this.

'Freddie's just a bit tired, aren't you?' Helen interjected.

Fred looked up. He had not heard a single word that anyone had been saying. Not since Carolyn's letter, at least.

'Fred?' Frank asked, 'What's wrong?'

Fred began to feel that prickling sensation all over his skin again, which was only exacerbated by the loud shouting as his father and Rosie burst into the house.

'Let go, Daddy, please!' Rosie wailed as George dragged her through to the kitchen, his hand tight around her arm.

'Get in there!' he growled and tossed her into the room. Rosie was hysterical as she tried to run back to the door.

'I SAID: GET IN!' George roared. 'And you, get off my land and never set foot on it again!'

The Tregiddens turned to see an anxious Jimmy hovering in the doorway.

'Da!' Rosie sobbed.

'Mr Tregidden, please—'

'Don't you "Mr Tregidden" me!' George shouted. 'Now get out!'

'George?' Helen gasped. 'What's happened?'

Inez ran to Rosie and held onto her distraught sister.

'I caught 'em together,' George growled. 'In the barn.'

'Wha—' Helen turned from Rosie to George. 'Not like— Oh, Rosie!'

'Taking advantage of my daughter!' George snarled as he marched towards Jimmy. 'My *little girl*!'

'Da!' Inez cried.

'Jus-just let me explain,' Jimmy begged. 'Please! I-I love her. I do, I love her—'

'All that you Worthings love, is causing upset!' George snapped. 'Now, clear off, I don't want to see you up here again!'

'Da, surely this ent helping!' Inez cried.

'I'm not going until Rosie says what she wants.' Jimmy stepped into the room, but was pushed back by George. Jimmy glared at him and stepped forward again. 'Rose? What d'you want? D'you want me to go?'

Rosie shook her head as she sobbed.

'I think you should,' Helen said. 'Just while ev'ryone calms down.'

'I'm not going until ev'ryone hears what I have to say,' Jimmy insisted. 'I love your daughter and would never hurt her!'

'She's too young to know what she wants,' George cried.

'I'm not!' Rosie wailed.

'You 'eard my daughter-in-law.' Frank shakily moved over to George, trying his hardest to create a barricade. 'I think you should leave, boy.'

240

'Rose—'

Fred stood up. He needed to act. He had failed Carolyn and would not do the same to Rosie now. Ralph was right, Jimmy could not be trusted. As he stepped forward everything went black until he was awoken by the sound of his mother and sisters' screams. Fred saw Jimmy in front of him, doubled over and holding his face, a stream of crimson blood running down his hands. Fred's fist ached and when he glanced down saw that it was red from impact. As Jimmy looked up, Fred realised that the blood was coming from his nose…he had hit him. Inez and Helen were still protesting while Rosie's cries had turned into shrieks. Even George seemed a little shocked, for he had placed a firm hand on Fred's back. The only one apparently pleased with what he had done was his grandad who kept on shouting. 'That's my boy! There's nothing wrong with you, is there?'

The anger still had not subsided and Fred found himself wanting to hit Jimmy again. To hit him so hard that he would crack him open like a walnut. However, this time he managed to refrain and simply said, 'Now fuck off.'

Dazed and bewildered, Jimmy turned and slowly walked away without another word, leaving the chaos of the Tregiddens' behind him.

Despite having always told himself that they would disapprove, there was a small part of Jimmy's mind which had clung desperately to the hope that the Tregiddens would accept him like one of their own upon learning about his relationship with Rosie. They had known him since childhood and were a few of the only people not to paint him with the same tarnished brush as his father. But now they were gone as well. The look in their eyes… Particularly Fred's; he had looked so angry and disappointed, even betrayed. He had been the closest thing that Jimmy had ever had to a brother and now he had lost that. All he had was that drunken excuse of a father who was most likely passed out in his armchair. He would not care that Jimmy had been hit or that he had been fired; all that Samuel cared about was where his next drink was coming from.

Sometimes Jimmy felt angry at his mother for dying; maybe if she had been around then she may have been able to prevent her pathetic husband from ruining their reputation. Then perhaps Jimmy could have lived a normal life, one where people did not assume that he was bad news and one where he was allowed to love whoever he wanted.

'Jim?' There was one person who Jimmy still had, the one person who always happened to be there no matter what. Throughout his childhood, during the war, Edward Pascoe was always there. Jimmy turned to see Edward walking towards him.

'Is ev'rything alright?'

Edward spotted the blood covering his face. 'Jesus! Jim, what happened?'

'It don't matter, sorry, Ed, I just wanna go home.'

'Hey.' Edward caught Jimmy's hand and lightly tugged him towards him. 'What's happened?'

'Ev'rything's ruined.' Jimmy could no longer keep it together and allowed the tears that he had been holding in to escape. 'I've lost Rosie and my job and Fred and…' He tried to catch his breath. 'I've lost ev'rything!'

'No you haven't.' Edward held Jimmy closer. 'You haven't lost me. Whatever happens, Jimmy, you'll always have me.'

Jimmy nodded and wiped his nose in his sleeve. Edward was different from the rest of his family. He did not judge him based on his father's mistakes but as himself and that was all Jimmy ever wanted.

Edward smiled as he ran his hand through Jimmy's hair and Jimmy realised that he was caught in Edward's arms. All of a sudden Edward leant in, pressing his mouth against Jimmy's, who recoiled in shock. 'What are you doing?'

Slowly, Edward smiled, 'It's OK,' he whispered and leant in again.

This time Jimmy was quicker and escaped from Edward's arms.

'Edward?' He wiped his mouth on his sleeve in disgust.

'You don't need to be scared, Jimmy,' Edward insisted. 'Not while I'm around, because I love you, I always have and I'll always take care of you.' He moved towards Jimmy, who stepped back.

'I love Rosie,' Jimmy said and Edward let out a laugh.

'No you don't. You don't love her, you love me, you always have – you told me!'

'When?' As far as Jimmy knew he had never declared his love for anyone other than Rosie.

'At war.' Edward's face dropped. 'When we were in Poland and were hiding. You told me—'

'That I loved you...' Suddenly Jimmy realised the huge mistake. 'As a friend! I thought we were going to die and was relieved to have you, my *friend*, by my side!'

Edward began shaking his head as though he could not comprehend Jimmy's words.

'No, no you don't mean that, you love me.' A fire began to rage within him. '*You love me, Jimmy!*'

'I DON'T!' Jimmy yelled, 'I have *never* loved you, Edward, and I never will! You're lonely because Kerenza left you so you want what me and Rosie have.' The word 'had' echoed in his head and Jimmy felt sick. It was all over.

Edward watched the colour drain from Jimmy's face and stared after him as he hastily walked away. He wanted to call after him, to insist that he was the one who was mistaken. But maybe he was wrong, maybe Jimmy had played him just like his mother said. Perhaps his mother was right, maybe Jimmy Worthing was the Devil?

Chapter 44

They did not need him, not anymore. All Fred was doing was causing his family trouble. His parents were arguing and Rosie hated him and Carolyn had run away. He had hoped that one day things would go back to normal, to how they had been before the war. That war. It had ruined *everything!* It had taken Charlie from Inez, caused Jimmy to seduce his little sister, driven a wedge between Carolyn and his father. Even his grandad seemed older since his return. Fred no longer recognised this world that he lived in. He was sitting at the kitchen table listening to the voices of Rosie and his parents as they argued and sobbed and swore. He no longer recognised them either.

'Where are you going?' Inez came walking into the room and Fred realised that he was opening the front door.

In truth, he had no idea, but answered regardless. 'For a walk.'

'Are you OK? I know all that arguing wasn't very nice.'

Fred hated the way he was being treated like a child.

'Yeah. Yeah, I'm fine,' he said.

'You should go and be with Rosie, make sure Mum and Da aren't killing her.'

Inez watched him carefully for a moment, as though she

was trying to read him like one of her books. Fred managed to work his face into a smile and a fleeting smile was returned by Inez.

Fred waited for her to return to the living room before stepping out of the house.

And, after that, he began to walk.

Eventually, Fred's legs could take no more and he found himself sitting on the edge of the road. The grass was damp under him, but he barely even noticed. The way from which he had come and the way that he was planning to head were both shrouded in a thick mist. It felt mysterious and isolating, yet strangely refreshing. As if his past and everything that he walked through was forgotten and everything ahead would not exist until he was ready for it. For the first time in a very long time, Fred felt in control. He waited for a while, sitting on the grass bank and taking in this moment and this very small piece of world around him. All that needed to exist right now was the grass and the hedge and the uneven road, full of potholes and mud. Fred began to believe that this was his, that he was the only person in this part of the world.

But that was until someone else came walking through the mist.

At first the character was nothing more than a distorted shadow, with a faint clattering. But as the clattering began to grow louder, the figure began to fall into focus.

He was a little shorter than Fred, with skin brown leathered from the sun. The hair that Fred could see from under his hat was grey and thinning and on his back was a heavy-looking pack. As he grew nearer, the man gave Fred a toothy grin.

'Having a rest are 'ee boy?'

Fred was unsure what to say, so merely nodded in reply.

'Reckon I'll join 'ee.' And before Fred could respond, his new friend had thrown himself down beside him, his heavy pack clanging as it hit the ground.

'Weird ol' day, enit?' The man struggled to pull his pack round in front and began rummaging it about in it. 'Weather, I mean,' he added upon seeing Fred's blank expression.

Fred hastily nodded. 'Yeah, s'pose.'

'Live round 'ere do 'ee?'

'Erm, yeah. Back that way a bit.'

'Penzance boy?'

'Yeah, basically.' Fred just wanted to be alone, but decided to be polite; clearly this man was not normal. 'What about you?'

The man shrugged, 'Don't rightly remember prop'ly.'

Fred let out a small laugh, 'What d'you mean? Surely you know where you live.'

'Well…' the man said. 'Nowhere – and ev'rywhere.'

Yep, Fred was right. This man was not normal.

'Cuppa tea?' the man asked but Fred declined, still watching in interest, however, as the man miraculously managed to produce a steaming pot of tea.

'I'm a walker,' he explained.

'I can see that.'

'No, what I mean is, my life is walking,' the man said. 'It's all I do. It's all I'm ever gonna do.'

'Why?'

'Cos there is nothing in this world that pleases me like walking does.' The man sipped his tea contently. 'There's nothing else in the world that I can imagine doing.'

'So…you just walk?' Fred asked. 'Where exactly?'

'I 'ave my places,' the man replied. 'The farmers always know when to expect me; I've just come from the farm run by them three brothers.'

'Galowva?' Fred asked and the man nodded.

'Tha's the one, I go visiting them ev'ry year – the youngest one told me it was even to the day this year! See, you don't wanna walk too fast, you don't want 'em growing sick of seeing you too much.'

'When did you start?' Fred asked. 'Walking, I mean.'

'Christ.' The man sat back and sipped on his tea as he tried to recall a date. 'Now you've got me. Must be…pushing thirty years I imagine.'

'You've been walking for thirty years?' Fred exclaimed and the man nodded.

'Not quite,' he corrected and squinted, trying his hardest to recall the dates. 'See, if I had my books then I'd be able to tell you exactly when it was.'

'Your books?'

'Oh yeah!' The man plunged a hand into his coat pocket and removed a small notebook and pencil. 'I write it all down, ev'ry little bit of it. Ev'rything I see, ev'ryone I talk to, all'a 'em go in 'ere. Then, when it's full, I send it to this nice farmer's wife I met in Kent; she keeps them all for me.'

'Can I look?' Fred motioned to the notebook, but the man's face darkened and he stuffed it back into his pocket.

'No.'

'Sorry,' Fred said. 'You were telling me so much about it…'

The two sat in silence for a while before the man said, 'Are you a walker?'

'No,' Fred answered hastily. 'No, of course not.'

248

'Oh.' The man nodded, 'Well, you'd make a convincing one, you fooled me when I saw you sittin' there in the grass with your head full of thoughts. I thought to myself, "now that there is a walker in his prime".'

'What made you decide to walk?'

Once again the man fell silent, but this time decided to answer, much to Fred's surprise. 'I came 'ome and looked around and realised that I did not recognise any of it anymore. I did not recognise my furniture, my friends, I didn't recognise myself.'

'Where did you come home from?' Fred asked and the man glanced at him.

'Where d'you think?'

Twenty-seven years. That was how long the man had been walking for. That was when the world had thought they were finally at peace again.

'It ent easy, is it?' Fred said quietly. 'Ev'rything's normal apart from you...you don't feel like you belong.'

The man studied Fred carefully before slowly nodding. 'I thought so,' he said, 'What's your name?'

'Fred.'

'Who do you have, Fred?' the man asked. 'You told me you lived back in Penzance, who do you have there?'

'My family, but they don't need me, they have enough of their own problems to worry about.'

'I'm sure that ent true.'

Fred fell silent and began pulling at the tufts of damp grass. 'How did you know when to walk?' he finally asked.

'When I looked in the mirror and no longer recognised myself,' the man said. 'When my old life no longer made any sense.'

'Mine don't!' Fred said, 'I don't belong here.'

'But you have ties,' the man said. 'You have a family. I bet you have a girl back there too, don't you?'

Fred nodded.

'See, that's where you and me are different,' the man explained, 'I didn't.'

Chapter 45

The blinding lights of London astounded Carolyn. She wanted to get lost within them and never be found again. In the city she could be whoever she wanted and no one would bat an eyelid. She was no longer Carolyn-Tregidden-daughter-of-George, but one face in a million strangers. She had never given life outside of the village much thought; even when the war was going on and the world felt smaller than ever, her life still revolved around Beacon Farm. But now it did not have to.

Ralph had been reluctant to bring her at first, but Carolyn gave him no choice and, before he knew it, the two of them were sitting on the train together. It was only when the train pulled into Paddington station that Carolyn realised that she had nowhere to go. She pretended that this did not matter and that she had been planning her escape for ages. The two of them walked side by side through the bustling and steam-filled platform, Carolyn trying her hardest not to bump into the busy strangers, while Ralph worked his way through them with ease and confidence.

'So where now?' Ralph asked.

Carolyn stalled. 'Sorry?'

'Well, I've brought you to London like you asked, so where

are you off to now?'

'Oh...' Carolyn tugged at the collar of her jumper as she tried to think on her feet. 'Well my uncle lives here and I know that he would be thrilled to see me and put me up for a while!' In truth she had not seen her Uncle Robert for a number of years – and the last visit had gone anything but smoothly.

'And you know where he lives?'

'Of course, he lives in London.'

Ralph laughed at this; something about Carolyn always made him laugh. She was so full of fire and bravado, but there was no fooling him, Carolyn was now a girl in a world that she did not belong. Her clothes – a thick woollen jumper and old baggy dungarees under her patched-up coat – and the way she bumped and stumbled her way through the crowds made her look even more out of place. Carolyn may have outgrown the village, but Ralph was not sure she was quite ready for city life.

Carolyn finally admitted that she had no idea where her uncle lived or how to get in contact with him, so Ralph inevitably invited her to stay with him for a few days.

Ralph's home was just a short bus ride away from Paddington, yet Carolyn had never been on a bus like it. People pushed and shoved and shouted and at one moment even sat on her! She tried her hardest to fight and argue back, but no one appeared to understand her accent, and if they did then they merely laughed. Even Ralph had to try his hardest to suppress a smile, which in turn earned him a crafty punch in the arm.

She had always imagined the people of London to all be incredibly rich – especially lawyers like Ralph. She pictured their houses to be huge structures and for each one to be immaculate. As they walked along the street towards Ralph's home, Carolyn felt as though her ideas had been realised. The street was long and lined with identically grand-looking townhouses.

'I've never seen anything like this,' Carolyn breathed and Ralph glanced at her with a laugh.

'Fortunately it was one of the streets that the Jerrys never bombed. Impressive, isn't it?'

It was a world away from the cobbled-together cottages that Carolyn was used to seeing every day.

'Here we go,' Ralph said as they turned up a path and began approaching a large black door.

'It's incredible!'

Ralph took a key from his pocket and unlocked the door. He opened it and stepped back, allowing Carolyn to enter first.

'Would Madame like to enter?' He mockingly bowed to her and Carolyn laughed.

As she stepped inside, she found herself in a vast and imposing hall; it had dark wooden floors and a steep flight of matching stairs.

A voice came from further back in the house. 'Hello?'

'Hello, Mrs Davies,' Ralph called as he closed the door behind them. 'It's just me!'

'Go!' he whispered and ushered Carolyn up the stairs. She hastily scampered up them and darted around the corner, glancing back down to see Ralph greet a round, middle-aged woman.

'Mr Howard?' she said. 'I wasn't expecting you back for another few weeks? How's your grandmother?'

'She's very well thank you, Mrs Davies.' Ralph began

backing up the stairs. 'I've had a bit of a change of plan though, I'll be back here more regularly if that's still OK with you?'

'Of course!' Mrs Davies beamed. 'You know I love having you here.'

'Well…' Ralph feigned a yawn. 'It's been rather a long train journey…'

'Then I shan't keep you,' Mrs Davies said. 'Goodnight, Mr Howard.'

'Night,' Ralph called as he watched her waddle back down the hall. He then turned and darted off after Carolyn.

Carolyn opened her mouth to speak, but Ralph held his finger to his lips.

'But—?'

'Sshh!' Ralph whispered. He took Carolyn over to another door and used the second key on his chain to unlock it. He then pushed Carolyn inside and hastily closed the door behind them before letting out a laugh.

'It's just as well Mrs Davies didn't look up,' he cackled. 'She would have gotten a shock seeing you watching us from the banister!'

'I don't understand?' Carolyn frowned. 'Why did you have to ask your staff if you could stay here?'

'Staff?' Ralph repeated blankly. 'She's not my staff. Mrs Davies is my landlady!' He then began to laugh again, 'You didn't seriously think the entire building was my house, did you?'

Carolyn felt herself blushing and grew defensive. 'Well, where else was I supposed to think you lived? You're a lawyer, ain't you?'

'Yes, and my wages are just enough to cover here.' Ralph unbuttoned his coat and hung it up on the hat stand by the door.

'Hang on…' Carolyn slowly turned around, taking in the room around her, 'This is your home? This one room?'

'Don't sound too disappointed, will you?' Ralph turned on the lights and Carolyn looked again. They were standing in a square room; at one end was a small kitchen and the rest of the room was taken up with two sofas and a coffee table.

'My bedroom is just through there,' Ralph nodded at another door. 'The bathroom is in there as well.'

'I…' Carolyn began, pushing her hair back in frustration, 'I don't understand. You are a lawyer, your granny lives in the biggest house in the village and *you*, you live…here?'

'Carolyn.' Ralph smiled as he carried their cases across the room. 'You aren't in Cornwall anymore, I live in the middle of the capital city. No one normal could possibly afford anywhere bigger than this!'

Carolyn blushed again. 'I'm sorry, I s'pose I don't know what I was expecting.'

'That's OK,' Ralph said, 'It's just…you do know what you've let yourself in for, don't you?'

'Of course I do,' Carolyn replied. Though, in actual fact, she really was not sure.

Chapter 46

Frank had seen many conflicts in his life, two wars that consumed the entire world, the death of his wife and grandson, his eldest son cutting ties with him, but he was certain that he had never felt an atmosphere at Beacon Farm as terrible as this one.

With Carolyn missing, Fred so unwell and now Rosie heartbroken, it felt as though his family had shattered like a piece of china.

He was a very private man who rarely shared his emotions with anyone else, but the one thing that he could not bear was seeing any of his family upset. So to see Rosie on the sofa, her head buried in the arm as she sobbed, broke his heart.

'There'll be other boys.' Frank lowered himself down beside her and ran his rough hand through her soft hair.

'No there won't.' Rosie's voice was a muffled sob.

'Course there will,' Frank insisted. 'You're a beautiful girl and you're only eighteen! You don't wanna go gettin' yourself tied down yet – 'specially to a boy like Jimmy Worthing.'

At this Rosie sat up, turning to her grandfather; her small face was red and tearstained and her eyes were puffy from crying.

'I don't know why ev'ryone thinks we're such a bad match,

no one's ever had a problem with him until now! Jimmy used to come here for tea, we used to take him to Sunday school!'

'I know, my sweet'eart,' Frank tried to sooth his grandaughter but Rosie only grew more irritated by the second. 'But that was before you fell in love with 'im.'

'I've been in love with him for a lot longer than that,' Rosie insisted. 'For as long as I can remember I've wanted to marry Jimmy, but he only ever saw me as Fred's little sister…but then he changed.' She gazed towards the empty fireplace, remembering vividly the first time that she knew Jimmy returned her feelings. 'He saved me at a dance. Peter Penrose was meant to be my partner but then he disappeared and suddenly Jimmy was there. He said that he saw me standing there in the middle of the room and couldn't bear to see me alone. When we danced…when we danced I knew. *I* knew, Grandad, I just did!'

'You're young, you don't know what true love is yet.'

'How old was Nana when she fell in love with you?'

Frank gave her a weary look. 'About eighteen, I s'pose.' Before Rosie had a chance to argue her point, he held his hand up. 'But it ent just about the age, it's *him*, why did you have to pick Jimmy Worthing out of all the boys?'

'I don't see why ev'ryone is against him joining our family, 'specially when he's practic'ly one of us anyway?'

'It's not about him being one of us.' Frank sat back and ran his hands over his lined face. 'We just don't want you becoming a Worthing.'

'Why not?'

'Cos they're bad news!' Frank took a moment to calm down. 'Just, believe me, Rosie, you don't want anything to do with them!'

257

'That ent fair, tarring them all with the same brush just because of what Jimmy's father's like?'

'You know nothing about Samuel Worthing, OK? You have no idea what he did.'

'Then tell me!' Rosie begged.

Frank looked at her for a moment that seemed as though it went on for a long time. 'D'you remember hearing about Mrs Howard's son, Michael?'

Rosie nodded, 'Charlie's father?'

'Yeah, he and his wife died in a road accident.'

'I know, they were hit by a bigger vehicle. I remember Inez telling me once.'

'It was a tractor.' Frank struggled to look at her. 'Our tractor.'

Rosie was unsure of what to say, so she said nothing. Just stared at her grandfather as he attempted to cobble together an explanation for the rest of the story. 'I sent Samuel out in it, I needed him to deliver some potatoes up to the pig farm only…when he showed up he was…he was drunk. But your father was busy and Michael had a day off and I just needed it to be done! So I thought, I thought that it might teach him a lesson, make Samuel work in that condition and he wouldn't show up pissed out of his mind anymore.'

Out of the corner of his eye, Frank could see Rosie staring at him, a look of utter horror in her eyes.

'I know what you're thinking; that it's my fault. I s'pose it is. I covered for Samuel, I told ev'ryone that the tractor was broken and that was why he had hit them, but they all knew, even then Samuel had a reputation… After that he got worse and I had to let him go.'

He turned to Rosie, who had shifted away from him. Her

wide eyes were shining.

'But Jimmy isn't like that.' She blinked them clear, 'He ent an alcoholic.'

'Jimmy slacks off work when he can,' Frank said flatly. 'He does stupidly impulsive things and chases after skirt, and that's how his father started out.'

'You're wrong!' Rosie leapt out of her seat. 'All of you are! You may have given up on Samuel, but Jimmy is nothing like him! He loves me; I know that he does! Nobody knows him like I do, not you, not Da, not even Fred! So don't you dare go telling me that Jimmy's following in his father's footsteps when you don't know the slightest thing about him! You are just a delusional old man!'

'I know you're upset.' Frank attempted to muster any kind authority that he was able. 'But remember who you're talking to.'

'I know *exactly* who I'm talking to.' Rosie was seething with anger as she leant over her frail old grandfather. 'The man who killed Michael Howard.'

Frank stared at her in shock.

'Because Samuel didn't kill him,' Rosie growled, '*You* did!'

Chapter 47

Things were changing, Madge could feel it. Edward had returned home in a very dark mood and retreated to his bedroom. He had been off for a little while now, ever since the revelation that he had been the one writing the letters to Jimmy. After that conversation, when her father had returned home, Madge had been asked to leave the room to keep an eye on Matty whilst her parents spoke to Edward alone. Since then her brother had barely uttered a word.

Though she did not understand Edward's reasons for writing those letters, she was willing to listen, if only he would speak to her. But she knew that he would not, for Edward rarely spoke to anyone about anything. That was the Pascoe way; keep up appearances and do not make a fuss. If there was a problem then you should discuss it with God and no one else; other people only made situations messier. Madge did not strictly believe in this philosophy; she preferred the phrase that the other teachers had always taught her at school: 'A problem shared is a problem halved'.

People kept too many secrets for her liking and it pained her to see her brother this way. Her parents had left a while ago to visit the church; both desperate to seek guidance in how to deal with Edward, but Madge had decided to stay home.

With Matty at school and Edward silently sulking upstairs, she had been left to her own devices and decided to clean the house; maybe coming back to a nice fresh home might put her mother in a better mood.

She began in the living room and swiftly moved through to the kitchen. The edges of the sink were still scorched black from where her mother had burnt the letters and Madge felt sick every time she thought about that afternoon and the sight of her mother, a crumpled mess, on the kitchen floor. She began to scrub the sink harshly, vowing to herself not to stop until the sides were unblemished and gleaming. If she could not prevent hurt and conflict, then she would try her hardest to fix it instead. Her parents, her brother, Fred, all of them needed mending and it looked like no one else would step up to the challenge.

By the time that the sink was clean, the cloth that she had used was little more than a cluster of grey thread, so Madge took it, along with the kitchen bin, outside to decant it into the dustbin. As she did, however, she spotted someone slowly walking towards her. He looked exhausted, as if he might drop to his knees and fall fast asleep at any given moment.

'Fred?' she called, walking into the street. 'Freddie? Are you alright?'

He looked at her and nodded.

'Fred?' Madge gently placed a hand against his cheek and recoiled. 'You're freezing! Come inside.'

Fred did not remember entering Birch Cottage, but soon found himself perched uncomfortably on the Pascoes' sofa as Madge handed him a cup of tea, which he took gratefully. He had not realised just how cold he was.

'Freddie.' Madge carefully sat down beside him. 'Tell me

what's wrong.'

'Ev'rything's broken, Madge.' His voice was choked and distant. 'My family, they don't work anymore and I can't fix them.'

'What d'you mean?'

'Carrie's gone…and Inez is always so sad…and Jimmy and Rosie…' Fred looked at Madge who had glanced away. He let out a small laugh. 'You knew, of course you did.'

'I'm sorry, Fred, Rosie made me swear not to tell anyone. She said, well, she said it would only make things worse for them.'

'It has.' Fred placed his mug onto the coffee table and buried his head in his hands. 'I just don't understand.'

'Well…' Madge tried to think of the best words to use. 'I think they really do love each other. I *know* that Rosie loves Jimmy, and, from what she says, it sounds like he really loves her too.'

'No.' Fred sat up, tilted his head back and began breathing in deeply. 'I don't understand *anything* anymore. I don't even understand how I'm supposed to make it through a normal day. Nothing about my life makes any sense anymore, no one makes any sense anymore.'

'No one?' Madge felt a little stung by this comment, but was not overall surprised.

'I feel like I'm a stranger like Ralph Howard. I don't think I belong here anymore.'

'Freddie.' Madge took his hands and held on to them tightly. 'This *is* your home, you've known us all your life and surely you have to know how much we all love and need you? I am so sorry that you have forgotten that. We've all let you down.'

Fred's face contorted in a confused frown as he looked at

her again. 'It ent your fault. You're the only one that I know won't hurt me, which is why I feel so guilty…'

'Guilty about what?'

'Fearing you.'

Madge stared at him for a moment. 'What d'you mean?'

'Ev'rytime I think of you and what you'll want from me one day…it scares me so much.'

'Fred, I don't want anything from you. I promise, I don't expect anything.'

She took his face in her hands and pressed her forehead against his. 'Freddie, you ent well.'

'I know.'

Madge felt tears touching her and was unsure of which of them they had come from. 'You need help, Fred.' She kept her voice calm. 'Not from me, or from your father. There are people who can help you, we just aren't qualified.'

'I can't do it by myself!'

'You won't be,' Madge insisted. 'You'll have your family and you'll have me.'

She took Fred's hand again. 'I will be the best friend that you have ever had.'

Fred looked at her, his eyes widening like a child's.

'Friend?'

Madge nodded. 'Because that is what you need.' She ran her hand over his face again and smiled, 'And that's exactly what I need too.'

Fred let out a breathy laugh as he hugged Madge, burying his face in her shoulder. 'I love you, Madge.'

'I love you too, Fred.'

Part of Madge wondered if it would have been this way if not for the war. Perhaps if Fred had never gone away then they would have happily married and had a family together, but perhaps not. Perhaps she and Fred Tregidden were just never meant to be.

Chapter 48

It did not matter that her entire family disapproved of Jimmy, it did not matter that they had all turned against him. Samuel Worthing had been shunned by everyone and left out in the cold and Rosie was determined that would not be Jimmy's fate.

The mist had lifted and left the afternoon cold and dry, yet Rosie would not have noticed even if it had started to hail, for she was on a mission and would not be deterred. Not even when a voice came calling after her.

'Rosie!' Edward called, spotting her marching through the village. 'Rose!' He started after her. If Jimmy had told her everything, then he needed to explain himself fast.

He caught up with her. 'Rose—'

'Not now, Edward.'

Madge and Fred had seen Edward running out of the house and decided to find out why. They were surprised, however, to see Edward running after Rosie and begging her to talk.

'Rosie, please, I need to talk to you!' Edward grabbed her arm to slow her down.

'Get off me!' Rosie pushed him away.

'Rosie?' Kerenza had noticed the altercation and ran to them from the other side of the road. 'Is ev'rything OK? Ed, what have you done?'

'Nothing!' Edward pulled at Rosie's hand again and whispered, *'Please*, Rose, can we go somewhere and talk, I can explain!'

Rosie looked at him blankly. 'Explain what?'

'Why I did what I did—'

'You told him?' The realisation struck Rosie and she pushed Edward again. 'You told my father about me and Jimmy?' She began hitting him as Edward tried to fight her off. If this was what she was angry about, then perhaps she did not know about his moment with Jimmy?

By now they had been joined by Fred and Madge, who, together with Kerenza, pulled Rosie away from Edward.

'Rose, let's go home,' Fred said.

'No,' Rosie cried, 'I am not going anywhere with you! You are a hypocrite, a *hypocrite*! Furious at Jimmy and all the while you're courting your other best mate's sister!'

Madge gave Fred a pained glance before looking away again.

'It's different…' Fred began, but Rosie had already begun storming away. This time, however, she had an audience as her brother and three friends decided to follow.

Even the Worthings' house was on its own. Laurel Cottage was a lot older than the majority of the village so therefore sat further away and looked different to the likes of Myrtle House and Birch Cottage. It had once, a couple of centuries ago, been part of Beacon Farm, though you would not know it if you looked at the house now.

Rosie, aware of her audience but not caring all the same, held her head high as she opened the rotten gate and made her way up the overgrown path. She had not had a chance to reapply her makeup, so before knocking on the door made sure to run her fingers under her eyes and lips, wiping away any excess makeup that may have run from her tears. She raised a hand to knock, before suddenly realising that she had not powdered her nose. How could she do what she was about to do if she had a shining nose? If she had been alone, then she might very well have rushed back up to the farm to make sure she was looking her best, but now that she had an audience, she knew what they would all think: *Vain Rosie, the silly little girl.* And she was here to prove all of them wrong.

She knew that Kerenza would have some powder in her bag – she never left home without it – and it pained Rosie that she could not ask to borrow it. Then, upon realising that she was merely trying to put it off, Rosie raised her hand again and knocked.

It seemed to take for ever for someone to answer the door and all the time Rosie felt her heart beating further and further up her throat. Finally she heard the sound of the door unlocking and Jimmy appeared from behind it. If Rosie did not know Jimmy better than anyone, then she would have assumed that he was fine. But she did, and therefore knew that Jimmy had been crying. His face was tinted red and his eyes seemed ever so slightly swollen in the corners. Upon seeing her, Jimmy took a long sniff before saying anything. 'Rosie? What's going on?' He nodded over her shoulder to the four spectators, all watching with intrigue.

'Ignore them.' Rosie fought her instinct to turn around. 'Let's play a game, our game, let's pretend it's just us.'

She combed her hair back with her fingers and could feel that it had grown in size from her flustering. 'But this time, let's play it differently, this time our game don't have to end, it doesn't have to end, Jimmy.'

'I...don't understand.'

'It can be just me and you for ever, nobody else matters. All I need in my life is you! If they ain't happy with us being together then I don't care. I love you, Jimmy Worthing, and that will never change.'

'I love you too.' Jimmy could feel Fred's eyes burning into him the entire time. He wanted to take Rosie's hand and lead her inside, but if they wanted a view, then that was exactly what they would give them.

Rosie let out a relieved laugh, and realised that her eyes were watering again. 'Thank God! That would have made this bit so much harder.'

'Made what harder?'

'Jimmy, I love you, I have always loved you and always will, but we'll never be taken seriously until we prove people wrong.'

Jimmy watched her anxiously as she continued, afraid of what might happen next.

'I know it ent conventional,' Rosie said, 'but nothing about us is conventional, is it?'

Jimmy hastily looked back at the others at the gate. Each of them had equally blank expressions on their faces.

'What's she doing?' Kerenza whispered to Madge.

'I think we should marry,' Rosie declared. Her smile faded at Jimmy's confused look. She combed her hair back once more and laughed. 'OK, I s'pose I'd better ask you prop'ly. James Samuel Worthing, will you marry me?'

'Rose.' Jimmy closed his eyes with a groan.

'OK, OK, maybe we are conventional. You ask me. Ask me!' Rosie begged. 'You love me! Ask me!'

'I can't!'

'Fine,' Rosie smoothed the skirt of her dress out and knelt down on the doorstep. 'Jimmy Worthing, will you marry me?'

Jimmy shook his head and stepped back as the others came through the gate towards them.

'But you love me.' Rosie began to sob. 'Jimmy, you said you love me!'

'I do,' Jimmy whispered, stepping behind the door. 'I do, Rose, it's just too hard.'

'JIMMY!'

He closed the door and the lock clicked again.

'Rosie?' Kerenza approached her friend carefully. 'Oh, come here, Rosie.'

She crouched down and placed her arms around her, attempting to guide her back to her feet. Madge joined them and finally managed to stand Rosie up again despite her sobs.

'Jim—' She lurched for the door again, but they hastily grabbed her and pulled her back.

Rosie pushed them away and turned to see Fred standing before her.

'Come on, Rosie,' he said quietly, 'Let's go home.'

Chapter 49

Carolyn began to find her feet in London, and, a week after her arrival, she was already starting to navigate the busy streets without Ralph's guidance.

In fact, despite living in the same cramped apartment, the two very rarely saw one another. By the time that Carolyn surfaced from her nest on the sofa most mornings, Ralph would have already left for work a few hours before. And their evenings very rarely coincided either. Ralph was a homebird who enjoyed returning to his flat as soon as his day at the office was over. He would sit at the kitchen table poring over files and books until his brain could take no more information and he would fall into bed and immediately into a deep sleep, so deep in fact that he never awoke to the sound of Carolyn returning from whatever bar or club she had discovered that night.

Despite them trying desperately to keep Carolyn's presence in the flat a secret, it only took a matter of days before Mrs Davies had discovered her. Carolyn had grown bored sitting in the flat alone waiting for Ralph to return – he had persuaded her not to leave without him in fear of Mrs Davies spotting her on the stairs – so she decided to look through some of his records. Upon finding one in particular, Carolyn could not resist putting on his player to have a little listen. She made sure to keep the volume low, but it was still loud enough to penetrate Mrs Davies' canine-like ears. The poor woman believed that there was an intruder in the house, for she had wished each of her tenants a good day as they had left the house that morning.

Upon her discovery, Carolyn had hastily explained that she was a cousin of Mr Howard who was staying with him while looking for work, a story that Ralph confirmed upon his return home. After that Carolyn had been treated as a very important guest and could do no wrong in Mrs Davies' eyes; she had been given the spare key to Ralph's flat and informed that she could go about as she pleased. During her days of wandering around the streets of London, Carolyn found that it was nowhere near as daunting as she had initially believed. Not everyone was rude or posh, but some were in fact very interesting. Everyone around her had a story that they wanted to tell; it was just that not very many people ever wanted to listen. Carolyn had met fighter pilots from the war, a woman who had run away from India in eighteen-sixty-seven, a man who claimed to have invented a brand-new kind of cheese, and that was just to name a few. She finally felt like she had found the place that she belonged.

While this was a blessing for Carolyn, Ralph viewed it as much more of a curse. He had only intended on inviting Carolyn to stay for a couple of nights at the most and had assumed that the hectic world of London might have driven her back home after that, or at least she would find somewhere else to go. This had not been the case and Carolyn appeared to be making herself *very* at home. Ralph liked Carolyn very much, but at the same time he found her incredibly exhausting.

His work kept him busy most days, for he was in the final stages of preparing for a case, so the last thing that he needed was Carolyn getting in his way and talking at a million miles an hour all of the time.

As the end of Carolyn's second week in London grew near, Ralph suggested they went out for a meal. Carolyn had readily agreed; there was a restaurant that she had seen a few streets away and thought that their menu was mouth-watering, like nothing she would have found back in Penzance.

So the two dressed up in their smartest clothes – for Carolyn that was anything other than her dungarees, and made their way there.

Ralph was someone who liked his food simple, so was slightly unnerved by the selection of unpronounceable dishes on the menu, and when he read through the ingredients, only grew more nervous. Carolyn, however, was in her element as she salivated over the words and spent a considerable amount of time attempting to decide between two dishes as the waiter and Ralph exchanged glances, but waited patiently.

As they tucked into their main courses, Ralph a little more tentatively than Carolyn, he decided to approach the subject that he had been waiting to talk about. 'How are you finding city life?'

Carolyn looked up from her plate with a bright-eyed smile. 'Great! I love it here so much, I just can't believe it's taken me twenty-two years to realise that London's the place for me!'

'So you don't miss home?' Ralph asked carefully.

'Not really, I think my whole vendetta against Da was just a way for me to express how bored I was with ev'rything there, just don't think I realised how boring I truly found that place.'

'It's not boring,' Ralph spooned up some of his strangely

aromatic soup. 'It's peaceful.'

'It's slow.'

'It's calm, much calmer than here.'

'And right now I want some excitement.'

'That's…fair enough.' Ralph sat back wearily. 'How long do you think you'll be visiting?'

'Visiting?' Carolyn's face broke into a grin. 'I ain't visiting, Ralph! I mean it, I ain't ever going back home.'

'I thought—'

'Well you thought wrong, my friend,' Carolyn laughed. 'I saw a man sitting on a street corner feeding a parrot earlier! You'd never see that in Cornwall, let alone the village.'

'But what about your family?'

'Why d'you think I left?' Carolyn asked bluntly, 'I'm sick'a them! Ev'ry single one of them, in fact I'm sick of ev'ryone in that bleddy village!'

'They're some of the nicest people I've ever met,' Ralph said. 'The people in the village – especially your family.'

'Sounds like you're the one who wants to go back.' Carolyn laughed, taking another forkful from her plate. She looked up at Ralph, who hastily glanced back to his soup. 'You want to go back, don't you?'

'Of course not. It was all too complicated while I was there.'

'With your granny?'

'Yes.'

'And with Inez?'

'I don't know what you're talking about.'

Carolyn watched him for a moment. She was right. She had been right all along.

'Yes you do,' she finally said. Ralph looked up. 'You know exactly what I mean.'

He closed his eyes; he had lost all control of the conversation. 'Carolyn, don't.'

'You didn't come here to escape your granny, you came here to escape my sister.'

'You make me sound like the villain.'

'Tell me what happened.'

'Inez *and* Granny couldn't see me as *me*,' he explained, 'All they saw when they looked at me was that I'm not Charlie.'

'I'm sure that ent true.'

'Granny so much as told me.'

Carolyn placed her fork down in order to give Ralph her full attention. 'Inez cares about you.'

Ralph shook his head dismissively as he stirred the remains of his soup around, his appetite long gone. 'She just misses Charlie.'

'No,' Carolyn insisted. 'She cares about *you*, you as Ralph, not as a Charlie substitute, but as Ralph Howard the grumpy lawyer.'

She watched as Ralph smiled slightly. 'Am I really that grumpy?'

'From what Inez has told me,' Carolyn replied jokingly. 'Didn't you steal her key and threaten my grandad?'

Ralph screwed up his face and cringed. 'I didn't realise that's what he and my granny were like with each other.' Then his face grew more serious and he added quietly, 'And I didn't realise that Inez was so upset about the key.'

'She's a funny one, my sister.' Carolyn sat back in her chair thoughtfully. 'She don't let much bother her, but a few things do.'

'And that did?'

'I think it was what the key represented more than anything;

Charlie gave it to her on their last night together.'

Ralph pushed his soup away, now feeling utterly sick. How could he have been so insensitive to her? All this time he had felt resentful that he was viewed as second-best to Charlie, but then he had not tried very hard to prove anyone otherwise.

'Like I said.' Carolyn looked at him. 'Inez cares about you.'

Chapter 50

As the weeks drew on, Helen's concern for her family only increased. She had been surprised when Fred confessed one night that he had been visiting Dr Drake privately and that the doctor had referred him to a psychiatrist. However, she was even more surprised when Fred revealed what the treatment would entail. 'I would have to go away, not for very long, maybe a few weeks? The doctor's at a clinic near Bodmin; he's one of the best in the country and knows all these new forms of treatments – Dr Drake showed me all these leaflets and information about it. He uses, was it called, *hypnotherapy*? And this thing with music as well – don't worry, Da, they're not going to cut my brain out!' he added to George, as he noticed the dark look on his father's face. 'But if you can't spare me, I understand, I know we've got a lot to do to get ready for next year.'

George leant forward, stubbing his cigarette out on the ashtray sitting in the middle of the table. He did not smoke much anymore, reserving it only for when he had a tough decision to make. He then sat back and crossed his arms over his round middle.

'The only thing you have to worry about,' he finally said, 'is getting better.'

George was not a man who showed his emotions openly very often, but after his son had thrown his arms around his neck, George had to excuse himself from the room for a moment.

Two days later, Fred was gone and Helen looked around the kitchen table that only she was sitting at. It felt alien to be the only one, but she supposed that it was something that she was going to have to get used to. Frank very rarely left his armchair in the living room these days, while Inez had been taking on extra shifts at work and Helen suspected that this was a way for her to take her mind off things. Rosie hardly left her bedroom either and could be heard crying from behind the door for most of the day. With Carolyn away and now Fred leaving as well, Helen realised that she was going to have to get used to these empty periods of time.

When she first came to Beacon Farm all those years ago as George Tregidden's bride, the noise and busyness of the farm life overwhelmed her. Helen had come from a small fishing family down in Newlyn, so had only ever been used to her parents, sister and two uncles. While at Beacon Farm, she spent her days with her mother-in-law Lizzie, as Frank and George spemt long days in the fields. George's brother had already run away to London, so Lizzie had viewed Helen as the daughter she had never had.

Even George's grandmother had still been around, though Mavis Tregidden had been confined to her bed by this point. It was not just the busy Tregidden family that she had to get used to, but all of the people coming and going. Not an hour went by that someone from the village did not pop up with some local gossip or in seek of advice, which Lizzie was always more than willing to give. Elizabeth Tregidden became Helen's idol and personified what it meant to be a Tregidden – always there for the village.

Despite her initial reserve, over time Helen grew to love this way of life and could not imagine any other home or family. By the time that Lizzie passed away, Helen knew that she had been taught well enough and was ready to become the matriarch of Beacon Farm.

Although this did not come without its complications, of course, and Helen had lately begun to wonder if she was in fact failing in her role as matriarch, for her brood was slowly dropping from the nest one by one.

The only one who appeared to not be going anywhere, but had still drifted too far away was Rosie, and Helen was desperate to make amends. There were things that Rosie did not know, and Helen felt that it was time that she finally learnt them.

She gave her daughter's bedroom door a knock, knowing full well that she would not answer, and entered the room. Rosie's room was never very neat, but full of character. Her clothes either hung from her white-painted wardrobe or over her dressing table and chair in the midst of being mended or tweaked. The rest of the desk was littered with pieces of cotton and fabric, along with her needles and thread. Although the piles of clothes had not changed since the last time Helen had visited the room and that was because Rosie had lost all enthusiasm for anything. She was curled up by her pillows on her bed and absentmindedly running her fingers through the thin fur of her teddy bear.

It struck Helen how young her daughter still looked. With

no makeup and clutching her bear close to her, Rosie still looked like the child whose hair she had tied in rags every night.

Rosie did not look up, even as Helen joined her on the bed. 'How are you feeling?'

Rosie's voice was quiet and weak as she replied, 'Sick.'

'Come here, sweet'eart…' Helen attempted to cuddle her in, but was rebuffed.

'I am sorry, Rosie.'

'What for? That you all rejected Jimmy? Or that because of that he rejected me?'

'We didn't reject Jimmy,' Helen said. 'I would *never* reject Jimmy.'

'Yet you'd rather I fell in love with the Devil than him!'

'There are things that you don't understand.'

'I don't give a damn about Samuel Worthing's guilty secrets,' Rosie snapped. 'Grandad told me.'

Helen looked at her carefully, 'Told you what?'

'That Samuel crashed the tractor into Charlie's parents.'

'Like I said,' Helen replied, 'there are things that you don't understand.'

'What d'you mean?'

'The story of Samuel Worthing doesn't end with that crash, it begins with it.'

'I don't understand.'

'You don't remember Jimmy's mother, do you?' Helen brushed her daughter's hair back over her shoulder tenderly. Rosie shook her head.

Helen smiled slightly as she remembered Imelda Worthing. She hated herself for the way things had gone, and hated that the world had forgotten her best friend. She had spent so long holding onto the story, that she finally felt ready to tell it. She was ready for Rosie to hear Imelda's story.

Chapter 51

Helen did not remember the first time she met Imelda Trevorrow, that was how young she had been. The Rowe and Trevorrow families had always been close, and had fished on the same boats for generations. When she thought about it hard enough, Helen's first memory of Imelda was a round-faced child with sandy hair down to her knees standing on the quayside as the two of them waved to their fathers' boat as it came back from a week fishing. Helen never enjoyed looking back this far into her life, she never enjoyed thinking of Imelda before Samuel.

As they grew up, both Imelda and Helen were very good girls, rarely putting a foot out of line. They had been together the day that the *Merry Lamorna* went down, standing beside each other on the edge of the quay, as they always did, although this time they did not see their fathers and uncles waving back to them, but the tiny boat being swallowed by monstrous grey waves. Helen's Uncle Bart had been on that boat. As had Imelda's father.

So, when everyone went to join the farm boys on their annual half-day swim, the girls refused to attend. They had vowed never to enter the sea again, for fear of what might happen if they did. In fact they took no interest in the half-day swim at all – until one particular year, Helen did.

She still remembered that day vividly; she had been seventeen years old and Janey Barker had come up to her. Janey always annoyed Helen; she was vain and flirtatious and everything that she ever did was in the hope that a boy might see her.

Janey strutted up to her, her red curls bouncing around and a sly smile on her bright face as she chirped, 'I know a secret!'

'Do you?' Helen asked wearily. She was in the middle of shopping for her mother and needed to carry the bags all the way back to the top of Newlyn. She attempted to walk away, but Janey followed.

'Don't you wanna know what it is?'

'Not partic'ly.'

'It involves you!'

At this, Helen stopped in her tracks. Gossip and secrets never involved her; in fact, she often wondered if people even knew that she still existed since leaving school. She turned back to Janey.

'Go on then.'

Janey gave her a childish smirk and started giggling. Helen rolled her eyes and continued on her way.

'Wait, wait, wait!' Janey begged and hurried after her. 'OK, George Tregidden fancies you!'

'No he don't.' Helen felt a rush of embarrassment flood her.

'He do!' Janey insisted. 'Yesterday, when we was all swimming he kept asking why you never come!'

Not too long after this conversation, Helen found out that – for once – Janey Barker had been right. As soon as she and George became a couple, things changed between her and Imelda. They saw less of each other and Helen got to know George's friends. Over time, all of George's wild friends quietened down and sooner or later found themselves attached to a local girl. George married her, while Michael Howard married Olive Martin from over in St Ives. In fact, the only one of the farm boys to never find a girl of his own was Samuel Worthing, which is why Helen suggested Imelda.

At first the couple appeared to work, despite their obvious differences. Samuel stopped drinking quite so much, while he in turn brought Imelda out of her shell. In fact, George and Helen were rather proud of their matchmaking skills, but then things took a sour turn.

The Tregiddens had begun a family, as had the Howards and even Janey and her husband Bernard Roskelley had baby Rowenna. This left Imelda and Samuel to their own company, which never seemed to last long before Samuel escaped to the pub. The Worthings became notorious in the village; Samuel Worthing, the man who couldn't last a day without getting drunk and his wife Imelda who never did anything but shout at him. It was almost humorous to onlookers, like a sketch you may have watched in the pictures about a long-suffering but comedic couple. However, a few years later, everything became a whole lot less comedic when Samuel's drunken antics suffered the first of its consequences.

When Helen learnt about the crash, she was heartbroken. Heartbroken for Michael and Olive, for the orphaned little Charlie, and for Imelda. She had encouraged her into the marriage with Samuel Worthing without realising where it could lead. While the village turned against Samuel one by one, Helen tried to stand by the couple – for Imelda's sake. Helen's little Fred and Imelda's little Jimmy were the same age and Helen could not stand the thought of Imelda being left alone raising her son.

But the rejection from the village had caused Imelda to grow bitter and untrusting. If she walked into a shop, people would look away. Henry and Poll refused to serve her or Samuel in the White Lion and the only person who ever gave her the time of day was Helen. Still, there was something in the back of Imelda's head; a little voice that told her not to trust her oldest friend. Helen had been the one to set her up with Samuel in the first place; she had been the one who signed her life away to an alcoholic. So over time, and, despite Helen's best efforts to prevent it, she too lost contact with the Worthings.

That was until one strange afternoon. It was the middle of September and a very bright and dry day. The children were out playing somewhere in the farmyard and Rosie had come in crying that Carolyn had thrown her doll into a tree. As Helen consoled her daughter, she was distracted by a knock on the door. Upon answering it, she was surprised to find Imelda on the doorstep with little Jimmy by her side.

'Oh!' Helen had not intended to sound so surprised, 'Imelda? Can I help you?'

Her friend had changed. She was as thin as a rake and her sandy hair had grown thin and lank. It was hanging in her gaunt face and every couple of minutes Imelda attempted to comb it back behind her ear.

'Is ev'rything OK?'

Imelda's mouth opened in a big smile, though one without an ounce of warmth or conviction.

'Course,' she replied. 'I were just wondering if you would be alright having Jimmy over for tea? I know I shouldn't ask, but I have to do something and no one else will 'ave him, not even Mrs Howard, d-d'you mind?'

'No,' Helen found herself saying. 'No of course I don't mind,' She then looked down at Jimmy with a smile. 'We've got cottage pie for tea.'

'Aw, you like that, don't you, Jim?' Imelda smiled and passed his hand over to Helen, who stepped back, allowing Jimmy inside the house.

'Listen.' Imelda smoothed her hair behind her ear again. 'If I, um, I'm not finished doing my thing until late, is it alright if Jimmy spends the night 'ere?' She forced out a laugh. 'I know that's cheeky. But I'd be 'ere first thing tomorrow?'

Helen looked at her carefully.

'Course.' She then turned to Jimmy. 'Tell you what, the others are outside, but I think Rosie's a bit upset with them, could you do an extra special job for me and look after her?'

Jimmy nodded and took Rosie's tiny hand in his own. Helen waited for the two of them to toddle out into the yard before returning her attention to Imelda. 'Are you sure that ev'rything's alright?'

Imelda nodded, though this time without a smile.

'I'll be back for him as soon as possible.' She then looked at Helen with her huge eyes and said, 'Thank you.'

Helen watched as her friend made her way across the farmyard, blowing her son a kiss as she did. The way Imelda moved was like a deer that had suddenly found itself in the middle of a city, anxious and flinching at anything.

Helen felt a strange feeling in the pit of her stomach. It was almost as if she knew that this would be the last time she would see her oldest friend.

Chapter 52

'I remember,' Rosie said quietly, 'I'd completely forgotten… but I remember that – Jimmy coming here. We went outside and he climbed up the tree and got Clara out for me. Her dress had torn and when they thought I was going to cry, Carrie laughed, so he pushed her over and she didn't laugh again.'

She looked up at her mother who was still wearing a strangely sad smile. 'Was that really the last time you saw her?'

'I saw her just once more.' Helen sounded numb. 'I saw her the next morning.'

She trailed off, so Rosie decided to prompt her. 'When she came to collect Jimmy?'

A tear fell from Helen's eye that she wiped away before taking a deep breath. 'She didn't come. Your father was furious at her for leaving Jimmy with us. You see, while I always tried to be there for Imelda, your father washed his hands completely of Samuel. Michael was his best friend and he held Samuel entirely responsible.'

She had not spoken about this for years, and even then only to George. 'I insisted that Imelda would be back after tea-time, but she weren't. I sent the five of you out playing and waited for Imelda to come back, but she didn't. I weren't too cross with her; she had said that she might not make it back in time, so me and your nana made an extra bed up in Fred's room and Jimmy spent the night in with him.'

Helen began playing with Rosie's hair, and this time her daughter did not pull away. 'In the morning I gave you all breakfast and sent you out playing again, but Imelda still didn't turn up. Well, you can imagine what your father was like. "What does she think she's playing at? Leaving her son with us when we're not responsible for him." So after lunch I decided to take Jimmy home.'

She released Rosie's hair and her daughter sat up again. 'When I got to Laurel Cottage, I knocked, but the door was unlocked.'

'Samuel never locks it,' Rosie added quietly.

'Me and Jimmy went into the kitchen and I told him to wait there,' Helen said. 'And I went into the living room calling after Imelda and Samuel…' She trailed off and Rosie was unsure of what to say.

'Mum?' She placed her hand on her shoulder.

'Samuel was on the sofa, passed out drunk,' Helen spat. 'And then…and then I turned around…I turned around and I saw her.'

'Mummy?' Rosie whispered.

'Imelda was at the bottom of the stairs.'

Rosie covered her mouth as tears began blurring her vision.

'They said,' Helen sniffed wetly and sighed. 'They said that it were an accident, that Imelda must have tripped down the stairs *after* Samuel passed out. He got away with it *again!*'

Rosie shifted slightly. 'Maybe she did? I mean, what's to say that Samuel…'

Helen looked at her innocent daughter and gave her a sad smile. 'At the top of the stairs I saw a suitcase.'

'Was she going to leave?' Rosie asked, 'With Jimmy?'

'I think she was going to pick him up from us on her way out of the village,' Helen explained. 'So, see? I don't hate Jimmy at all, I love him like he's my own son. He didn't have a mother so *I* stepped into that role. And I am scared ev'ryday that Jimmy goes home that he might not come to work the next morning,' She tenderly ran a hand across Rosie's cheek. 'And I can't bear to think of you being in that position. If you were with Jimmy, you would have Samuel in your life as well and that, *that* scares me.'

'Does Jimmy know?'

'No, he thinks that it was an accident.'

At this Rosie let out the sob that she had been holding onto. 'So he's been left in a house with a man who's killed three people?'

'We didn't have a choice!' Helen insisted, 'Imelda's death was ruled as an accident, just like the crash! There was no reason for anyone to take Jimmy away from him!'

'D'you remember when Fred forgot to lock the chicken coop one night and you told him that he may as well have fed them to foxes?' Rosie asked, 'That is exactly what you have done with Jimmy!'

Down in Laurel Cottage, Samuel had witnessed Jimmy turning down Rosie's proposal and could not stop himself from goading him about it.

'So you 'ave t'get the girls to ask you?' He grinned, 'An' even 'en you turn 'em down!'

288

Jimmy curled up further in the armchair, trying to block out his father's slurring voice.

'You're pathetic,' Samuel laughed, 'Ain't yeh?'

'No I ain't!' Jimmy spat at him.

Samuel held his hands up in surrender. 'Don' shout at me, ain't meant as an insult! 'Parently I'm pathetic 'swell, jus' makes two of us, don' it?'

'I'm nothing like you!' Jimmy growled at him before turning to the comfort of the chair. He could not stop thinking about Rosie's face as he closed the door on her, her shouts from outside as the others took her away. That was days ago now, yet Jimmy still felt sick. He was now unemployed, with no friends or life at all. Maybe he was not so different from his father after all.

'You look down on me,' Samuel said. 'Don' you?'

Jimmy did not reply.

'Cos you're *so* much better?' Samuel asked. 'Jimmy Worthing prancing round the village wiv all the girls and all 'is friends! You dunno what it's like bein' me! Livin' in my 'ead all day bleddy long!'

Jimmy rolled his eyes and closed them. *Maybe if he went to sleep this would all be over?*

''Avin' to raise you all on my own!' Samuel continued. At this Jimmy sat up.

'Raise me?' he laughed, 'You didn't raise me! Half the village raised me, but you didn't!'

'I tried my 'ardest! I din't 'ave what all those other people did!'

'What? What didn't you have? A job? That's cos you couldn't keep hold of one. A wife? Well look at Kerenza! She might be grown up, but her little sisters ain't! Mrs Roskelley's been

289

raising them on her own and seems to be doing a pretty good job! And what about Charlie Howard? He didn't have either of his parents and he turned out alright!'

'Don' talk about them!'

'Who?' Jimmy asked. 'The Howards? Why?'

'I dunno.'

Jimmy sat thinking for a moment. Mrs Howard's other grandson, that Ralph, he never seemed to like him very much. And Mrs Howard had always looked at him with a slight sadness in her eyes; he had always been invited to play with Charlie or in for a biscuit, but his father was never welcome. It was as though Mrs Howard had been trying to make a point. 'Did you…?' Jimmy looked at his father who was crying and suddenly felt horrifically sick. 'No…'

'Don' look at me like that!' Samuel slammed his hand down, 'I din't mean to! An 'en they all 'ated me out there and made our lives 'ell! I mean it. *'ell!* If it weren't for them, your mother—'

Jimmy stared at him coldly, 'My mother, what?'

'I need summin' to drink.' Samuel went to stand up, but Jimmy was on him in a second and had slammed him back into his chair. 'What were you going to say about Mum?'

'Nuffin'!'

'WHAT WERE YOU GOING TO SAY?' Jimmy roared. Samuel drew away from him, shaking with tears. Jimmy stepped back, crossing his arms over his chest. 'What did the village do to her?'

'They made 'er 'ate me,' Samuel mumbled. 'Those Pascoes with their bleddy preaching, and *Helen Tregidden*, they all kept whispering things to her an-an' turned her against me!'

Jimmy slowly lowered himself back into his seat.

'When she died I was at the Tregidden's house, weren't I? I

remember her taking me there and saying that she was gonna come back in the morning, I was having a sleepover with Fred... Where did she go?'

'Don't.'

'Dad, I want to know—'

'DON'T!' Samuel roared.

'Did she run away?' Jimmy asked, tearfully, 'Did she run away and ev'ryone told me that she died?'

Samuel pressed his face into the side of the chair. His voice was so muffled that Jimmy could not hear him.

'Speak up.'

When his father continued mumbling, Jimmy marched over to him and yanked him back up, pushing him onto the back of the chair.

'Sit up straight and tell me the truth!' Jimmy ordered.

Samuel looked as though he was a child that had just been scolded by a teacher.

'She 'ad a bag, it were 'idden under the bed. I walked into the room and she were filling it with more clothes.'

'Then what?'

'I tried to convince 'er to stay.' Samuel stared at the wall across the room. 'But she left.'

'She left?' All this time Jimmy had been led to believe that his mother had died. He had cried for her and wished for her to come back time and time again, but now he was supposed to accept that she just walked out on him, left him alone with his father?

'Yeah...' Samuel replied slowly. Jimmy shook his head, attempting to get his thoughts straight.

'No,' he said, 'No, no, I want the truth! Swear to me that she left, that my beautiful mother left me with *you*!'

291

'We argued and she left the room,' Samuel insisted, 'And then it were just me and you! Wh-what more d'you need to know?'

'Ev'rything!' Jimmy shouted, 'I need to know ev'rything, of course! So we've established that she left the room, but did she leave the house?'

Samuel shrunk back and shook his head.

Jimmy ran his hand over his chin, getting an explanation out of him was like pulling teeth. 'So she *did* die?'

Samuel nodded.

'How?'

'She fell.'

'Where? Down the stairs?' Jimmy asked. 'Dad, answer me.'

'Yeah.'

'Did she fall…?' Jimmy could not believe that he was about to ask this, 'Or did *you*—'

'SHURRUP!'

'Did you push her?'

'I din't want her to go!' Samuel sobbed. 'She left the room and I went after her an—'

'And what?'

'She ended up at the bottom of the stairs.'

Chapter 53

'I'm gonna be sick.' Jimmy sprinted across the room and into the kitchen where Samuel heard him retching into the sink.

'Jim?' he called and shakily stood up. He stumbled across the sitting room, grasping his way along the furniture to keep himself up. He felt like a walking corpse.

As he entered the kitchen, Jimmy wiped his mouth on his sleeve and spun around to face him.

'*You* keep away from me!' he warned. 'You're a murderer.'

'I ain't!' Samuel sobbed.

'Why are you still allowed to be here?' Jimmy cried, 'You killed Mrs Howard's son and his wife and you killed *my mum!*' He ran his hands over his face, which was drenched in sweat and tears. 'Was she going to take me as well?'

Samuel began making his way across the room.

'Was she going to take me with her?'

'I need a drink.' Samuel reached for a bottle, but had his arm snapped back by Jimmy.

'I need you sober for this!' he shouted. 'Was my mother gonna take me away?'

'Yes!' Samuel yelled. 'That's why I couldn't let her! I couldn't lose you! My boy!'

Jimmy paced around the room, turning on his heels as he pulled at his hair.

'She was gonna take me away from you.' He was barely breathing. 'I'd never have had to see you again.'

'You're my little boy, James.' Samuel reached out and pulled Jimmy towards him, pushing their foreheads together. 'My son.'

Jimmy lurched away, pushing Samuel, who drunkenly stumbled back and hit his head on a shelf, sending an array of bottles shattering onto the kitchen floor.

As Samuel gathered his bearings, he ran his hand over the back of his head and looked at his son. For a moment, Jimmy wondered if his father might be about to cry. But then Samuel stepped forward and swung his fist, sending it colliding with Jimmy's jaw.

Jimmy moved to defend himself, but was hit again. This time his knees buckled and he fell onto the floor. He looked up to see his father standing over him, a wild look in his eyes. Samuel clutched at his chest as he said breathlessly,

'I ain't a bad person!'

Rosie frantically knocked on the door, hoping that he was in. As soon as she and her mother had finished their conversation, she had left the house and run all the way here. She had to get Jimmy away from his father. Finally she heard movement and the door opened, revealing Edward.

'Rose?' he gasped upon seeing her distraught face. 'What's wrong?'

'It's Jimmy! Edward, we need to help him. Samuel's dangerous and Jimmy's been left with him all on his own!'

'Hang on, hang on.' Edward frowned. 'I don't understand?'

'My mum just told me...' Rosie could barely believe Helen's tale herself. 'That Samuel Worthing killed his wife – and he killed Charlie's parents too!' She watched as the colour drained from Edward's face. 'Jimmy's alone with him and thinks that ev'ryone's abandoned him. Please help me, we need to get him out of that house!'

'Why me?' Edward asked, 'Why d'you need my help? Where's Fred?'

'Freddie's gone away and I know that if you thought Jimmy was in danger then you'd do whatever it took to save him, I know you love him.'

Edward stared at her, unsure of what to say.

'He's your best friend, ent he?' Rosie asked. 'Of course you love him.'

'Yeah.' Edward slowly nodded. 'Course I do.'

'Then come with me please!' Rosie was already halfway down the path before Edward joined her.

'What makes you think that Samuel would hurt Jimmy?' he asked as they made their way through the village. 'Jimmy's lived with him for twenty years, surely if he was going to do anything then he would have done it by now?'

'My mum said that the reason why Jimmy spent so much time at our house was because she didn't want Samuel drunkenly hurting him.'

'Ev'ryone's parents used to hurt them a bit when we were young though, didn't they?' Edward pulled the sleeves of his jumper further down to hide the burns. 'I know mine did.'

'I'm not talking about a smack ev'ry now and then,' Rosie said. 'I'm talking about life or death. Don't you remember? Jimmy spent all his time at the farm or with you and Madge?

Mrs Howard even gave him his tea once a week, that's how much the village don't trust Samuel; this is the first time that Jimmy has had no one around.'

Edward felt a racing in his chest. The very same racing that he had felt that day in Poland, hiding in the barn as enemy soldiers marched past, the day that Jimmy had crouched so close to him behind the bales of hay that he could feel his breath on the back of his neck, the day that Jimmy had whispered, 'I love you, Ed.'

Those words had calmed him then and now all that Edward wanted was to be there to calm Jimmy.

The two sprinted their way through the village until reaching Laurel Cottage. It was hardly surprising now to Rosie that the door was not locked. She pushed it open and ran inside. The kitchen, which was usually dark, seemed darker than normal. Two of the chairs had been tipped up and there were smashed bottles of alcohol everywhere. Rosie felt Edward draw up next to her in the doorway and place his hand on her shoulder.

'Jim?' Rosie called. 'Jimmy? It's me?'

In the corner of the room she spotted him hunched up, with his knees beneath his chin.

'Jimmy!' Rosie ran to him. As she crouched down, she saw that he was covered in blood, some of it was his own and some was not. Jimmy's nose was now red, as was his chin and one cheek.

'It's OK,' Rosie whispered. 'Ev'rything's going to be OK. Jim, I'm here. We both are, me and Ed, you're not on your own.'

Edward watched the way that Jimmy looked at Rosie. As

296

soon as his eyes met hers, Jimmy relaxed, sinking his head to her shoulder. He never looked at him like that – and *would* never look at him like that.

'Jim?' Rosie asked, 'Where's your father?'

Slowly Jimmy's gaze shifted across the room. And Rosie and Edward followed his gaze.

'He cried out in agony…and then collapsed. I-I couldn't wake him up. I tried!'

Slowly Edward approached Samuel; he was a very small man and looked even smaller now. As Edward crouched down and pressed his ear against Samuel's chest, he was scared of crushing his fragile bones. Samuel was completely still. Edward sat up and looked at them both.

'He's dead.'

Rosie drew Jimmy in closer as she wrapped her arms around him.

Samuel-the-drunk was gone.

Chapter 54

The time that it took for Samuel's body to be removed from Laurel Cottage felt like an eternity. First of all there had just been an ambulance crew and Rosie thought that would be it. But then the police arrived and began asking questions. Jimmy was incredibly quiet, barely saying a word and unable to take his eyes off the sheet-covered mound that had once been his father. Rosie was at his side the entire time, holding his hand and trying her hardest to prompt him to tell them what had happened. But then they took him away.

'Just for questioning,' a police officer explained, but also said that Rosie would not be permitted to attend with him. Rosie had protested as Jimmy numbly left the house and climbed into the police car. He was so shaken and she did not want to leave him on his own. As the officer left the house, however, Edward held her back.

'Rose, it's all going to be OK,' he promised, although more to himself than to her.

Jimmy was kept in the station for a very long time. He was questioned and then questioned again, having to live through

298

the details of that afternoon over and over. They asked him why his father collapsed. Jimmy told them that they had been fighting. But why had they been fighting? At this Jimmy had struggled to speak.

'Mr Worthing,' the officer had said. Jimmy knew him a little. He had been at school with his daughter. 'I'm just trying to piece together exactly what happened.'

'He was drunk,' Jimmy said. 'He was always drunk.'

The officer was very much aware of this.

'He told me things…confessed to them, I dunno.' Jimmy shifted in his seat. That anger he had felt towards his father had still not gone, if anything it had increased; dying was an easy way out of his sentence.

'Confessed to what?'

'He killed her,' Jimmy whispered, 'My mum, he killed her.'

The officer looked up at him.

'Are you sure?'

'Yes, and he killed other people too. Michael Howard and his wife.'

The officer then informed Jimmy that he would be back shortly.

After many more hours of questioning, Jimmy was informed that he was free to go. A massive heart attack had killed Samuel Worthing – brought on by his life of excessive drinking.

The walk from the police station was strange, for Jimmy felt as though he could not hear, let alone take in anything that was going on around him.

He was the final Worthing. The very last one. His paternal

family had passed away years ago, and the only member of his mother's family that he assumed was still alive was a distant aunt in St Just, but he hardly counted her as family – and she did not bear the name Worthing. He could not decide how it felt being the only Worthing. There was no one else to drag the name through the mud, but then there was no one else to bear the cross from all of the damage the Worthing family had caused, or all the damage that *Samuel* Worthing had caused.

There was no need for him to return home immediately, for there would be no one waiting there. No mother ready with a kiss and his tea, and now no father lying passed out on the sofa, having set fire to the kitchen cupboards whilst trying to cook.

Instead, Jimmy walked. He made his way slowly through the town, thinking about nothing, nothing at all. Maybe he could leave just like Carolyn had done. But where would he go? His great aunt was a strange woman so he would not be going there.

Not many shops were open now. By the time that he had left the station, the sun was already beginning to set and now the darkness was setting in. As Jimmy reached the next shop, he found himself pressing his face to the window to get a better look inside. The cool glass against his forehead felt relaxing and Jimmy began to breathe. He was not sure when he last breathed properly, not since his father's death, though maybe not since the war. Perhaps he had not breathed in years, since he was a five year old boy and learnt that his mother had died. As Jimmy's eyes skirted around the dim shop, they stumbled across a mirror. Then Jimmy saw himself. His eyes were tired and dark, while his skin appeared to hang from his face in exhaustion. His hair stuck to his head in a tangled mess and he was shivering as he stood slumped against the window. It was not the eyes of Jimmy Worthing looking back at him, but Samuel. Jimmy drew back with a cry and stumbled across the street. People avoided him; they would not look. To them, he was Samuel Jr, and looked as though he was going the same way as his father, traumatised and unhinged, just another helpless drunk. Jimmy's throat felt dry and he desperately craved a drink. As he reached the other side of the street, Jimmy felt himself falling into a metal chair outside a cafe. The chair squeaked and scraped against the pavement as he buried his head in his hands.

Everyone was watching him, he could tell, the final Worthing, and wondering when he was going to fall off the wagon. But then Jimmy heard a voice.

'Jim?'

Inez Tregidden's hands felt safe as she placed them on his knee, crouching down beside him. There was no other way that Jimmy could think to describe her other than 'kind'. Her eyes widened with concern as she moved her hands from his knees to his own shaking hands. She was wearing the nice red coat that he had seen her in recently and two books were poking out from the top of her bag.

'Jimmy, what's happened?'

'There's no one left.' It was as though Jimmy's voice had not come from him and Inez stood back up, slowly guiding Jimmy to stand as well.

'Ev'rything's OK,' she whispered, 'I'm going to take you home.'

And, by home, Inez meant Beacon Farm.

Chapter 55

'What's wrong with him?' was the first thing Frank asked when he saw the boy sitting on his sofa. Jimmy was still pale, but no longer shivering, and had Rosie sat close to his side.

'Come into the kitchen, Grandad.' Inez took his arm and hastily led him from the room. By the time that she had bought Jimmy home, Rosie had already relayed the afternoon's events to their parents. She had waited for Jimmy at the station, only to learn that he had already left. As soon as he had entered the farmhouse, Rosie had thrown her arms around his neck and had not left his side since.

George and Helen abruptly ended their conversation, until they saw that it was only Frank and Inez who had joined them in the kitchen.

'So he knows now?' George turned his attention back to his wife. 'Jimmy knows exactly what his father did.'

'That's what Rosie told me,' Helen said, ''Parently he and Samuel were fighting about it when Samuel – you know…'

'Died, Mum,' Inez pulled a chair out for her grandfather, before sitting in the one beside him. 'You are allowed to say the word.'

'I know, but I hate it!' Helen said, 'It's been said too much these last years.'

Rosie and Jimmy could hear every word coming from the kitchen, despite the family's hushed voices.

'I'm sorry.' It made Rosie jump, for these were the first words that Jimmy had uttered since arriving at the house.

'Sorry?' she frowned, 'Sorry for what?'

'For humiliating you,' Jimmy said. 'For making you think that I didn't care. I do.'

'Course I know that.' Rosie took his hands and squeezed them, 'Jimmy, I love you so much and I am so sorry for ev'rything that's happened.'

She truly was the most beautiful person that Jimmy had ever met. But not in the way that most people thought. Yes, Rosie was pretty, but the way she cared and the way she fought for the people she loved, *that* was beautiful to Jimmy. He looked back to the warm fire that was burning in the hearth and relaxed his fingers from Rosie's grip.

'Do you ever think that maybe we just aren't supposed to work?' he asked. 'Surely if we were supposed to be together then things would be so much easier.'

'Not at all.' Rosie tightened her grip, 'I thought you were the one who didn't believe in fate or destiny? You told me that you don't feel God at all.'

'I don't,' Jimmy said. 'But there are things that I do feel instead.' He turned back to her with a smile. 'I feel you. I feel you ev'rywhere, Rose, it's like you're running through my blood, and if what you asked me is still on the table, I would be mad to say no.'

Rosie only realised that she was crying when she let out a

laugh and hastily wiped the tears away with the back of her hand.

'You mean it?' she asked.

'I'm sure it won't be easy,' Jimmy said. 'Things never are, but I want to marry you, Rosie Tregidden.'

Inez was in shock when Rosie and Jimmy came into the kitchen to announce their news. Delighted for them of course, but still in shock. She exchanged hugs and kisses with them both and stepped back, allowing her parents to take charge of the conversation.

'Oh, my darlings, I'm just so pleased!' Helen beamed tearfully over and over again. George had been quieter, finally deciding to speak to Jimmy face to face.

'Worthing,' he said. 'I've said things about you. I've assumed things about you as well. I've always suspected that you were like your old man.'

Jimmy glanced away, not wanting to make eye contact with his boss. 'But I think I've been wrong,' George confessed, 'And I'm sorry.'

'It's fine,' Jimmy said, 'Mr Tregidden, it's fine.'

'No it ain't.' George looked at Jimmy. 'It's not Mr Tregidden, it's George.'

He held a hand out to Jimmy, who shook it in disbelief. Maybe things did not have to be so complicated after all; maybe the Worthing way was not the only way.

Inez felt a tug on her arm and glanced down to see her grandfather looking at her with concern.

'What's going on?' he whispered and Inez started laughing.

'Rosie and Jimmy are engaged.'

At this Frank demanded his turn to hug the bride-to-be and grill the groom-to-be and Inez stepped back, still with a smile etched onto her face.

This was not the way she had imagined the first engagement to be, with Carolyn and Fred away and Rosie being the first to fly the nest. Six years ago she had imagined things in such a different way, so different to now that it was hard to remember a time that she had believed in those things. The celebrations were so loud and boisterous that only she heard the knock on the door.

It was a welcome relief to escape the warmth and noise of the Tregiddens for a moment and just to be alone. Of course Inez was pleased, of course she was. Carolyn was apparently very happy in London, and Fred finally had a chance of getting better, now even Rosie was getting her happy ending. Inez could not help but think that her Nana Lizzie had a hand in it all. This was the kind of story that she liked, the kind where everything tied up nicely. A fairy-tale.

As Inez opened the door, she was shocked to see the person standing there. 'Hello?'

'Hello,' Ralph Howard said.

'I don't—' Inez stepped outside and into the night, 'I don't understand – what are you doing here?'

'I missed the quiet Cornish life,' Ralph said. 'And I missed Granny.'

Inez tucked her hair back behind her ears and crossed her arms, trying to trap some warmth from the kitchen back inside her. 'How's my sister?'

'She's fine,' Ralph said. 'Carolyn's fine, she loves it in London.

I think the two of us are opposites to be fair; she just wants to be in the city, while I just want to be here.'

'So you're back for good then?'

'Yes.'

'And what are you doing here? At the farm, I mean?'

'Oh.' Ralph scratched the back of his neck, he had not thought this far ahead. 'Just to let you know.'

'OK.'

'And to ask a favour from you.'

Inez let out a sigh and leant against the doorframe. 'And what would that be?'

'Could we start again?'

Inez looked at him. 'For the third time?'

'I know.' Ralph gave an embarrassed laugh. 'I'm sorry, I should go, it sounds like you're having fun in there.'

'Rosie's just got engaged.'

'To Jimmy Worthing?'

Inez nodded.

'Tell her congratulations from me,' Ralph said. 'I'm sorry for disturbing you. Goodnight, Inez.'

He turned and started walking away as Inez found herself running out into the yard.

'Ralph!' she called.

Ralph turned to face her and she smiled, holding her hand out.

'I'm Inez,' she said, 'Nice to meet you.'

Ralph began to laugh and shook her hand.

'Thank you.' He beamed.

The two remained standing in the yard for a moment, until Inez glanced back at the house where her family were still chatting and laughing; even Jessop had joined in with gleeful barks.

'I'd better get back in there,' she said. 'I'll see you soon though, Ralph.'

She began walking away when she heard footsteps and turned to see that Ralph was following her.

'Inez, I have something for you,' he said and Inez frowned. 'Hold your hand out.'

Inez obliged as Ralph placed something cool and metallic in her palm. He then gave her a smile and walked away. Inez opened her hand and looked down to see it lying there.

A key.

The Tregidden Family Will Return in…

THE TREGIDDEN FAMILY WILL RETURN IN...

About the Author

Tal Macey grew up in the house that was once Beacon Farm. Cobbled together with his grandmother's diaries, written as a teenager during World War II, the idea for this story came to life.

When not writing, Tal can be found exploring the countryside and coast of his native West Cornwall searching for inspiration and stories waiting to be uncovered.

Printed in Great Britain
by Amazon